Finding the Perfect Mate just got way more complicated.

When Perry pledges abstinence until he meets a Perfect Mate—a rare mortal perfect for a vampire—he doesn't expect to be tested. Especially by another vampire. But Mandy smells like heaven. Has a sexy British accent. And is the smartest person he's met. She's just so … perfect. If he holds on to his fantasy, will he lose his chance at love?

Finding the perfect vampire was never on her radar.

Mandy hasn't seen her father in 500 years but when he goes missing she drops everything and heads for the States, only to discover the Russian vampires kidnapped him. She insists on being involved in his rescue and suggests she and Perry—who's sexy as sin and makes her laugh—infiltrate as lovers. As they pretend, she realizes he's just so … perfect. But she's got a secret that will mean her death. Can she trust him not to turn her over to the authorities or does she keep mum and let him go?

Other books by Stacy McKitrick

Bitten by Love Series:
My Sunny Vampire
Bite Me, I'm Yours
Blind Temptation
A Vampire Wedding
Biting the Curse
Finding the Perfect Mate

Ghostly Encounter Series:
Ghostly Liaison
Ghostly Interlude

Short Stories in the Following Anthologies:
Home for the Holidays
Love's a Beach

Short Stories:
Forever Thirty-two
Savannah's Destiny

Finding the Perfect Mate

(Bitten by Love #6)

Stacy McKitrick

Dayton, Ohio

Mythicalpress.com

Copyright © 2020, Stacy McKitrick
Edited by Michele Stegman and Stephanie McKitrick
Formatted by Enterprise Book Services
(www.EnterpriseBookServices.com)
Cover designed by Maria Zannini (BookcoverDiva.blogspot.com)

All Rights Are Reserved. No part of this book may be used or reproduced in any manner whatsoever without written permission, except in the case of brief quotations embodied in critical articles and reviews. The unauthorized reproduction or distribution of this copyrighted work is illegal. No part of this book may be scanned, uploaded or distributed via the Internet or any other means, electronic or print, without the author's permission.

This book is a work of fiction. The names, characters, places, and incidents are products of the writer's imagination or have been used fictitiously and are not to be construed as real. Any resemblance to persons, living or dead, actual events, locale or organizations is entirely coincidental.

Published in the United States of America
First print edition: April 2020
Print ISBN: 978-1-7331762-1-7

Dedicated to Perry's Fans
It's because of you he got his own book

Prologue

Barnet Groves, Head of the Committee for the United States vampires, sat on the cement bench next to a cement table in a rest area off I-71 between Cleveland and Columbus, Ohio. He'd been sitting there for an hour watching truckers park for the night. Sitting and watching the few travelers dodge snowflakes as they stopped to use the facilities. Sitting and watching traffic drive by. But mostly, just sitting. After having actually touched Janie, an unbonded Perfect Mate, he was still feeling the effects. Or rather, one part of his body was.

What an insult to his late wife, Rachel. How many times had he jacked off in the woods since he'd touched Janie? Too many to admit. And every time he'd thought he had it under control, one tiny memory of Janie's scent or the warmth that had spread throughout his body when he'd touched her would poke him in the gut—or rather, his libido—and it would start all over again.

Was it just a coincidence that every Perfect Mate he'd been in contact with had the same wild meadow fragrance as Rachel? The Perfect Mate story indicated that every unbonded Perfect Mate of the desired sex would smell like home to a vampire and since he considered Rachel home, maybe not so coincidental.

"Forgive me, Rachel. You deserve better than this." His people deserved better than this. He was the God-damned Committee Head. He had to set an example. If he couldn't control his urges, how could he expect the same from other vampires?

Were Perfect Mates a God-send or were they an enemy? Barnet believed the former, especially after having met several. Just because they couldn't be controlled or turned, and no vampire could read their minds, didn't mean they were an enemy. Just meant they were different. And boy, what a difference.

His libido was still giving him fits.

This Perfect Mate business was going to get worse before it got better unless he could locate Alexi Popolov, the vampire credited with writing the Perfect Mate story. A story that had been considered a myth up until a year ago. But Alexi had gotten himself buried alive somewhere in Russia and Barnet's notes from the few Perfect Mates they'd discovered were inadequate at best. Certainly not enough to convince the other Committee Heads that Perfect Mates were not a threat. He just hoped their existence didn't bring about another vampire war. Vampires had survived discovery after the last one, but social media hadn't existed. Neither had television nor radio. And the population hadn't been near as large. It had been so much easier to hide back then.

His phone vibrated in his pants pocket. He'd been talked into trading in his old flip-phone for this newfangled smart phone that he still didn't trust. He pulled out the device and frowned at the screen. The number belonged to Dimitri Kalashnikov, not that Barnet saved any number in his phone. Owning one of these contraptions meant being safe with it, which meant he'd delete any call he received, too. He didn't need a record of calls and his vampire memory was more than adequate to remember phone numbers.

Was the Russian Committee Head finally ready to talk? Barnet had only called their Headquarters ten times in the last week. Each time the call had been answered by Felicks—one of the members—and each time he asked to take a message. Whatever the reason for the call, Barnet relished the distraction so he could head back to Dayton erection-free.

He pushed the accept button. "Hello, Dimitri. Glad to see you finally got my messages."

"Barnet. I hear you're looking for Alexi Popolov. You need to stop."

Maybe it wasn't the ten messages that got Dimitri to call. Maybe it was the snooping. "I know you've had issues with him in the past, but did that warrant burying him alive?"

"That is a lie. Who told you that? I want his name."

Funny how Dimitri always assumed a man was responsible. In this case he was wrong, but Barnet wasn't going to correct him. "So you can bury him alive, too?"

"The man lies. Alexi is missing. His last meeting was over five years ago."

Yeah, a meeting he couldn't make because he was buried. Barnet rubbed the back of his neck. Time to take a different approach. "Dimitri, Alexi's story about Perfect Mates is not a myth. We've discovered them. I only want to talk—"

"You have discovered freaks. Nothing more. Popolov lies. He lies about everything."

"He didn't lie about this. They're out there and once they've bonded—"

"They are freaks and must be killed! Do you not understand? Go on back to your committee. Destroy the freaks and stop poking around where you are not wanted."

"Dimitri…" Barnet hung his head. "They aren't a threat." If anything, they were the most wonderful creatures on Earth.

"Anyone who cannot be controlled is a threat. Are you a threat now, too?"

The words, "go on back to your committee," kept running in Barnet's head. Two cars had been in the parking lot for almost as long as he'd been here, but he'd been too frustrated to notice until now. "What is that supposed to mean? Are you willing to start a war over this?"

"Are you?"

"You can't bury the truth. And you can't just kill innocent people."

The cars were empty, which meant the occupants could be anywhere. Damn it. Why hadn't he paid attention?

"We do not kill innocents. We destroy threats."

"Is that what you're going to do with Alexi? Destroy him?"

Dimitri sighed. "Popolov is missing. He either dead or rogue. But if alive and foolish enough to be caught, yes, he will be destroyed. Is that not what we all do to rogues? But first he will suffer. Be set as example."

Suffer. Yeah, that was Dimitri's modus operandi. So was spying. And apparently he'd sent people here to spy on, or rather, follow Barnet. Unauthorized Russians. In the US. He should have noticed.

But his mind had been so consumed with Perfect Mates he never even considered the consequences.

"So you're saying even if he's found, I won't have a chance to talk to him?"

"If you do, it would be the last words you ever spoke."

"Okay, now *that* sounded like a threat."

"Is not threat. Is fact. You are not allowed to interfere."

"You're right. My apologies. But this Perfect Mate business is not over. I'll just have to find another way to convince you. Good day, Dimitri." Barnet disconnected the call and shoved the phone in his pocket. No one lurked around. He made a dash for the car.

Barnet collided with a wall, or rather a man resembling a wall. Pain lanced from his belly and he crumpled to the ground.

A tazer. He'd been tazed. A vampire's second worst nightmare.

Wall Man turned Barnet onto his back. Another bruiser stepped up and smiled just before he drove a stake into Barnet's heart.

Yeah, that was the worst. Being staked.

One good thing: he no longer had an erection.

Chapter 1

Perry Davenport, occasional helper of the Committee, rolled a trunk into a holding cell of the Committee Headquarters. He opened it, exposing one piece-of-junk vampire. Perry itched to leave the guy there, like a staked pretzel. Better yet, scramble his brain for good. It wouldn't take much. Perry's sire had taught him all sorts of neat tricks.

Tricks, for the most part, Perry had been told to keep hidden. Made life simpler that way. And wasn't that the truth.

So with cameras stuck in each corner of the cell, capturing every movement Perry would make, he kept to his orders: remove the stake and secure the prisoner.

Although, leaving the stake in could be constituted as being secure, which was probably why Victoria Martin, a Committee member and an occasional thorn in his side, had been so specific. However, she did not say he needed to remove the duct tape from the guy's mouth—just because a vampire was staked didn't mean they couldn't talk, and this guy talked way too much—so that would stay. If Bozo managed to get enough strength back after the stake removal, he could untape his own damn mouth.

For a holding cell, the accommodations were pretty nifty. Not much different than staying in one of the many rooms offered to vampires during their annual check-in. Recessed lights, a couch, a TV built into the wall, and a shower and sink for those that wanted to stay clean. The differences? No bed—like Bozo would get conjugal visits—electrified bars for a door, and no way out without help.

Oh, and the cameras. Couldn't forget the cameras.

Perry dumped the vampire onto the floor and tossed the trunk aside. Using his foot, he straightened Bozo out on his back and stepped on his torso. Perry avoided skin contact. He so did not want to hear Bozo's pleas again. As if the guy didn't deserve this treatment or worse. Perry grabbed the stake and yanked.

Bozo wailed behind the tape covering his mouth, but otherwise remained still. Without blood, it would take a good hour before the guy could move. Perry locked the cell door behind him and turned toward the prisoner. "You know, Tucker, if more vampires were like you, we'd be in a world of hurt. Maybe next time you use that noggin of yours before you try mating with someone who doesn't want you. If there is a next time. Enjoy your stay. If the Committee sees fit to feed you, they'll feed you. But I wouldn't hold my breath if I were you. It could be a long wait."

How long a wait remained to be seen. And apparently Perry would have a say if what he'd been told was true: that he'd been named the tie-breaker voter in case something were to happen to the Head of the Committee. And apparently something had happened to Barnet Groves since he was supposed to be at Headquarters by now. Perry had tried to convince Vic that Barnet was merely embarrassed being caught with a boner after meeting an unbonded Perfect Mate and went to cool off somewhere. But even Perry was beginning to doubt that. Barnet never needed to cool off. He was always cool. Then again, he'd never met an unbonded Perfect Mate before he met Janie. And she could have been his if someone else hadn't found her first.

Like if that someone else had been Perry. But it wasn't. He'd been too late, too. Damn it, why couldn't he have found Janie first?

Not that they'd had a connection. But she would have been better than any mortal, and definitely better than a vampire. Who's to say the connection wouldn't have eventually kicked in? That was neither here nor there since Janie was now bonded to Sam.

Lucky bastard.

"What'd he do?"

Perry spun toward the hallway at Suzie-Q's voice. Susannah Martin, the newest member of the vampire community, and Vic's sister-in-law, was a lovely sight to see. She actually smiled and spoke to him, so maybe she'd forgiven him after all. He flipped on the switch, arming Bozo's door. "He tried to force a bonding with an unwilling Perfect Mate."

"That woman in Detroit?"

"No. The man."

"Oh."

Perry closed the door to the holding cells and nodded for Suzie-Q to follow. "How've you been?"

"I'm not heart-broken, if that's your worry."

That was a relief, although he'd been sure he'd hurt her feelings after their disastrous date. He'd been going for honesty and instead sounded blunt. Heartless, in fact. "I didn't mean it as an insult."

"I know how you meant it. And it's true. I'm not a Perfect Mate. Never was."

Yeah, because if she was, she never would have been controlled or turned. Perfect Mates were immune to vampires and their venom. Still, Perry hadn't meant to hurt her feelings. Maybe he shouldn't have bothered going out with her in the first place, but she had intrigued him as a mortal. He just assumed she'd keep intriguing him. But then, no other vampire ever had—which was why he'd never considered turning a mortal—so why had he thought differently then?

She gestured to his new garb. "Where'd you get the Hawaiian shirt and cargo pants?"

"You like?" The familiar wear made Perry feel like his old self. Those polo shirts and khaki pants just hadn't done it for him. Much too constricting and…normal. Who wanted to look normal? "I now have pockets for my lock picks and knife. I really missed my pockets. Couldn't believe I found these at Walmart. They were on sale, too."

"You bought them?"

"Of course I bought them. I'm not a thief. I have money." Why did people always assume that about him? Couldn't be the clothes. They thought that when he was dressed like a golfer. Was it his ponytail? He'd hate to think he might have to chop it off to get some respect.

At least he didn't wear it in a bun. He'd chop his hair off first before that happened.

"I'm sorry. It's just… How do you get money? Do you have a job?"

Okay, maybe she didn't think he was a thief. And hadn't he considered finding a more respectable job to impress his future Perfect Mate? "Sort of. I do work for the Committee at times and they actually pay me."

She lowered her head. "Do you think I'll ever get to work again?"

She used to own a driver's training school, but now that she lived off blood and had to stay away from the sun, she couldn't risk keeping the business. Not while she was still learning how to be a vampire. Maybe in a few decades she could chance it, provided she hired mortals to do the work during the day, but now? She just wasn't ready.

"If you want to work, you can. Just gotta find a job that fits your needs and talent. Maybe we can look together. I figure I need a better paying job if I hope to snag a Perfect Mate. Be respectable and all that."

"There's nothing wrong with you, Perry. I'm sorry the woman up north wasn't for you, though."

"Ah, no worries. She wasn't my type anyway." But if not for Janie, he would still be walking around in the wrong wardrobe. She'd mentioned that what he'd been wearing didn't suit his personality, and for that he was grateful to have met her.

Suzie-Q grabbed his arm. "Is it true? Barnet's gone missing?"

"Missing? Where'd you hear that?" Perry played it cool. Vic had given him strict instructions not to say anything to anyone. Not even Suzie.

"I overheard Ben and Victoria talking. I thought maybe you knew."

Of all the ding-dong days! Those two were bonded. They didn't need to speak out loud to talk to each other. And what was Vic telling Teach anyway? He wasn't part of the Committee.

"Overheard them talking, huh?" Perry offered his elbow. "Why don't we go find your brother and see what's up?"

"He's with Richard Daugherty. Told me to stay away."

"Did he now?" Perry had escorted the male Perfect Mate to Headquarters. An unbonded Perfect Mate at that. Why wouldn't Teach want his sister to meet one? Maybe once she got a whiff of one, she'd understand what all the fuss was about. She hadn't taken his elbow, so Perry lowered his arm. "Do you want to meet Ricky-boy? I mean, Daugherty?"

She shrugged. "I don't know. Should I? I've heard stories of how some vampires go a little crazy around them."

Suzie hadn't heard wrong. Perfect Mates in the process of being bonded could make their vampire mates irrational whenever another vampire so much as looked at their Perfect Mate. And then there was Tucker. He was in the slammer because he'd been sure he could bond with Ricky-boy, regardless of how the Perfect Mate felt. Only five Perfect Mates have been found so far, but the Committee had learned so much from each one.

"If you approach one prepared, you won't have a problem."

"Then what's your excuse?"

"You saying I'm crazy?"

She placed her hands on her hips and raised one shapely eyebrow. "What do you think?"

"I haven't laid claim to any Perfect Mate yet, so no, I'm not crazy. I'm merely obsessed with finding one. Big difference. If you approach Ricky-boy knowing his scent will be intriguing and touching him will set off some warm tingles, or even give you a lady boner, you'll be okay. Aroused, but okay. Hell, maybe he's yours. Won't know unless you see."

"But Ben said—"

"I thought you were the older sibling." It was probably the wrong thing to say, but Suzie needed to grow a backbone if she were to survive in the world as a vampire. She'd done nothing but cling to people at Headquarters.

"What does that have to do—"

"And you're a vampire. Way stronger than him. He can't stop you. Not unless you want him to."

"I don't want to hurt Ben."

"Who said anyone was getting hurt? Come on." Perry offered his arm again, and again she didn't take it.

"How old is Richard Daugherty?"

Perry shrugged. "Mid-twenties? Maybe? Why?"

"He'll think I'm too old."

Sure, she'd been turned at 40, and the grey she'd apparently covered up when she was mortal was now showing, but she still had a killer body.

"Honey, you're closer to his age than any other vampire. And if it turns out he's your Perfect Mate, he'll probably keep aging until he catches up."

"Right. Like he would enjoy that. Doesn't seem fair that Ben gets younger looking every day and I'm stuck at…this."

Yeah, he'd made the mistake of telling Teach that he now looked more like his sister's son than younger brother, and boy did Vic chew him out for that. And for good reason, as Suzie had overheard him. Not one of his finest moments. "Because Teach is a Perfect Mate bonded to a teenaged-looking vampire and you *are* a vampire. Don't you think Vic wishes it were in reverse, too? That she would have matched his age? You know we don't write the rules, don't you?"

"I wish I'd never been turned."

"And if I could turn you back, I would. Don't let being a vampire stop you from experiencing life. And don't let this opportunity slip by. There aren't that many unattached female vampires. I promise you, they'd all jump at the chance at meeting an unbonded Perfect Mate."

She still wasn't budging. Maybe it was time to play the "B" card.

"If you can't do it for yourself, do it for Barnet."

She lifted her head. Her eyes wide like saucers. Her mouth in a frown. "He'd want me to do this?"

Well whaddya know. No wonder she wasn't mad at him. She was hung up on Barnet. "Suzie-Q… Does he know?" Which was probably the stupidest question ever. Barnet was oblivious to things right in front of his face, especially when it came to women.

"Does who know what?"

He bumped her with his shoulder. "Don't play dumb with me. Does Barnet know you like him?"

She lowered her head. "Doesn't matter. He's like you. Looking for that Perfect Mate. Which you already said I wasn't." She straightened and took a deep breath. "Fine. Let's go. I'll meet him."

"That's my girl." Perry offered his arm once again, but she took off down the hall. By the time he caught up with her, she was opening the door to the library.

Teach and Ricky-boy were sitting at one of the tables. Teach looked up. "What are you doing here? I told you to stay away."

Ricky-boy turned around. "Oh wow. Your mother is a vampire?"

Perry facepalmed. Maybe he should have sent a warning first.

t

Mandy Groves pulled into the parking garage of the Committee Headquarters with minutes to spare. She leaned back and reveled in the adrenaline rush. Next time maybe she'd cut it closer. Beating the sun was about the only way she'd get her heart racing nowadays. Kind of hard to fear that which couldn't kill her.

Although her heart rate *had* jackrabbited when she'd gotten that message from Victoria Braeden. No, scratch that. Victoria Martin. She'd gotten married last year.

Mandy was supposed to have gotten married once. Thank God she'd discovered his true nature before she said "I do." Might have been better if she'd discovered that little fact before he'd turned her into a vampire, though.

Yeah, one of many mistakes of the past. And ones she'd been living with for centuries. Hell, she wouldn't even be here—in the States—if it weren't for Victoria's message. A person just didn't go where they weren't wanted, now did they?

She climbed out of the car—still feeling weird sitting on the wrong side—grabbed her purse, and straightened her skirt. She opened the boot. *Take the bags or leave them?* She'd packed a week's worth of clothes, but if this was all a misunderstanding, why bother taking them? She closed the boot, leaving the bags inside.

Her heels clip-clopped on the cement floor of the practically empty garage—just her car and another van. No need to be quiet when her visit was expected. And she loved the way her shoes echoed in the enclosed space. One good thing about being a vampire: her feet didn't get tired from wearing four-inch heels. And she did love the heels. The higher, the better. Being five-foot five wasn't all that intimidating. Five-foot nine, or ten, made a hell of a difference.

She punched in the code she was given. One click and green light later, she opened the door. Stairs led down, not up, to Headquarters. Then again, it wouldn't be called the Underground if it were above ground, now would it? No lift here. Didn't really need one. No vampire would tire climbing stairs. But she wasn't going to use the stairs. Not when there was a perfectly good handrail.

Planting her bum on the rail, she slid to the next floor. No big rush, but fun all the same. Once she wrapped up everything here, maybe she'd check out an amusement park before heading back to London. Provided they were open after the sun set.

She liked adrenaline, but she wasn't stupid.

Mandy opened the door to a vacant reception area. Sign on the wall said Vantage Accounting Management and Personnel Services. Their Headquarters acronym was VAMPS? She broke out laughing. She'd have to shake the hand of the vampire who came up with that. And apparently had talked the Committee into it. Brilliant.

The Atlanta Underground could be seen from the big windows in the reception area. "Be still my heart."

She should have done more research. And maybe brought more suitcases. The Underground was one big shopping center. She'd have to check out the shoes and other lovelies.

"Amanda?"

She spun around. The door on the other side of the room stood open and a petite blonde, wearing a pink business suit with practical, low-heeled pumps, smiled at her. "Yes. But I prefer Mandy."

"I'm Victoria. Won't you come in?"

Victoria, huh? Not Vicky? For a teenage-looking vampire she was all seriousness, as was her wardrobe—with the exception of the pink. Then again, maybe she had to appear serious to be taken seriously. Men could be such pigs.

Mandy followed the sprite, feeling like a giant beside her. Maybe the heels weren't a good idea. "Is the business real or fake? And can people see inside those windows?"

"The windows are reflective on the other side, but the business is real. We even had a manager—they don't like to be called receptionists—but she just quit. Happened at the worst time, too. But we'll manage somehow. The mortals don't ever stay that long anyway and vampires just don't want to work here."

"You had a mortal working here? At Headquarters?"

"Well, they worked out there. In the reception area. But yes, we hire mortals as well as vampires. Most of the jobs require mortals and we really don't care who manages the clients. Just that they get managed." Victoria stopped at a door with a keypad on the wall beside it. "The code is vampire."

"Well, that's easy."

"It's not like we'd forget it anyway. Right?" She entered the code. The door led to another set of stairs going down.

Mandy had studied the layout of their Headquarters. All underground under the Underground. The mortals none the wiser. Brilliant.

Victoria opened a door marked LL1. Indicated they go to the right. "You really didn't need to make the trip out here. Like I told you on the phone, we don't have any information."

That was the problem. The lack of information and being so far away. "I understand. But sitting idle is just not my thing. I prefer to be where the action is."

"I don't mean to sound rude, but until yesterday, none of us knew you even existed."

Mandy didn't know whether to feel hurt or surprised. Maybe a little of the former and none of the latter. "So how did you find out about me if he's not here to tell you?"

"He had instructions to be read upon his disappearance."

Interesting. So not a loose end. Then what was she? "He thought I should know he disappeared? Wow. I was pretty sure he hated me."

A woman appeared from another hallway, running toward Mandy as if her life were in danger. A man chased her and yelled, "Suzie-Q. Wait up."

The so-called Suzie-Q skidded to a stop when she saw Mandy and Victoria.

"Susannah. Is everything all right?" Victoria asked.

Suzie-Q, or Susannah, shook her head. She wiped her eyes as if something had leaked from them. Vampires couldn't cry, so it was probably a reflex.

Ahhh, newbie vamp. It'd been awhile since Mandy had met one. That scared look would eventually go away. Once the newbie realized how un-scary the world was when it couldn't hurt her anymore.

Victoria glared at the handsome man. "Perry, what'd you do to her?"

Mandy stifled a chuckle. Was Perry a bad boy? Hmmm… He might be kind of fun. Except he called Susannah by a nickname. Only the attached did that, right? Yeah. Too bad.

He raised his arms and rolled his eyes. "Why does everyone automatically blame me? I went to introduce her to Ricky-boy—"

"You did what?"

"And nothing happened. She ran off when he thought she was Teach's mother." He then turned those gorgeous green eyes Mandy's way and smiled. "Well hello there. Who are you?"

About time Mandy had caught his eye, even if he was involved with someone else.

Victoria answered. "This is Mandy Groves."

Perry scrunched his forehead. It was very cute. Hell, he was cute. All long and lean with one sexy ponytail. Mandy especially loved his beach shirt.

"Groves? As in Barnet?"

Astute, too. Nice to know he hadn't changed his last name. Maybe he wasn't ashamed of her after all.

Susannah lifted her head at that, her eyes wide. "Are you his…wife?"

"Wife? Oh hell, no," Mandy said. "I'm his bloody daughter."

* * * *

"Barnet has a daughter?" Perry wasn't proud that those were the first words he uttered to the most beautiful woman he'd ever laid eyes on. And she was a Brit. God, he loved her accent.

Mandy's electrifying blue eyes brightened. "I know! Shocking, huh?"

Would it be bad manners to plant a kiss on those luscious lips of hers? He sure loved the words coming out of her mouth. But getting involved with her would be the worst of all bad ideas. Not because she was Barnet's daughter—although that was pretty bad, and weird—but because she was a vampire. His eyes might be happy with the scenery, but the rest of him rejected her. One touch and he'd hear everything he didn't want to. Been there. Done that. Too many times.

"So it's true?" Suzie-Q asked. "Barnet's missing?"

Vic glared at him. "You told her?"

Again with the accusations. Would he never get a break? "I did no such thing. She overheard you and Teach talking. You know, if you want something kept a secret, maybe you shouldn't blab out loud with a person you could talk to telepathically. If you get my drift."

At least she had the audacity to lower her head in embarrassment. "You're right. I'm sorry." She placed her hand onto Suzie's shoulder. "Yes, he's gone missing, but we don't want to alarm the vampire public. Please, don't spread this news."

"Like I have anyone to tell." Suzie-Q lowered her head and walked away. He should probably follow, as much as he'd like to stick around with Beautiful here, but when he took two steps Suzie's way, she stopped. "I want to be alone, Perry."

Decision made, he let her walk off alone.

"How old is she?" Mandy asked.

He knew she didn't mean Earth years. Not when it came to vampires. "Seven months."

"Seven months? She doesn't seem happy. Why'd you turn her?"

Vic giggled. Perry fumed. Was Vic rubbing off on Mandy already, or was he destined to be accused by every female on the planet? "I didn't. She was turned by a psychopath when she didn't even know vampires existed."

"She's my sister-in-law," Vic said. "We were hoping being near her brother would help motivate her, but it doesn't seem to be working."

"Because you're all babying her," Perry said.

"Maybe now wasn't a good time to dump her."

"I didn't dump her. We went on one date. One. Date. I can't help it if I'm not into her." And he really thought she'd be different. But no, once she'd turned into a vampire, the desire just poofed away. "If anyone can help her, it's Barnet."

Beautiful's eyebrows raised. "My father? Why is that?"

"Because she's hung up on him."

"Does he feel the same?"

"I have no idea." Did anyone ever know what the big guy thought? He had a daughter no one knew about. Talk about keeping secrets. That man was a rock. Perry turned to Vic. "So what's the plan? I can't imagine you wanted to chit chat in the hallway." Although, he could chit chat with Beautiful all day long. Her voice was totally alluring.

"You'll find out. Follow me."

Vic led them to the major conference room. Four monitors hung from one wall. Three tables were situated in a U-shape with the monitors at the open end and Barnet's seat opposite. The few times Perry had been in the room, one or two members were displayed on the monitors. But today all were dark as the other three Committee members—Hilde, Jack, and Abe—were physically seated at one side of the table, side by side by side. Guess important news couldn't be left to the airways. Or would that be fiber optic cable?

Perry nodded at the three. Were they just as surprised as he was for becoming the tie-breaking vote? He'd been in Detroit helping Sam and Janie when Vic had told him. And then went and told him to keep it a secret. Man, that was tough. Him and secrets just didn't always mesh. Well, except his own. But that was different.

Jack and Abe stood as the newcomer entered the room.

Vic took over the introductions. "Mandy, this is Jack VanAllen, Abe Ross, and Hilde Meyer. They are the other members of the Committee. This is Mandy Groves. Barnet's daughter."

Abe's eyebrows raised, making him seem taller than his six-six height. "Barnet has a daughter?"

"I know, right?" Perry winked at Beautiful. At least he wasn't the only one in the dark. And it felt kind of good to mimic her.

"I told you to read the memo." Vic shook her head and pointed to Barnet's chair. "Please, have a seat."

Beautiful glanced at the chair and looked around. Took the seat beside Victoria.

Well, if she wasn't going to sit there… Perry planted his butt in Barnet's chair. Ooh. It swiveled? Sweet. How hadn't he noticed before?

"Really?" Vic said. "You're going to sit there?"

"No one else is." And it also gave him a good view of Beautiful. Oh sure, he could have sat beside her—the spot was open—but then he'd be obvious when he stared. And he was definitely going to stare—even if she was a vampire—because his eyes enjoyed the scenery.

But why'd she have to be a vampire?

Abe sat. "Did the paperwork state how Barnet became a father?"

Beautiful laughed. "Well, I would assume he made love to my mother."

Perry slapped his knee and cackled. "That's a good one." When the four Committee Members glared at him, he stopped laughing. "Well it was."

But Beautiful hadn't glared at him. Oh no. She beamed. Hmmm… No. Bad idea. Bad idea.

"Obviously, he fathered you before being turned," Jack said. "But his letter didn't mention how you were turned. Did he turn you?"

"No. Quite the opposite. I turned him."

Oh, Great One. The sired was the sire. And not a breath could be heard. Until now, Perry had thought he was the King of Speechlessness with the Committee. Seemed he'd been dethroned.

Chapter 2

Perry twisted in his chair and nearly burst out laughing. He'd never seen the Committee look so shocked before. Even Abe's mouth hung open.

Perry had always wondered who had turned Barnet. He'd always been tight-lipped about that. And to find out his own daughter did the turning? Was he ashamed or just mad? It had to be one of those for him to never mention a daughter. And what happened with his wife—Mandy's mother? So much Perry wanted to know. Hell, the whole Committee probably wanted the same thing.

Mandy leaned her elbows on the solid oak table. "I understand you have questions about me. But that's not why I'm here, is it? What have you found out about my father? And what are you doing about it?"

More questions Perry would like the answers to, too. Barnet was like a second father to him. Actually third. Would that make Beautiful his sister? Ewwww. Why'd he go there? Just because he had no intentions toward Mandy didn't mean he'd stop dreaming about her. Because then he could pretend she was a Perfect Mate and resistant to vampires.

Hilde said, "Ever since we discovered the first Perfect Mate, Barnet has been obsessed with finding the origin. So we've been quietly searching for Alexi Popolov."

"The author of the Perfect Mate story? So, you've actually found one? A Perfect Mate?"

"We've found five," Victoria said. "I'm married to one. In fact, there's an unbonded male here now. In case you want to see him."

Perry stopped twisting the chair. "Hey, what gives! You were mad I was going to introduce Suzie-Q to him."

"You don't think Mr. Daugherty would be interested in Mandy?"

"I don't know who Ricky-boy would be interested in. That's not the point."

"Excuse me, but I'm not looking for a suitor," Beautiful said. "But you found five? Do the other Committees know about this?"

"Barnet has been slowly addressing the issue with them, but hasn't reached them all. Wanted to do it one-on-one. But then he heard about Popolov. Seems he's been buried alive."

Mandy leaned back in her chair. "Dimitri."

Perry straightened. "Dimitri? Dimitri who?" It couldn't be the same guy. Could it?

"Dimitri Kalashnikov, Head of the Russian Committee," Hilde said.

Perry breathed easier. Okay, so not Dimitri Rodchenko. Whew. That would have been awwwwkward. Well, only awkward if Perry had intentions of going to Russia, which he did not.

"We don't know why or if the rest of the Russian Committee is aware," Hilde continued, "but they claim Alexi failed to show at his scheduled meeting, nearly five years ago. That's when they put out a notice. When he failed to show at the next meeting, they deemed him dead or rogue. Basically what any Committee would do. But Barnet was determined to find Alexi, so we sent out some inquiries to people who knew Alexi. One such acquaintance witnessed Dimitri stake Alexi and put him in a coffin, later burying him. Five years ago. She hasn't said anything for fear the same would happen to her. And she hasn't tried to rescue him because his grave is under surveillance. She's afraid and frankly, I don't blame her."

Perry didn't blame her, either. Being buried alive was no joke. But how common was the name Dimitri? Or was it just a coincidence that his Dimitri and this Russian Head Dimitri both liked to bury their subjects? Maybe it was a Russian thing.

Hilde continued, "That didn't stop Barnet from calling Dimitri several times this past week. But Dimitri never took his calls. Instead, we believe he kidnapped Barnet."

Perry kept twisting the chair when everything inside him wanted to stand up and scream. Kidnapped! Holy hell. That was way worse than being missing. He'd do anything to help Barnet. He owed the man his life.

Mandy leaned forward. "Kidnapped? Over a man who might possibly be the author of a story we all believe to be a myth? That makes no sense."

Hilde nodded. "It makes no sense, but these are the facts. Three days ago, two of Dimitri's men flew out of Moscow on a private jet. They arrived in Atlanta. Unannounced. That right there is in violation of our treaties. Barnet drove to Dayton, spent the day there and the next night continued to the Cleveland safe house to meet an unbonded Perfect Mate. The jet then traveled from Atlanta to Cleveland. Barnet was supposed to drive back to Dayton after the meet. He never showed. We found his rental at a rest stop and that Russian jet returned to Moscow the same night."

Victoria turned toward Mandy. "We were hoping to hear something from Barnet or Dimitri, that maybe Dimitri finally scheduled a meeting without our knowledge. Then we heard from our contact. Barnet is in Russia. Being held in what she calls *podzemel'ye*. Roughly, it means dungeon."

"How did they find him?" Mandy asked. "It almost sounds like they have a mole here."

"It does, except very few people knew of his trip. The Committee, John and Sarah Pennington in Dayton, and the four people in Cleveland, including Perry."

Perry stopped twisting when his name was mentioned. "I can vouch for them. There's no way they're involved."

"I agree. I can only assume the Russians tracked his phone." Vic lowered her head. "I finally convinced Barnet into upgrading to a smart phone. He was sure they weren't safe. That they would be the demise of all vampires. He wasn't totally wrong, there. Just not in the way he thought."

Jack jumped to his feet and paced the room, smacking a fist into his hand. "Dimitri has to know this is an act of war. You just don't grab a Committee Head without consequences."

"And if we went to war," Abe said, watching Jack, "how do you think that would turn out? Dimitri knows exactly what he's doing and he knows we won't risk exposure."

Jack flopped back into his chair. Perry stared at the two members. Were meetings like this all the time? Jack would lose his cool and Abe would calm him down? Or did Barnet keep things under control all the time?

"So what's the plan?" Mandy asked.

"That's what this meeting is about." Vic turned toward Perry. "We need to send someone over there to bring him home."

"I'll do it." Anything to help Barnet. So what if he had to go to Russia. It was a big country, right? The odds of running into Dimitri Rodchenko had to be nil. The man came from St. Petersburg, not Moscow. And the Russian Headquarters was in Moscow.

"I'm not asking you to go. I'm asking for a recommendation. You know the vampires better than we do."

That remark stung, but Perry resisted rubbing his heart. "What's wrong with me?"

"We were thinking of sending someone who can distract Dimitri while our contact helps him escape. According to our contact, the man never leaves Headquarters and he monitors them all the time."

Sounded like an upstanding Committee Head—not. "And you don't think I can distract him? He speaks English, doesn't he?"

Hilde placed her hand on his arm. "He does but you have to admit, you can be very frustrating. We don't want to anger the man."

Yeah, to his friends. Not an enemy. That's what Dimitri was, right? An enemy.

"And," Vic continued, "we're using Oscar and his jet."

"Oscar the Grouch?" Perry had only met the vampire twice. A potato had a better sense of humor. But had he heard Beautiful snicker? She was covering her mouth.

Vic pounded the table. "Will you stop calling him that?"

"But he's always grouchy."

"Seriously. Stop."

"I can bring him home." Mandy looked at him. "You don't need to involve Perry. They don't know he's my father and I'm not even an American. I probably have more experience in espionage than Perry does."

Another stinging barb. They'd barely met and she already knew that about him? What else did she know?

"We don't need a spy. Just someone to distract Dimitri."

"I can do that," Perry said. Really, how hard could that be?

"What reason would you have for going over there? We need someone who is not associated with the Committee."

"Like I'm associated with you guys. I'm the lacky. Gopher. Errand boy. Hell, none of you even knew I was designated the tie-breaking vote until now, am I right? I could go over there looking for a new job because you guys banned me here." Hell, he'd ask for a vote now if he thought he'd get at least two of them to agree.

"In a country you don't even know the language?"

"I could learn it. I'm not stupid."

Mandy tapped the table. "How about Perry and I go over there as a couple. Wanting to move to Russia. The Committee Head would have to meet us then, correct? And we'll use aliases so there won't be any connection to the Committee."

"A couple?" Perry could get behind that. Then maybe the Committee would show him some respect and see him as the hero instead of the fuck-up.

Hilde nodded. "That could work. But to make it more believable, you should have several destinations in mind. But I could see it, Victoria. Perry's from the US, Mandy's from Britain. They could be a couple searching for neutral ground. Dimitri is always complaining about losing vampires to other countries. He just might become so focused trying to sell Russia to these two that our contact will be able to help Barnet escape."

"Could you do that, Perry?" Beautiful asked. "Pretend to be my boyfriend?"

"Sure." It wasn't like he'd found his Perfect Mate yet, so it wouldn't be cheating if he was pretending, right? Not that anything would happen. Oh, maybe a little PDA, but nothing more than that.

Because she was a vampire.

But hot damn. Was he actually going to pay back the man who'd saved his life? He never thought this day would come because Barnet never needed saving. He was always the level-headed one. The cautious one. The one vampire who never did a stupid thing in his life, like get buried alive. And now Perry was going to Russia to save him.

To Russia.

Oh Great One, please don't let me run into Dimitri Rodchenko.

* * * *

Barnet landed on the hard ground with a thump. Dust blew around him and he coughed. Wall Man from the rest stop stepped on Barnet's chest and yanked out the stake. Pain ripped through Barnet's heart and he screamed.

Wall Man smiled as he closed the door to the cell he'd dumped Barnet into. Said something in Russian—Barnet only caught Dimitri's name—and turned away, laughing. The laughter died when the door to the dungeon shut. At least Barnet assumed it was a dungeon. Besides the barred cells, it had that earthy, ancient smell. And he wasn't exactly lying on carpet.

The flight to Russia—and he assumed that was where he landed—had been more pleasant than his new quarters. And he'd been stuffed in a trunk.

He couldn't move, not yet, but the shuffling sounds across the walkway told him he wasn't alone down here.

"*Chto ty sdelal?*" The male sounded weak. As if he hadn't fed in weeks.

"I'm sorry. I don't speak Russian." He probably should have learned it. As the Head, wasn't it his duty to know the languages? Instead, he'd become complacent. Mainly because the other Committee Heads knew English.

"What you do to Dimitri? He not usually throw Americans in dungeon."

So the man spoke English. A blessing, but an embarrassment, too. When Barnet got out of this, he would start with learning Russian. "Searched for Alexi Popolov. You?"

"Alexi?" The man's laughter barely reached Barnet's ears. "Well, that is unfortunate. You may be here longer than me. And all I did was make suggestion. Maria, she told me to keep mouth quiet. I should have listened."

"How long have you been in here?"

"What day is it?"

"January sixteen. Or seventeen. I might have lost a day somewhere."

"Is new year already? I missed Christmas. Three months. In dungeon almost three months."

Three months? That didn't sound good. "What kind of suggestion did you make?"

"That if Committee wanted to keep people from defecting, that maybe they relax on some of the rules. Let us travel like mortals. I only wish to take Maria to her homeland. On a trip, not to defect. I miss her."

Would he be stuck here that long? Even Dimitri wouldn't be that stupid. Would he? "What do you know about Alexi?"

"That he is more fool than I."

"How so?"

"Oh, he writes those stories, or he coerces people to write them. Crazy stories about vampires. As if we are monsters. Then taunts Committee when the stories are published."

Barnet had heard those rumors and had thought they were false. "Do you think he wrote the Perfect Mate story?"

"The myth? I suppose is possible. Why do you ask?"

"Because it's not a myth. Perfect Mates are real."

The man laughed. "Okay, now you sound crazy like Alexi. But that could be why—"

The opening of the dungeon door cut off his words. A large man strode inside wearing a three-piece suit. Seemed excessive for a prisoner visit so Barnet could only assume he was Dimitri Kalashnikov, having never met the man before.

He peered inside Barnet's cell and frowned. "You are Barnet Groves?"

"The one and only. Dimitri, I assume?"

He nodded. "But you are old. And short. Who would ever turn a person like you?"

Five-nine wasn't all that short and he certainly wasn't considered short when he was mortal. As for who had turned him, that wasn't up for discussion. "Is that why you brought me here? To question me about my sire?"

"Maybe some other time. Have you not healed already?"

Barnet could only move his hands and twist his head. He hadn't fed since before his meeting with the Perfect Mate in Cleveland. "You caught me a little low on blood."

"Ahh, that is too bad. I might be able to remedy that." He turned toward the other prisoner. "*Kto ty?*"

"*Mikhail, ser.*" Mikhail continued speaking in Russian. Either it was easier, or he was protecting Barnet. Dimitri would not have taken kindly to having his disciplinary actions known.

Dimitri nodded to someone at the door. Wall Man. He inserted a key in Mikhail's cell and opened it.

Mikhail bowed. *"Spasibo, Dimitri. Spasibo."* Hunched over, he hurried out of the dungeon.

Seemed as if Barnet had been the prisoner's ticket out of here. Good for Mikhail. Not so good for Barnet.

"We need to talk." Dimitri turned toward Wall Man. *"Vy mozhete idti seychas."*

Wall Man nodded and left. Closed the door behind him.

"You couldn't do this over the phone? Or even video conferencing? I left you ten messages."

"There are ears on phone line. On Internet. No ears here."

Barnet couldn't refute that fact. Hadn't he told Victoria how much he distrusted smart phones? He hated having his point proven in this instance, though. But if what Dimitri said was true, at least Barnet's conversation with Mikhail had been private. "You could have also sent me an invitation. Staking me was uncalled for."

"But did it not get your attention? We have serious problem and you are not helping."

"Are you talking about Perfect Mates?"

"You need to stop calling them that." Dimitri rubbed a hand down his face. "I want to know what you know about Popolov."

And get his contact in trouble? Barnet couldn't risk that. "Not much. Just that it's likely he wrote the Perfect Mate story. And that he's been a pain in your ass."

"He is difficult one, yes. But story is not true."

"The characters may not be true, but the actions they experience are. I know this as a fact. I've met one. Touched her."

"You touched a freak. And is a miracle you survived. They cannot be trusted."

"That's not true. Victoria is married to one. They're bonded. He'd do anything to protect her."

"Yes. While she lives. But when she dies?" Dimitri shook his head.

Barnet couldn't believe what he was hearing. Dimitri knew more than he'd let on. "What would happen if she dies first?"

"Armageddon."

Chapter 3

Would today be the day she finally, after all these centuries, confronted her father? Or would that be tomorrow, with the time changes and all? And was she making a huge mistake coming on this mission? Mandy slowly boarded the small jet. Turned out she wasn't in such a hurry to find out. She couldn't imagine her father would be happy to see her, but it was what it was. She wanted—no, needed—to see him. It was time. Long past time.

Not a window in sight in the small jet's seating area. Perfect. Then again, a vampire owned the plane, it only made sense. She took a seat in the first row and placed her backpack and coat in the seat beside her. Slipped off her shoes and stretched her legs.

Perry boarded and whistled in awe. "How'd you come about owning one of these, Gr—Oscar?"

She could see why Perry deemed the man "Oscar the Grouch." Not because his hair was shaggy like the Muppet—a person could see their reflection in his bald dome—but he had yet to smile. At anyone. Even her. The audacity!

Oscar folded his arms across his chest. "I didn't steal it."

Perry tossed his backpack and a leather jacket on a seat. "I figured that. But what kind of job do you do to pay for one of these things? I can't imagine the Committee charters this out regularly."

"I'm a CPA."

"What's that?"

Mandy laughed. "Certified Public Accountant. It pays that well?"

"During tax season, it does. I have a lot of happy clients."

"What do you do?" Perry asked. "Fudge the records so they get money back?"

Oscar placed his hands on his hips. "Are you for real?"

"Hey, I don't know how it works."

"I can't believe I have to do this with you. Now take your seat and buckle up."

Yeah, Oscar the Grouch was a suitable nickname. Although, it was highly possible Oscar was only grouchy around Perry.

"Wait a minute." Perry strutted to the back of the plane as if he knew she was looking at his bum. And what a fine bum it was. "Got any weapons on board?"

"I have a taser. In the cockpit."

He swung around, eyebrows raised. "That's it?"

"Why would I need more than that?"

"I don't know. We're on a mission here. Figured you'd be more prepared." Perry opened the door to a compartment. "You have one taser but three snow shovels?"

"It's winter. Of course I have snow shovels. Now shut that cabinet, sit your ass down, and buckle up." Oscar grumbled a mumble as he headed to the cockpit.

Perry bowed. "Yes, your highness." He shut the door and sat across the aisle from her. "Bossy, isn't he?"

"He just wants you safe for takeoff." Which seemed the nicest thing she could say. She couldn't imagine Oscar cared if Perry were safe or not.

"Oh no he doesn't. He just doesn't want me bouncing around and damaging stuff." He secured his seatbelt. "So what'd you do all day? Did you check out Ricky-boy? The Perfect Mate?"

Actually, she'd gone shopping with Victoria. In addition to all the clothes she'd bought, she gotten another suitcase to take them back home in. The Underground was a wonderful place. "Do you have a nickname for everyone?"

"No. Just most people."

"I get 'Ricky-boy,' 'Vic,' and 'Suzie-Q.' Why 'Teach'?"

"He was Vic's driver's ed teacher."

"Victoria had to go to school to drive?"

"Well, no. Barnet made her. Long story."

"No nickname for him?"

"I usually call him 'Boss,' but only after he became Head of the Committee. Before that, I called him Barney once. That didn't go well."

She laughed. No, she couldn't imagine it had. Her father never was the nickname type. Never called her Mandy. It was always Amanda. "What'd he do?"

"He didn't do anything. The rest of the Committee put me in the slammer for about a month."

"For calling him Barney?"

"For disrespecting the Committee. Granted, this was back in 1799. Barnet had just become a member and they were a bit stricter. Accommodations nasty, too. Nothing like what they have going on now. But I wasn't going to risk it again. Especially since Jack became a member. He can be kind of mean."

Jack had seemed a little hot-headed during the meeting. But had her father actually mellowed out? The man she remembered had a bit of a temper. Blimey, he'd been mad at her for over five hundred years.

"You don't have a nickname for Jack?"

"Nope. Like I said. Mean."

"So if the person isn't mean, you give them a nickname? Oscar doesn't seem all that friendly, yet you gave him one. Why?"

"See, now, he can't put me in the slammer. And frustrating people is fun. Else, why do it?"

She couldn't argue with that. She did a lot of things for fun.

"So, did you? See Ricky-boy?"

"No." She had no desire to lose control over a mortal. Or anyone for that matter. That wasn't why she was on this mission.

"How come? He might have been yours."

"I'm not looking for a suitor."

"You say that now, but if you had met him…"

"You believe that myth. That Perfect Mates exist." She'd heard various versions of the story, but they all ended the same: happily ever after. Which told her right there it couldn't be true. There were no happy ever afters. For anyone.

"I know they exist. I've met the two females. Unfortunately, they'd met another vampire before they met me."

"And that matters?"

He shrugged. "Maybe. Maybe not. But that seems to be my case anyways. Day late, dollar short, you know?"

"And you want one of these Perfect Mates?"

"Of course. Shouldn't every vampire? I mean…they're perfect!"

Perfection was also a myth. Although Perry seemed rather perfect. The perfect hair. Perfect body. Perfect attitude. She just hadn't found his flaw yet. "Too bad you're looking for a Perfect Mate. I thought we might have some fun on this trip."

"Who said we can't have fun? I haven't found her yet. Could be decades. Hell, she might not even be born yet." He frowned at that.

Mandy contained the laugh that threatened to escape. He wouldn't be able to tell if a child was his Perfect Mate or not, since vampires couldn't control children. "You're not too worried she'll be old?"

He shook his head. "Have you seen Teach?"

"Yes. Why?" Ben Martin was cute. A little young for her, but cute. Victoria had found the perfect match.

"Would you believe he turned forty this year?"

The man looked barely old enough to drink if the legal age was still 21. "Forty?"

"Yep. He was blind and had grey in his hair when Vic met him. They bonded. He got his sight back, the grey disappeared, and, well, you saw him. Young. Like her. So, no. I'm not worried she's old. I'm just worried I won't find her."

"You don't strike me as the sort who wants to settle down."

"Settle down? Who said anything about settling? My Perfect Mate won't want that. That's why she'd be perfect."

Ahhh, but was anyone really perfect for someone else? Although, her father would probably say that her mother had been perfect for him. "Does my father feel the same as you? Is he looking for his Perfect Mate, too?"

"I don't know. I've known the guy for centuries and didn't know about you. Why is that? Why hasn't he ever mentioned you?"

She could give him a list, but why ruin a nice trip. "You'd have to ask him."

* * * *

Nine hours on a plane with a beautiful woman and all Perry did was watch movies. This would have been the perfect opportunity to experiment. But if touching led to kissing and kissing led to more fun, intimate aerobics, it'd be nice if there was a bed in the back. What kind of jet didn't have a bed in the back? Groucho's kind, that's what.

Even if there was a bed in the back, Groucho would have put a stop to anyone using it. The chairs were comfortable—reclined, even—but Groucho left the cockpit every now and then to check on them. Or rather, check on Perry. Like he couldn't be trusted or something.

So no hanky-panky experiments on this flight. Figured. He'd never done it with another vampire before. Never really cared to, until now. But he got the impression Beautiful was fine with making this couple-thing look real. And what couple wouldn't join the Mile High Club if given the opportunity? But he wasn't an exhibitionist and didn't wish to start now.

Once the plane landed and shut down, Groucho joined them in the seating area. "We'll be safe here until it's time to leave. In about nine hours."

Perry had always wanted to see London. "No time for any sight-seeing?"

"Sight-seeing? Our Head is missing and you want to sight-see?"

"Okay, okay, don't get all huffy. How long does it take to fly to Moscow?"

"About four hours."

"So we'll have time to feed, right? Maybe buy a souvenir?"

"You want to feed, feed. There are mortals out there. I suggest you hurry, the sun rises in thirty minutes." He headed for the desk area in the back and pulled out a laptop. He had a desk, but not a bed? The guy's priorities were all screwed up.

An accountant. The guy was an accountant and could afford this plane? Perry could never swing a job like that. It just sounded…boring.

"Are we in the Committee hangar?" Mandy asked.

"That we are. It's why we're safe here."

She nudged Perry. "Come on." She stood and turned toward Groucho. "We're going to take a little walk."

He waved them on. Or was that away?

Perry followed Beautiful down the stairs. Mmmm, mmmm, mmmm. Her skirt hugged her butt juuuuuust right. Wonder what she had in mind? "I can't imagine there's much to do here."

"Who says we're staying here? He said we have thirty minutes. I can make it to the terminal and back in less time than that, can't you?"

Thirty minutes to dash, feed, and maybe buy a souvenir before dashing back? Sounded doable. "Lead the way."

She headed for a door off to the side. An office. She waved him inside. Grabbed a grey coverall off the wall and tossed it to him. "Here, put this on."

As he stepped into a pant leg, she grabbed another and did the same. "What's this for?"

Her skirt was going up, up, up. Before he got a peek at heaven, or her panties covering heaven, she turned. "So we can walk out there without being noticed. No offense, but that beach shirt just screams unofficial."

Hmpf. The woman had no sense at all. "It's not a beach shirt. It's an Hawaiian shirt."

"There's a difference?" She stuck her arms in the sleeves and zipped up.

He looked down at his shirt as he zipped the coverall closed. "Of course there's a difference." He wasn't sure what, but it sure sounded better than beach shirt.

"My apologies. Then Hawaiian shirt, it is. Still won't work around here if you want to blend in." She grabbed two lanyards. Tossed one to him. "Now we look official. Ready to have some fun?"

He put the lanyard around his neck. "How'd you know these were here?"

"This is my home. I know where the UK Committee keeps all the neat stuff."

Shit. He worked for the US Committee and didn't know where any of the neat stuff was. If they even had neat stuff.

"What about your shoes?" While the four-inch heels looked sexy as sin, he was pretty sure they didn't go with the outfit.

"Oh, bollocks." She slipped them off and padded over to a drawer.

Damn, but she was a petite thing. He could easily pop his vampire cherry on her. Now, if she were mortal, Perry would do her against the wall then over the desk. Oh yeah. But she wasn't and yet, his dick didn't seem to mind at all. In fact, it was getting kind of hard. Good thing the coveralls were on the baggy side.

Maybe she'd be willing to experiment. He could ask after they returned. This office would definitely be private and out of Groucho's view.

She put on some work boots. "They're a little large, but they'll have to do."

The terminal was farther away than Perry had anticipated. And pink tinged the eastern horizon. He'd been caught in the sun before and would prefer not to experience that again. "You sure we have time?"

"I thought you'd be fun, but if you'd rather stay here, stay. I'm going." She took off toward the terminal.

Well, hell. He was fun. No one had ever said he wasn't fun. He took off after her. She smiled when he caught up.

* * * *

It had been decades since Mandy had let loose with another vampire. Even longer with one who was willing to risk a little sunlight. Not that she planned on getting burned. Feeding was bad enough for her without having to risk that kind of exposure. Still…Perry followed and she liked it.

She led him to the lower portion of the terminal. Workers were busy loading and unloading luggage and paid no mind to them. She turned to the right, toward the stairwell, where they climbed to a closed door.

"Our cards will get us back in here through this door, but try not to use it more than that one time. If you use it too many times, it'll look suspicious and they could deactivate them and then I'd have to explain to the UK Committee what we'd done."

He looked at his card and laughed. "Right. Because I definitely look like old Basil here—not."

"Oh, and I look like Roderick?" She held the ID inches from his face.

"Well, maybe with a little more makeup." He chuckled. "What's the plan?"

She rubbed her hands together. "I don't know about you, but I'm famished. Think I'll find me some hunky footballer. The athletes always taste best. Meet you at the restrooms by this door? And then we can go find you that souvenir."

"You don't want to feed together?"

Oh hell no. "Feeding time is private time. Sorry."

"What are you afraid of? That I'll get horny watching you feed? Because—news flash! I'm already horny. Kinda hoping you'd be interested in a little fun back in that office when we return."

Oh my. That would have been fun, except he was taken and she never poached on another woman's man. "You plan on being unfaithful to your Perfect Mate?"

He stepped into her personal space. "Beautiful, kind of hard to be faithful to someone I haven't met yet. I thought we went over this on the plane."

She loved the nickname he'd given her and his musky vanilla scent was definitely yummy. But even she had her limits. "I'll not be some kind of placeholder for you. And when you do finally meet her, and I'm still around, I won't be that woman from the past. I can't be that woman. So I'm sorry. To me, you're taken. Now, if you want to get that souvenir, you better hurry."

She turned from the sad expression on his face and opened the door to the terminal. Still early in that fewer people milled about the restrooms, waiting on their companions. There really wasn't time to find that hunky footballer and a private place, so she'd settle for private.

She walked into the ladies room. The last two stalls were unoccupied. She entered one. Ugh. Some kid must have been in here. Toilet paper was strewn all over the seat and floor and the smell was anything but clean. Just her luck to find the messy stall. She'd wash up once she could leave. She locked the door and carefully crawled into the other stall, leaving that door open. Crouched on the toilet seat and waited.

The woman who entered wore way too much perfume. Mandy almost sent her away, but time wasn't her friend, so she held her breath as she manipulated the woman to lock and face the door. Mandy sank her fangs into the soft flesh of the neck.

Feeding was always an unpleasant experience, but today was doubly so. The perfume had permeated the blood making for one distasteful feed. Or maybe it was remembering the sad look on Perry's face that made this so much worse.

Not that she was looking for anything permanent. She wasn't. And how could a woman he hadn't even met yet expect him—one sexy man—to remain celibate? Hell, they were supposed to be a loving couple. They probably should start acting like one. And that office back in the hangar would be ideal to start practicing.

Practice made perfect, didn't it?

After getting her fill, she licked the site on a shudder—it really was nasty blood—and healed her fang marks. Now the fun began. She crawled back to the other stall and released the woman.

She placed her hands on the outer walls of the stall, lowered her head, and waited. If she wasn't careful, she'd leave indentations behind, but sometimes that couldn't be helped. Thankfully her stomach hadn't cramped before this feed, so maybe her body wouldn't go into full seize mode.

"Bloody hell," she muttered under her breath. Fire-like pain shot through her limbs as the fresh blood pumped through her heart. She gritted her teeth. Red splotches formed on her hands as if she were burning from the inside out. The coveralls covered most of her body, but what was happening with her hands was happening all over. If she had a mirror, she'd see the splotches on her face.

This was why she fed alone. This was why she had to feed privately. Because she was a freak in the vampire community.

The one thing she needed to survive was the one thing she was allergic to: blood. Vampires were supposed to be immune to such things. But no, not her.

The only vampire who knew of her affliction no longer lived: Frederick, her sire. She had her father to thank for his death, not that he'd done it for her. No, not even close.

At first she'd thought all vampires went through the same thing when they fed. But Frederick had told her otherwise. That if another vampire discovered her flaw, she'd be put to death. Used that information to insist she stay with him. That he'd keep her secret and protect her. When it was more like he'd wanted to control her.

Still, she knew of no other vampire who was allergic. And she wasn't about to ask another vampire if what Frederick had said was true, because what if it was? It would only put the spotlight on her. So she kept mum.

Ten minutes. It took ten minutes for her body to heal. Some days those minutes went by quickly. Others, like today, had trudged by like hours. But no way would she be seen in public like this. The mortals would definitely fear their safety thinking Mandy was contagious. Or a monster. And what if she missed wiping a mortal's mind? Not worth the risk.

Five minutes later, the burn subsided. Another five minutes and her rash faded. She exited the stall, washed her hands, and headed to the meeting place. Perry was sitting on the floor, waiting for her.

He stood on her approach. "Man, you took your time. I guess he was good?"

She let him think what he wanted. Probably better that way.

"There's a gift shop that way." She pointed away from the gates.

Perry's shoulders slumped. "That's okay. It's getting late. We should just go back to the plane."

"Do you always sulk when you don't get your way?"

He chuckled. "Probably, but that's not it. I get what you said. And you're right. I should be faithful, even if I don't know who she is right now."

Well, bollocks. She never should have turned him down. That was what she got for not thinking first. "Yeah, but I was wrong, too. Like you said, it could be decades. You're going to be celibate for all that time?"

"Why not? It hasn't been all that fun for me lately anyway. I'd rather have it mean something. I'd rather have it with someone who means something to me. That's what I want."

Sounded good on paper, but was it realistic? "That's very commendable of you. But what does that have to do with getting a souvenir?"

"I just figured you didn't want to do anything with me. I don't want to force you."

"We can be mates, can't we? In the friendship way, that is."

He blinked several times as if she'd spoken a foreign language. "Wow. Yeah. Sure. Can never have too many friends."

"So let's get that souvenir."

He smiled. "Thanks. Lead the way."

The first store she found was definitely souvenir-worthy. "What did you have in mind? Keychain? Magnet? Shirt?"

He zeroed in on the Union Jack T-shirts. "Cool! Perfect thing to wear when we meet Dimitri, don't you think?"

"You'd wear that? Why?"

"Because you're supposed to be my girl, right? Why wouldn't I wear it?" He turned toward her, concern all over his face. "It's not cheating if I have to kiss you for this assignment, is it?"

Oooh. Kissing Perry. There was a thought. She wouldn't mind testing those lips of his. "I'd say no. You plan on kissing me?"

"Isn't that what mates, or rather, suitors do? Kiss a lot?"

She shrugged. Like she knew anything about having a suitor.

"Well, Johnny and Sarah are always kissing. So are Vic and Teach. I even caught Sammy kissing Janie numerous times and they weren't even bonded yet."

"Those are Perfect Mate couples. We're not Perfect Mates."

"True, but Jack kisses Sunny every chance he gets and they're both vampires." He waltzed into her personal space. Those enchanting green eyes of his luring her in. "Is it cheating if we have to practice? I want it to look real to Dimitri. To any Russian vampire. People tend to notice when I lie."

His vanilla scent was hooking her in, too. Practice kissing Perry. Now there was a thought. She wouldn't need any practice to make it look real. Oh no. One kiss and it'd be real to her. But if he kissed her in private, she wasn't so sure she could control herself. Or if she wanted to. So maybe public would be better. "We could always practice in front of Oscar the Grouch."

His eyes widened and he let out a high-pitched laugh. It caught her off guard and was so contagious she joined him in his jocularity.

"That is the perfect name for him, isn't it?"

It was. But would he call her Beautiful again or consider that cheating, too? Bloody hell. Why'd she have to make Perry think that being interested in her was cheating? *Idiot!*

Chapter 4

Perry paid for his purchase and picked up the bag containing his Union Jack T-shirt. At least now he had proof he'd been in England, because he wasn't throwing away the receipt.

The clock on the wall displayed 7:55. "We'd better hurry if we want to get back before eight."

"Oh, we have time. Don't worry," Mandy said.

Don't worry? They had five minutes. Five minutes. Would Oscar the Grouch be pissed if his passengers didn't return until sundown? Probably. But he'd also report them to the Committee, and Perry hadn't been joking when he said Jack was mean. That man hated rule-breakers.

True, he'd softened some since his marriage to Sunny, but not completely. And if anything happened to Barnet that he couldn't be the Head of the Committee anymore, Jack would be more than happy to step into that position. Hell, he'd been targeting it ever since he joined the Committee. Perry disliked change in general and life was good right now, not that it wouldn't remain so with Jack. But Jack was an unknown—in a way—so Barnet better be all right.

Perry stuffed his bag inside his coveralls and followed Mandy to the door leading below. She swiped her card and opened it. More people were down there than before. She acted as if they belonged, so he followed her example.

He couldn't keep his eyes from zeroing on her ass, though. This celibate thing was going to be hard. But he would do it for his

Perfect Mate. He owed her that much, since he wasn't the best vampire specimen she could choose.

Now, if he could only get his eyes to focus on their destination instead of Beautiful's ass. Or maybe he should stick to calling her Mandy. Yeah, that was probably best. Giving her the nickname of Beautiful wasn't conducive to being faithful. Besides, wasn't Mandy a nickname for Amanda anyway?

But as his eyes kept being deceitful, he hadn't realized she'd stopped and he bumped into her. "Sorry."

"Excuse me." A man with an Irish accent stood in front of Mandy. He wore some kind of security uniform with the name North imprinted on a nametag. "Who are you?"

"We work over there," she said, pointing. "Just heading back to our hangar."

"I need to see your ID."

Perry waited a moment. Was she going to manipulate the man or what? North hadn't moved.

Perry whispered so that only she could hear him, "What are you waiting for?"

She whispered back, "He's not listening to me."

"ID?" North held out his hand.

Perry sent a command, "*Stand aside and let us pass.*" North stood rooted. "*Flap like a bird.*" North rose an eyebrow and shook his hand.

Oh shit. Nothing worked on the guy. Which could only mean one thing.

"Is there a problem?" North reached for his weapon.

Whether it was a gun or a tazer, Perry didn't want to find out. Praying for no witnesses, he sucker-punched the guy. He collapsed as if he didn't have a bone in his body. But at least he was down.

"What'd you do that for?"

North's heart was still beating, so Perry hadn't killed the guy. His jaw may be a different story. Something might have crunched. Perry couldn't worry about that now. There was a cart by the exit. Perry lifted North, tossed him on the cart, and covered him with a tarp. "Let's go."

Those pink tinges had turned orange. Sun would be out soon. He moved as swiftly as he could without drawing attention.

"Are you going to answer my question? And where are we taking him?"

"We couldn't control him." Just his luck he'd found another male. A male. What were the odds?

"I got that. You couldn't just leave him there for someone to find?"

He glanced at her. She was joking, right? Apparently not. "Why would I do that? He's a Perfect Mate."

She rushed ahead and opened the door. Perry maneuvered the cart inside and not a moment too soon. His face had been getting a little...tight.

"How do you know he's a Perfect Mate?"

"Well, I don't. Not yet. But touch him. Does he feel warm to you?"

She stepped back and held her hands close to her chest. "You touch him."

"I'm not gay. He won't work on me. Go on. He's not going to hurt you. But fair warning, you might like it. A lot."

"I don't know..."

"You're the only one who can verify what he is. If he doesn't cause you a reaction, then I guess I was wrong." But he wasn't wrong. He'd bet his...well, if he had anything to bet, he'd bet it.

"Fine." She uncovered the tarp. Stared at his hand longer than she needed to. Perry was about to encourage her to grow a pair when she touched North. Gasped and snatched it back as if he were fire.

Perry let the smile take over his mouth. He knew it! "Warm, huh?"

Using two fingers, she touched North again. Her eyes widened. "How is that possible?"

"Because he's a Perfect Mate. Maybe he's yours."

"Will you quit saying every male Perfect Mate might be mine?"

"Well, they might. What does he smell like? All Perfect Mates will smell the same to you. Something that reminds you of home."

She glanced between Perry and North. "All Perfect Mates smell the same?"

"For each vampire. I've met two. They both smelled like jasmine. All the Perfect Mates Vic had met before she bonded with Teach had smelled like the ocean. It'd be nice if I could smell him, then I would have known what he was right away, but apparently it doesn't work that way. So whatever you're smelling, that's what all unbonded, male Perfect Mates will smell like to you. So what does he smell like?"

"My mother's kitchen, I suppose. Huh." She shook her head and stood back several steps. "What's your big plan? He shouldn't be here."

Big plan? That was a good one. When had Perry ever planned anything? "Well, first, we should probably tie him up and blindfold him. Stick him in the office. Then you need to call your buddies at the UK Committee. But before we do that..." He pulled out his phone and snapped a picture of the man and his name tag.

"Why are you taking his picture?"

"So I can send it to Vic. For some reason his name looks familiar, so maybe Vic can figure that out. Better yet..." He checked the guy's front pocket and pulled out his wallet. His ID was on front. Perry snapped a picture of that, too. "She's gonna love me for this, I just know it."

* * * *

Mandy hung the coveralls back on the hooks. Placed the IDs back in the desk. All the while, staring at the tarp-covered body on the cart.

She hadn't lied about the stranger smelling like her mother's kitchen. Just hadn't elaborated that her kitchen had always smelled like vanilla. And right now the scent was strong. But was it coming from Perry or the security guard? And what did it mean that they smelled the same?

Mandy daren't speak. And touching the guy was definitely crossing into the strange and are-you-stupid range, but the urge wouldn't go away. Because she had felt heat. It had spread across her hand.

No wonder Perry was searching for one of them. They could make a vampire feel almost human. The last thing Mandy wanted was to feel human, though.

Fighting her urges, she left the office and quietly closed the door. And just like that, the urge left. What a relief. She'd been afraid that it would have stuck with her the rest of this trip. Perry was sitting on a step of the plane, staring at his phone.

"Did you send your pictures?"

He looked up at her and nodded. "You gonna call the UK Committee?"

"I can't. They don't know I left the country or that I'm on this mission. And I'd rather they didn't know any of that yet, either. Can you call Victoria and ask her to contact them?"

His phone rang and he looked at the display. "Seems I won't have to." He pushed a button. "Hey, Vic."

"What is this you sent me?"

"I thought I made myself clear on the text. Did I mis-send it?"

"No, I got the text. I got the pictures. Where was this taken?"

"Here. Oh… We're at…" Perry looked at Mandy and raised his eyebrows.

"Heathrow," Mandy finished. "The UK Committee's hangar."

"And he just happened to be there?"

"No. Perry and I were at the terminal. Ran into him on our way back."

"Yeah," Perry said. "He wanted to see our ID and we couldn't control him so I bopped him one and brought him here."

Groaning, or maybe growling, came from the phone. "*Scheisse.* Perry, what have you done?"

"What do you mean? He's a Perfect Mate."

"Have you learned nothing from Richard Daugherty? You should have left him there."

Mandy really didn't want to say it. No, she wanted to say it. "I told you so."

He slumped in defeat. "I thought I was doing the right thing."

"Where is he now? He better not be on that plane."

"He's not," Mandy said. "We tied him up, blindfolded him, and covered him with a tarp. Left him in the office of the hangar. When he comes to, he won't know where he is. Would you please contact the UK Committee so they can take care of him? They don't know I'm on this mission and I'd rather they didn't. Not yet, anyway."

"I guess this is one way to break the news to the UK Committee. Did you leave the heater on for him?"

Heater? Oh shit. Mandy shook her head.

"Of course we left the heater on." Perry chuffed. "We're not imbeciles."

"Could have fooled me." The line disconnected.

Perry shook his head and pocketed his phone. "She does that all the time and she wonders why I don't like phones."

"When did you turn on the heat?"

"I didn't, but she didn't need to know that."

Right. Because they were imbeciles.

"Do you know where the thermostat is?" he asked.

"No. I don't even know if there is a heater."

He stood and headed for the office. "Come on. I'm sure there is."

"I'd rather stay here if you don't mind."

"Why? Afraid you might molest him or something? Because if you're getting that urge..." He jerked his hips forward several times.

"I'm getting no such urge." Not for the security guard, in any case. "Is that what they do to you? Make you horny?"

He patted his chin. "I've only met the two. One did. The other didn't. But their mates? Oh yeah, that's what they want to do. All the time." He shook his head. "They are so lucky."

"You make it sound like you can't have that with another vampire." Because hey, she wouldn't mind being an experiment if he was doing the experimenting. She had needs, too.

He shrugged. "Wouldn't know. Never did it with another vampire."

"Never? Not even Suzie-Q?"

"Suzie? No, not even her. She's so new, you know? And her thoughts, well, she doesn't know how to hide them."

At least that wasn't an issue with her. No one listened in unless she invited them. "I'm sure with practice, she'll be okay."

"I don't know... Her mind was very open as a mortal. Very easily manipulated. It would take someone with more patience than me to...not so much fix her, but help her become a stronger vampire."

"Someone like...Barnet?" She almost said Father, but wasn't sure if Oscar was listening or ignoring them.

Perry glanced toward the plane's opening as if he understood her pause. "Yeah. Someone like him. But I'm not going to be the one to tell him. She'll need to do that herself." He stood. "So, you coming with?"

"You just want to see if I get horny, don't you?"

"Who me?" he said in a high-pitched squeak, placing his hand on his chest. "Whatever gave you that idea?"

And he wondered why people knew when he lied? She laughed. He was impossible. Impossible to resist. Never did it with a vampire, though? That was crazy. How could he make a decision about a Perfect Mate without knowing his options? Not that she wanted to be an option. Just an example. Because vampire sex? The man did *not* know what he was missing. Maybe she could change that. Weren't they supposed to be a loving couple?

43

Chapter 5

Barnet sat on the bench inside his cell. After Dimitri's little bomb about Perfect Mates causing Armageddon, he'd been called away. Said to think about it.

That had been several hours ago.

Not much to think about since Dimitri hadn't given any examples. Barnet couldn't even imagine Justin, Sarah, or Ben going off the deep end if any of their vampire mates were to perish. Sure, they'd grieve. But Armageddon?

Shortly after Dimitri's departure, Wall Man had returned with a female mortal he controlled. She had stuck her arm through the bars. Barnet had feared his secret would have been exposed, but with a cramping stomach and a weakened body, he really had no choice, so he fed. His long-sleeved shirt hid the rash on his arms and he'd sat in a ball in the corner to hide his face. Wall Man's indifference had made Barnet suspect his seizure went unnoticed.

It would have been nice to place a command into the woman's head to send word out to his people that he was okay—because his phone had been confiscated and destroyed—but one, he didn't know Russian, and two, Wall Man had control of her during the whole visit. Dimitri still hadn't trusted that Barnet would do something to escape. And frankly, he wasn't sure he wanted to. He wanted to get word to his people but he wanted answers more. Answers Dimitri and maybe some of his people had.

The door upstairs opened with a squeak. No hiding the fact someone was coming down the stairs and, sure enough, Dimitri appeared. Barnet stood and approached the bars.

"I see you are feeling better. I was afraid something was wrong with our donor. Yevgeni told me you seized."

Apparently it hadn't gone unnoticed, but he wasn't about to elaborate. "Your donor was fine and I thank you for her. But is it really necessary to lock me up?"

"Is necessary for my people. I do not need them to hear your lies."

"I'm not lying."

"Your misconceptions, then."

"Can we just talk about it? Somewhere more pleasant?"

"You not like my accommodations?" He laughed as if he'd heard a good joke. "I was about to suggest such a thing when I got word of your rescue attempt."

"My what? How does anyone know I'm even here?"

"Oh, don't play innocent with me. They must know or they not send these people. Do the names Perry Davenport and Amanda Groves mean nothing to you?"

Barnet squeezed the bars but relaxed lest he give away the rage that flowed through him. What the hell was *she* doing here? Had the Committee thought he died? That had to be it. It wasn't a rescue mission. It was a retrieval mission. And that's why Perry accompanied her. "Doesn't matter what I say. You're going to believe they're here for me."

"Because I am not a fool. I do find it curious, though. Amanda Groves is part of UK. But her name… Is it not same as yours?"

"Groves is a common enough name. As is Kalashnikov."

"That may be true, but you know more than you say."

"And you know more about Alexi Popolov than you say, too. You want to share information?"

"I have nothing to share. But I will make deal."

As if Dimitri could be trusted. Any kind of deal Barnet would make with the Russian Head would probably be unfair. "Okay, I'll bite. What kind of deal?"

"I will let you go home with them if you promise to stop spreading lies about Perfect Mates. That you kill any of these freaks you discover. We are better off without them. How can we trust someone we cannot control?"

Yep. One-sided. The man was all about control. Barnet had learned long ago to lead by example. No uprisings. No headaches. "How did you trust someone when you were mortal?"

"I trusted no one. That is how I survive so long."

And led with an iron fist, apparently. "Can we discuss this with the rest of your Committee? Because I get the feeling it doesn't matter what I say. You don't trust anyone. Not even me."

"I trust that when you give your word, you keep it. You have not failed in that regard."

"But giving you my word that Perfect Mates are not a threat isn't enough, is it? Why do you think they will bring Armageddon? What proof do you have?"

"You want proof? Here. See for yourself." Dimitri extended his hand through the bars.

Barnet hesitated. If he linked with Dimitri's thoughts, he could leave himself open to being probed. He'd built a strong barricade—a necessity being the Head of the Committee—so the risk would be minimal. Maybe. This would certainly test his ability. Sure, he could decline the offer, but if Dimitri offered proof, real proof, Barnet couldn't not see it. It just wasn't in his nature.

So as he fortified his barricade, he placed his hand on top of Dimitri's and connected with his memories.

A male vampire wearing a peasant outfit was led to a guillotine and beheaded. A female screamed, speaking in Russian and wearing clothing from another century. She attacked the henchman with a sword and lobbed the man's head off. Dimitri yelled at someone, who loaded a flintlock pistol and shot her. They placed her body beside the vampire and left them. Probably for the sun to burn. Later, she returned and attacked Dimitri. Screamed more Russian. His guards chopped her head off. Dimitri checked on his people. Found body after body of dead vampires.

More than ever Barnet wished he'd learned Russian. But this was no recent event. Perfect Mates went back that far? How? There was so much to learn and Dimitri held some of the answers. He pulled to disconnect, but Dimitri grabbed his wrist. God damn it.

"Let me go." Barnet focused on barricading his thoughts.

"Why are you fighting me? What do you have to hide?"

"You have no right." Barnet yanked Dimitri against the cell's bars and became free.

Dimitri rubbed his forehead. "You are older than I thought."

"Lucky me." Barnet rubbed his wrist. "You know I don't understand your language, so what did you hope to accomplish? Are you going to tell me what they said? What his crime was?"

"What does it matter? She could not be controlled. Bullets could not stop her. She killed my people."

"But what did he do? There has to be a reason she came after you."

"She came after me because her mate died. She killed my men because her mate died. That is why. Do we have a deal?"

Barnet shook his head. "No. You killed her mate. He didn't just die. Why did you kill him?"

"See? Even when I give proof, you do not believe. Maybe you will when I send your friends down here with you. And if your Committee sends anyone else, I will bring them here, too. There is plenty of room."

"If you bring them here, you're declaring war. And if you think Perfect Mates are a threat, what do you think a full-blown war will do?"

"Your people are soft. It would be an easy annihilation."

"It would most likely become a public one, too. Are you ready to be outed?"

"No one will be outed because we are that good. You have two and a half hours to change your mind. That is when I expect your friends to arrive."

"I'm not going to change my mind. I will not kill innocent people."

"Then you leave me no choice."

Barnet grabbed onto the bars. "You have plenty of choices. You just refuse to listen to them. Did your people even know what kind of person you are when they voted for you?"

"I am exactly what they need. I protect them from the likes of you. If you should change your mind, let Yevgeni know."

Dimitri ascended the stairs leaving Wall Man, or rather, Yevgeni, behind. Barnet sat on the bench. He'd known the Russian Committee would be difficult, but not willing to cause a war. The only way to diffuse the situation was to get the other Committees on board with the US. But he'd have to escape first in order to do that.

Seemed all he had to do was sit tight if indeed a retrieval team was imminent. Would they be surprised to see he was actually alive, though?

* * * *

Perry hiked the backpack on one shoulder and stood at the plane's hatch. He was actually in Russia. Well, he could only assume he was in Russia. This hangar looked the same as the London hangar, except for the signs. They were all written in a language he couldn't read with letters he couldn't pronounce. Thus, the assumption.

He could pronounce the Russian words for "stop" and "sleep" so he could feed from a Russian. Because if he tried to control someone in English and they didn't understand the language, he might as well attempt to control a brick wall. Or a Perfect Mate. He'd get the same results. But reading those words were a whole different matter. Maybe he should have studied the language during the flight. Then again, hindsight was always twenty-twenty.

If everything went according to their plan, he wouldn't need to learn the language. And now he would have to put on the show of his life. Mandy had written out a play of sorts. How they should act toward one another. He'd be the goof-off—as if that were a stretch—and she'd be some giddy idiot—as if he'd ever be interested in someone like that.

They'd never gotten around to practice kissing, which was probably just as well. Being close to her in the plane during their trip was bad enough. If they'd started kissing, he might have jumped her bones.

Which lead to the question: why was he attracted to Mandy? He'd never been turned on by another vampire. Never. Oh sure, Suzie-Q had turned him on…when she was mortal. Once she became a vampire, he'd lost interest. Or rather, his libido lost interest. He should have never asked her on that date and just stuck with being her friend.

So Mandy couldn't be any different. It had to be the mission. It was messing with his brain. He would just have to remind himself of that every time Mandy's ass came into view.

He had texted Vic that they had landed safely. She was responsible for alerting their contact and if all went well, he and Mandy would be back in London tonight with one more occupant.

Vic had also texted that the airport security guard Perry had punched was taken care of. Since no one could plant any false memories in the Perfect Mate's head, the UK vampires had come up with a story that some crazy bastard and his girl were on the run and that North had just been caught in the middle of it.

In any case, the UK now had confirmation that Perfect Mates existed—where before they'd been skeptical—and they were taking measures to monitor them. So Vic could be mad at Perry all she wanted, but he still thought he'd done the right thing.

He replaced his cellphone in one of his cargo pockets. It was so nice to have his old style pants back, where he had a pocket for almost anything. He even had a place to store his charger cord, not that he needed to charge his phone. He'd done that during the flight.

He chuckled. Him. With a charged phone. Would wonders never cease?

Rubbing his hands together, he turned toward Groucho. "With any luck, we'll be back here with—" Mandy kicked his leg. "What was that for?"

She took his hand and a shot of desire zinged up his arm. Now not only were his eyes and dick being traitorous, his hand was, too? What the hell. How would he ever stay celibate with all these temptations? Or was he being tested by the Great One? To see if he was worthy of a Perfect Mate? Holy shit. All the more reason to resist.

"Sweetheart. He knows his job. You don't have to keep reminding him." Telepathically she said, *"There are cameras everywhere, which means there can be ears, too. We have to start playing. We can't even mention my father's name."*

No other inadvertent thought snuck through. Just her message. Hmmm… Was she older or just talented? *"Thank you. Maybe I should let you do all the talking."* It wasn't like he always thought before speaking anyway. "You're right. Guess my excitement has gotten to me. My apologies."

She hugged him and kissed his cheek. "We're still going to check out other places, aren't we?"

Other places? Oh, their mission. "I said I would. Quit being a nag."

She swatted his arm and giggled. "Will you stop?"

Groucho rolled his eyes. "I'll be back to pick you up around four. Call if that changes."

"Right." Perry winked. "Because you have another customer." When really, Groucho was supposed to move the plane to another location.

He rolled his eyes again and headed back to the cockpit.

Perry almost blurted, "Watch out, your eyes will stick that way," but caught himself in time. He didn't need another kick from Mandy.

She grabbed her backpack and descended the stairs. "I can't wait to see the city. Do you think they have shoe stores here? I'd like to buy a pair of boots." When she reached the bottom, she stuck out her foot, clad in a pump with a four-inch heel.

Perry bit his knuckle and groaned. Oh Great One, why did she have to have sexy feet, too? Good thing she wanted to get boots. Less feet to see. Right?

She palmed his cheek once he reached the ground. "You okay, baby?"

There went that zing again. He wrapped his arms around her waist and twirled her around. Anything to get her hand off him. "Couldn't be better. Let's go get us processed and out of here."

As they stepped outside, where the airport looked like any other airport, a black Rolls Royce parked in front of them. The male driver—or rather, chauffeur, because hell, he was dressed like one—exited the car and opened the backseat door. "Mister Davidson. Miss Groves. Please come with me."

While Mandy had suggested they use aliases, the Committee decided against it. Not enough time to make them investigative-proof.

"I guess they got the message we were coming." Perry bowed and swung his arm toward the car. "After you, m'lady."

The driver moved to the trunk. "Where are your bags?"

"We travel light. Just have the backpacks. We'll keep them with us."

"Very well, sir."

Sir. Listen to that. Someone called him sir. Was this an awesome trip or what?

She climbed in and he enjoyed the sight. Ass, feet, whatever. He didn't will his boner away because he was supposed to be her mate.

And mates were turned on by their mates. At least he didn't have to fake that. He just wouldn't do anything about it.

Perry sat beside her and the chauffeur shut the door. What service. He could get used to this.

Mandy glanced at Perry's crotch and grinned. Snuggled beside him and kissed him. On the lips. With tongue, even.

Man, she tasted good. All cinnamon spice and everything nice. He pulled her onto his lap. If she wanted to put on a show, he was going to make it a good one.

Keeping her lips locked with his, she flipped her skirt and straddled his legs. Ground into his aching boner.

Oh Great One. Are you trying to kill me?

The scent of jasmine filled the interior of the car. He froze. No, not now. Not while he was in this situation. Perry broke the kiss and spoke over Mandy's shoulder. "Is someone sitting up there with you, Mr. Chauffeur Guy?"

"No, sir. I am alone."

He relaxed. Okay, so he didn't have to explain what he was doing. But that scent. He gazed into Mandy's mesmerizing blue eyes. "Are you wearing a new perfume, snookums?"

She snickered. "Snookums. You're so funny. But what happened to Beautiful? Aren't I Beautiful anymore?"

"You are. You definitely are. But that didn't answer my question."

"The only perfume I'm wearing is my desire for you. Is it good?" She rubbed her nose against his.

It was not only good, it reminded him of home. Just what kind of test was the Great One pulling here?

* * * *

Mandy ground into Perry's lap. The man was hard. For her. And she was pretty turned on herself. Time to take advantage, because when would she have this chance again? She spoke over her shoulder toward the chauffeur. "How far is it to Headquarters?"

"I am not taking you to Headquarters. I take you to Hotel. Dimitri will not be able to see you until two in morning. Drive to hotel is twenty minutes. You like privacy?"

Two a.m.? That was cutting things close. "Yes, please."

A partition between the front and back rose. She took his hand. *"Might want to let Victoria know we're being delayed."*

"You gonna get off my lap so I can get my phone?"

Hell, no. He started this and she was having so much fun. *"Which pocket?"*

He pointed down his right leg. She leaned over, making sure to rub him just right, unbuttoned the pocket, and pulled out his mobile. The man was definitely hard and definitely no teeny-weeny. Well, they might not have sex, but she sure could torture him some. Because he was certainly torturing her.

He leaned his head back against the rest. His eyes closed. Yeah, she was torturing him all right. She'd kiss those lips of his again, but since they had privacy there really wasn't a reason she should. No one to perform for. But if for some reason he saw fit to start another round of kissing, she certainly wouldn't stop him. Oh no. Using his mobile, she tapped his shoulder.

He opened his eyes. Those green orbs had to be the most beautiful eyes she'd ever seen. He took the mobile and texted.

They might not have sex, but they did have roles to play, and that chauffeur could easily report back to Dimitri. She smiled and put her mouth beside Perry's ear. "Let's have some fun."

"Fun?" The word came out on a squeak.

She almost laughed. Would he catch on soon or not? Did it matter? Hell, no. "Yeah. Haven't you ever done it in the back of a limo?"

His eyes widened. "He can still hear us, you know."

"So?" She unbuttoned his slacks. "You did it on the plane."

He placed his hand over hers, stopping her from unzipping his pants, not that she had planned to go that far. Not without encouragement from him anyway. "Yeah, but that was different. The pilot wasn't on the other side of a partition. And the plane was loud."

Okay, he was playing the part now. She laid it on thick. "Aww, come on. Be a sport. I came here for you. Please, please, please?"

He touched her face. "Wouldn't you rather be on a comfortable bed, where I can take my time loving that beautiful body of yours?"

Bloody hell. Her heart might have melted a little. No one had ever said anything like that to her before. And technically, he hadn't either. He was playing a game.

She re-buttoned his pants. "You're right. That sounds heavenly."

"There is something we can do. Right here."

"There is?"

He kissed her. Devoured her mouth. The man definitely did not need practice in that department. Nope. None whatsoever.

He grabbed her hips, but didn't grind into her. Being a gentleman or afraid of the consequences? She played nice and settled for sucking his tongue and playing with his pony tail. She could kiss this guy forever. He knew exactly how to set her body on fire. Damn him and his celibacy, though. She could use some sex about now.

He nuzzled her neck. Tongue, whiskers, and threat of fangs. She was riding a cloud over the mountains. His mouth would probably feel wonderful anywhere he wanted to place it on her body. If he ever had a desire to do so. Unfortunately—

He bit her and her thoughts froze. He sucked on her blood.

Holy crap. She came. Hard. And he hadn't even touched her down there. The man had talent. Definitely had talent. And he was saving himself for someone else.

For some stupid Perfect Mate.

But he was hers for now. If only for pretend. And she could pretend with the best of them. Once she recovered.

* * * *

Perry nearly groaned as the sweet taste of her blood covered his tongue. She not only smelled like home, she tasted like Heaven. And he'd only gotten a sample.

A vampire. And not an inadvertent peep from her. Damn. Maybe his problem had been finding ones that were too young. Or not strong enough.

But this was just a game. A job. Not real. He had a Perfect Mate in his future and he didn't want to cheat on her.

Mandy's orgasm had seemed pretty damn real, though. Oh Great One, was that considered cheating? No, no. Not his fault she got off on his bite. Not his fault at all. He licked her neck, not that he needed to heal the marks he'd left behind, but so he wouldn't waste any of that sweet elixir. Her blood wouldn't sustain him, not like a Perfect Mate's, but did dessert ever sustain a mortal? Nope. It was just tasty. And that's what Mandy was. Tasty.

So very, very tasty.

What did that mean? What did that mean?

"Oh my God, Perry. You are a wonder, aren't you?"

"Did I please you?"

"Oh, very much so." She licked his neck. Ran her fangs along the skin. Damn. That felt good. Would she bite him, too? "Should I please you, too?"

"No, that's not necess—"

She bit.

He lost it. He grabbed onto her hips as he emptied into his pants.

Daaaaaammmmmmnnnn. What had he just done?

She palmed his cheek and kissed him. Deep and delirious. "*You okay, Perry?*"

"*Sure. Fine. Peachy.*" He hadn't cheated. No. No. It was like a wet dream, right? He couldn't be responsible for those. And he was on a job. Doing a job. He couldn't control how his body functioned while on the job, right? Right. He licked his lips.

Funny. There was no lingering taste of his blood on his lips or from her tongue. She had bitten him, hadn't she? His dick certainly thought so. He shook his head and got with the plan. "Did I pass for your limo experience?"

"You were perfect. Thank you, baby."

Was she saying that for real? Because the orgasm sure seemed real. She hadn't faked it, had she? Damn. Maybe she had. Well, he certainly hadn't. He had the mess in his pants to prove it, too.

She climbed off him and looked out the window. "Moscow's a big city. Do you think Sydney is just as big?"

What the hell was she talking about? Oh yeah. Their mission. Their roles. "You haven't even been here an hour and you're already thinking about Australia?"

"All I asked is if Sydney was as big. I didn't say anything bad about Moscow. I said I would give Russia a chance and I will."

There were tissues in the seat back. Apparently it was common for vampires to have sex back here, why else the tissues? Mr. Chauffeur Guy could probably tell lots of stories.

Maybe it would be best not to find a Perfect Mate here. Mr. Chauffer Guy could be a blabber mouth.

Perry shoved some tissues down his pants, hoping to keep the mess to a minimum. Good thing he had another pair in his backpack. These would need to be cleaned. He was not giving up these pants. She watched and smiled. And man, what a smile. Was she hoping to get a peek, was that it? Well, some things were meant to stay hidden. From her, anyway. But how far in this game would she go? They basically had an audience—albeit a blind one—so he put her to the test.

"After we check out the hotel room and muss up the bed a little," and he wagged his eyebrows for emphasis, not that Mr. Chauffer Guy could see him, "we should go find a place to feed. I'll pick some hunky guy for you to watch and you pick some sexy girl for me to watch. What do you say?"

Mandy's eyes widened. Ha! He got her now. Feeding time is private time, indeed. Not when two vampires were together they weren't. He knew for a fact that Jack and Sunny did exactly that. Then had sex after, or so Sunny had confided to Suzie one night. Perry couldn't help it if the conversation had leaked out of Suzie when he'd held her hand.

Which had been the last time he'd done that. Lesson learned.

But the feeding and the sex after seemed like some kind of a vicious cycle for vampires. Thankfully when Perry found his Perfect Mate, he wouldn't have to do such things. Not that it didn't sound like fun.

Feeding and sex? Two best things in the world.

"Well?" Perry tucked a strand of Mandy's silky hair behind her ear and waited for her to speak. Would she stay in character or not?

"Whatever you want, sweetheart. I'm here for you on this trip."

She was good, he had to give her that. Her voice never wavered. But Mr. Chauffeur Guy couldn't see that she averted her eyes when she'd said those words.

The limo pulled into the hotel drop-off zone. The partition lowered. Mr. Chauffeur Guy turned around. "I will return here at one-forty five."

Mandy leaned over the seats. "Are there any stores open late at night?"

"Most stores close at eight in this area. But there is one." He pulled out a card. "Owned by one of us. She keeps store open twenty-four hours. Is not far from hotel."

She took the card. "Thank you." She smiled at Perry. "You ready?"

Oh, he was about as ready as he was ever going to be in a country he could not communicate in.

Chapter 6

Mandy followed Perry into the elevator. Just a typical hotel. With a typical check-in counter. She hadn't been sure what to expect. Thought it might be run by vampires, but that wasn't the case.

Anxious to check out the store, she wouldn't even bother going to the room if not for Perry. She couldn't imagine he'd want to walk around with a wet stain in his crotch area. And what a nice crotch it was, too. The Hawaiian shirt covered most of her view, so she could only go by what she remembered as she sat on him—on it—and had probably one of the best orgasms ever.

A bite had never been so exciting.

Damn, she'd almost sunk her fangs in him, too. Thankfully she'd stopped in time. Or had he come before she could pierce his skin? Either way saved her an explanation and a lot of pain. But he must have noticed, why else had he mentioned feeding together?

She might not ever have sex with Perry, but she sure got him to lose control. Could she do it again? She took his hand. *"Remember. This whole place can be bugged."*

"Really? This is a chain hotel, not a vampire one."

"And he knows we're staying here. I'm sure it's no problem for him to get the room number."

"A distrustful bastard. Got it." He shook his head and unlocked the door to their suite. "Holy shit. This—Wow. What a room, huh?"

Could the man be any less subtle? Sure, he had no idea what kind of room the US Committee had reserved, but he was supposed to have made the reservations. She almost laughed. "You've gone all out, I'll give you that. Thanks, sweetheart." She closed the door and placed her bag on a table. The bed was in another room off to the left. A room that would most likely not get used since vampires didn't sleep.

And she couldn't imagine Perry would be willing to use it for other fun things. Hell, she was still shocked he'd gotten her off with just a bite. A bite. Imagine if they'd been making love? She looked at the bed with a sigh.

"You okay there, Mandy?"

"I'm fine. But I do want to check out that store. You wanna come?"

"I think I did that in the limo."

Now she did laugh. "I meant to the store."

"Ohhh. Thaaaat." He grinned. "Sure. After I change." He grabbed his backpack and headed for the loo.

She checked the room as discreetly as she could. If there were listening devices or cameras, they were hidden well. But she couldn't believe they were not bugged. Dimitri knew they were coming. Which meant they had to stay in character. Oooh. Maybe they'd get use of the bed after all.

She sat on the soft mattress. Beds like this hadn't existed when she was mortal. She almost envied them the luxury. To fall asleep and forget about…everything. The most Mandy could do now was zone out. And even that wasn't enough. Wasn't like sleeping.

Perry emerged from the loo. Stopped when he saw her on the bed. Was he just now realizing that they might have to do more than kiss if their roles were to be believed?

She ran her palm against the silky spread. "I'm looking forward to you making slow, sweet love to me." Smiled when his eyes bugged out. "But let's go shopping first."

To say he was visibly relieved was an understatement. The man practically deflated onto the floor.

Ohh, he was like putty in her hands.

While she wouldn't mind playing around in the bed for Dimitri's sake, she wanted to check out the store. At least the trip there would be stress free. Dimitri couldn't have eyes everywhere. Could he?

She took a quick look in the mirror. Lipstick had smeared—gee, wonder why?—and her hair needed a good comb-through. "Why didn't you tell me I looked a mess?"

"You don't look messy. You look sexy."

"I look used."

"Exactly."

She shook her head. "Men."

Once they were both presentable, they headed to the concierge and got directions. The shop was only two blocks away. She'd never been to Moscow—or Russia, for that matter—and the walk to the shop would give her time to see part of the city. The streets were empty of people and few cars were out and about. But the trees were all strung with white lights, making for a lovely evening with a lovely man. She took Perry's arm.

"You think Dimitri has cameras out here, too?" he asked.

She glanced at all the CCTV cameras in the area. "He may not own those, but I wouldn't be surprised if he didn't have access. There could be vampire eyes on us, too. If we're to be a loving couple, shouldn't we play it all the time?" Hell, right now she'd take any excuse to touch him.

"Yeah?" He stopped. Turned to face her. Took her face into his hands and kissed her. On the lips.

Soft. Tender. She nearly melted on the spot. Kissing Perry was probably the best thing she'd ever done. And then he pulled away and it was over.

Holy mother of all things good. He gazed at her with loving eyes. Loving? No, that couldn't be right. "What was that for?"

"Just being a boyfriend." He grinned. Took her hand and placed it back on his arm as they resumed walking.

Being a boyfriend? Well, he was doing a superb job. "Did you have a lot of girlfriends? Before you started looking for that Perfect Mate?"

"Me? Nah."

"Oh that's right. Because you don't date vampires."

"Not just that. I'd find someone. We'd have fun. But then they just wanted to change me into something I'm not. That's why I want a Perfect Mate. She'll accept me for who I am. Plus, I won't hear her thoughts."

"That bothers you?"

"Let's just say that no one ever lies in their thoughts. And I don't always want to hear the truth. Not when it's just a thought. Thoughts are private. Or at least, should be."

"I completely understand. It's hard to unhear a thought."

"Exactly." He nodded up ahead. "I think that's your store."

In a way she was disappointed the walk had ended so soon. They wouldn't be able to talk this freely in the hotel room or inside the store unless they touched, and he seemed to avoid touching her for some reason. Such a pity. But they would revert back to their roles and frankly, that wouldn't be so hard. Or bad. She enjoyed being his girlfriend. Even for pretend.

* * * *

Perry had thought being buried alive was torture. That wasn't even close to what he'd just gone through with Mandy.

And not because she was shopping. Nope. Not at all. It was because of *what* she was buying.

Was there any outfit in that store that didn't make her look sexy? Apparently not. And then she went and picked probably the sexiest outfit she could have picked out.

A black leather skirt that barely covered her thighs. Thigh-high boots that barely reached the skirt. A red blousy top that revealed more cleavage than he needed to see. Topped off with an awesome, black, sparkly sweater-thing she called a duster.

He'd never been so turned on before.

And the wench decided to wear it out of the store. Yeah, under her winter coat, but still.

He may never get soft again. And what did that say about his future Perfect Mate? Or rather…him? If an outfit—okay, an outfit on one beautiful woman—could do this to him, would do this to him, then how could he ever hope to win over his future Perfect Mate?

Oh, he was so screwed. He looked to the ceiling. *You* are *testing me, aren't you, oh Great One.*

"What are you looking at?" Mandy asked.

"Just admiring the construction." Which was probably the stupidest thing he could have said but she'd startled him and he just blurted out the first thought that came to mind. Was he so far gone that he couldn't hear her approach? Then again, the store was fairly busy. Whether all the customers were vampires or not, he didn't know. It wasn't like he knew any Russian vampires and they didn't go around dropping fang.

"It's a ceiling."

"But it's—" What? Plaster? He couldn't make his stupid remark any better. "Never mind. You ready to go?"

"Don't you want to get anything?" she asked. "Maybe a souvenir?"

He wanted to strip her of her clothes and bury himself deep inside her. But hell, he couldn't do that. "If we're going to live here, why do I need a souvenir?"

"We don't know we're going to live here yet. You should get something. Maybe some boots? They'll look more…commonplace than your trainers."

Now she was picking on his footwear? "Well, I certainly want to look…*commonplace*. Now don't I?"

"I just meant you'll blend in easier. You should really replace this shirt." She flicked the collar.

He backed away. "You can't mean that."

She ran her hand down his arm and grabbed his hand, making skin contact. "*I don't mean it,*" she said telepathically, "*but your pretend girlfriend does.*" Aloud and with a wink, she said, "Wouldn't you like to get a sweater? Or a vest to wear under your leather jacket?"

He shivered. He actually shivered. No job in the universe could force him to wear one of those. He yanked his hand away. "If you think I'd wear either, you don't know me very well."

"I'm just trying to get you to play around with your wardrobe."

"No. You're trying to change me. But I suppose I could use some boots. I wouldn't want my *sneakers* to get ruined in the snow."

Mandy smiled at that. Took his hand again. And whaddya know, she found some boots that looked pretty awesome with his cargo pants. Hell, with all the snow on the ground, they would probably come in handy. Hopefully he wouldn't have to need handy, but better to be safe and all that.

He took his bag and her three—because that's what boyfriends did, right?—and held the door open for her. They headed back to the hotel and she grabbed his arm once again. Yeah, it was all a show, but it still felt nice having her there. And that kiss he gave her earlier? Holy shit. He'd only meant for it to be a light peck. But once his lips touched hers? He just wanted more. More that could happen in their room, was probably expected even, if Dimitri had bugged the room like she suspected. And really, why wouldn't Dimitri bug the room? He probably didn't believe their cover story. Too coincidental after Barnet's abduction.

"You okay there? You tensed up."

Perry glanced around. No one was lurking. "He's going to expect us to make love when we get back."

"Probably. It's not cheating if you're pretending."

But would he be pretending? He liked her. A lot. She turned him on more than any mortal had.

She rested her cheek on his arm. "It's also not cheating when you're doing a job. If you can't do the job, then what are you doing here?"

"I owe Barnet my life. I can't let him down."

"Are you willing to do anything to save him?"

Perry used to think that meant giving up his life for another. And while that was true—Barnet was the best thing that happened for the vampires—it held a completely different meaning now. Was he willing to cheat on someone who didn't even exist in his life yet to save a man who he considered his father?

He lowered his head. "I just want to be worthy of her."

"You think saving the Head of the US Committee isn't being worthy?"

Well hell, when Mandy put it that way, it made sense. He chuckled. "Maybe the Great One is testing me."

"The Great One?"

"Yeah. The one who made us. Not a God. Not a Goddess. Someone who is both sexes or all sexes or no sexes. Whatever. The Great One."

She nodded. "Hmmm… Never thought about it like that. What makes you think you're being tested?"

"Because…" Holy shit. He couldn't say why. Not to her. "I just do."

She squeezed his arm. "Hey, I know this isn't easy for you. But it is just pretend. You don't have to worry about me being clingy or anything. And it's not like I can get pregnant, right? This is a job. Like acting. Actors pretend to make love on the screen all the time, right?"

He nodded. Everything she said made sense. But this would have been so much easier if he'd never met Sarah, Johnny's Perfect Mate. If Perry had never sampled her blood.

Barnet had accused Perry of being obsessed with finding a Perfect Mate because of that one tiny incident. Because Barnet believed Sarah's blood was still in Perry. Still affecting him. And she wasn't even his Perfect Mate. She was Johnny's, the lucky bastard.

"You got quiet. What's going on in that brain of yours?"

"Nothing." When she laughed, he grasped his blunder. "Yeah, yeah, yeah. Yuk it up."

"When this mission is over, I could help you. If you want."

"Help me with what?"

"Finding your Perfect Mate. I assume I look for someone I can't control, right?"

"Why would you do that?"

"Because we're mates. Friends. Isn't that what friends do?"

None of his other friends offered. Even the ones who'd already found their own Perfect Mates. Oh sure, maybe they would help if he asked. But he hadn't asked her. "You amaze me."

"Do I now?" She smiled.

Perry could think of worse things he'd be forced to do on this mission, as she liked to call it. And maybe that's how he could picture it, too. A mission. It's not like he had to kill anyone. And it wasn't like he was a virgin, so he wasn't giving up anything like that.

They reached the street of their hotel. She stared at the building. "So, what's it gonna be? Back to the room or more sight-seeing?"

Perry wasn't about to let Dimitri even wonder if their story was legit. He dropped their bags and shoved her against the wall. Cupped her face. That beautiful, beautiful face. And kissed her as if he wouldn't get this chance again. Relished every bit of her mouth.

She wrapped her arms around his neck and pulled him in close. Her tongue tangoed with his. She tasted sweet and savory. Her jasmine scent intensified and he grew hard for her.

If he was going to pretend, he might as well enjoy it.

* * * *

Mandy resisted the urge to wrap a leg around Perry. They were, after all, outside. Not exactly private. Not exactly public, either.

They hadn't passed one pedestrian on their walk back to the hotel, but those cameras…

He pulled away and picked up the dropped packages. "Here, hold these."

She took them just as he swept her into his arms. "What are you doing?"

"I'm doing a romantic gesture. Showing everyone how special you are to me."

Oh, if only it were real. She could get on board with that too easily. But she'd promised not to be clingy and she wouldn't.

He carried her to the elevators. She pushed the up button. When the doors opened, he still held her, so she pushed their floor button. As they rode upward, she kissed his lips. Just lightly. In play. But he took it as an invitation to do more. He devoured her mouth. And damn, if that didn't get her all excited for him.

It had been too long since she'd last had sex. Too long. She didn't care if it was all just pretend, she would cherish this moment forever.

The elevator doors opened. He strode to their door and stopped. Chuckled.

"What is it?"

"It almost worked. But my key is in my pocket."

She palmed his cheek. "Put me down."

He lowered her legs. She dropped the packages and ran her hands down his chest. To his waistband. Palmed his erection. "Which pocket?"

He gasped. "Top right."

She extracted the key card and straightened. Brought his face to hers and kissed his lips. "Key?"

He took it from her hands and opened the door. She retrieved the packages. He scooped her up again and carried her inside. Thankfully the door was the kind that closed on its own because they were in the bedroom when it finally clicked shut.

He tossed her on the bed. "While I love seeing you in that outfit you bought, I'd rather see you naked right now."

She knew she'd gotten a reaction from him when she'd tried it on. It was the main reason she'd bought it. That, and it was awesome. "You want to see me naked, then undress me. But don't ruin my new clothes."

His green eyes grew a bit darker. He grabbed her hand and pulled her upright. Gripped her hips and moved her to the edge. Kneeling on the floor between her legs, he slowly unbuttoned her blouse. Slipped the material off her shoulders, baring her bra. Red and lacy, it was one of her favorites. She hadn't worn it for him—hell, she hadn't known she was going to strip for him, let alone have sex—but wearing sexy undergarments always made her feel sexy and confident.

He palmed her breasts—keeping the bra in place—and kissed the parts exposed. "Pretty bra."

"Thank you. The knickers match."

Closing his eyes, he groaned. "I assume I can't hurt the underwear, either?"

"You assume correctly."

The blouse landed on the floor. He brought her to her feet and lowered the side zipper. "Do you always wear skirts?"

"I like them. Easier to move around." Easier to fuck in, too. But hey, why go there when he was doing such a splendid job of undressing her.

He pushed her onto the mattress and pulled the skirt free. "Ah fuck. You're so beautiful."

"You say that all the time." She liked that he was into this, but he had to remember, they weren't supposed to be strangers. This wasn't supposed to be their first time.

He blinked several times. Then it seemed to hit him. "Because it's true. It's always true."

He jumped on top of her and kissed her. His clothes rubbed against her skin, a delicious feeling of being dominated. And while she could go for something like that, she really wanted to see him naked. When would she have this chance again?

She removed his shirt and tossed it to the floor. What a fine chest he had, all smooth and muscular. She broke their kiss and took a nipple into her mouth. Sucked.

He groaned. "Damn, woman. You want me to come in these pants too?"

No, she most certainly did not. She rolled him onto his back, straddled him, and unbuttoned his pants. As she lowered the zipper, he practically popped out. What a magnificent erection he had. Was he pretending she was his Perfect Mate or had she done that to him? She'd like to think the latter, even if this didn't mean anything. Because it didn't. It couldn't.

He attempted to kick off his boots, but they were laced higher than his trainers and wouldn't budge off his feet. Growling, he crawled out from under her and proceeded to unlace the boots while she giggled in her hand. The humor died when he finally kicked the boots and his pants free and stood for her inspection. Damn, what a fine specimen of a man. And that dick was going to be in her. She couldn't wait.

Slowly, he crawled up her body, kissing her toes, her feet, her knees. "I love your undies, but they really must go."

She unhooked her bra and he pulled her knickers off. Both items ended up on the floor.

"Yes. Beautiful." He ran his nose along the inside of her thigh. Licked her core.

She arched. His tongue played with her clit and she closed her eyes. Rode the sensation wave. He fucked her with his tongue and she came.

Oh, bollocks. Giving him up would be difficult.

* * * *

Perry closed his eyes as the orgasm took her. She tasted better than he expected, and he expected her sex would taste pretty good after getting a sample of her blood.

He kissed his way up her body. Palmed one breast as he savored the other with his mouth. Using his tongue, he flicked her nipple. Then he bit her breast.

Sweet ambrosia.

She arched. "Oh God."

If she were mortal he'd have to be careful. But she wasn't mortal. She was a vampire. He could take more and she'd be okay. She'd need to feed, but she'd live. Still, he didn't need to make a mess in the hotel room. So he licked her—cleaning her, healing her—and kissed his way up to her neck.

He inhaled. Had her scent changed or was he being more observant? Jasmine dominated the fragrance, but there was something else mixed in with it. Something earthy. Something so delicious. None of the Perfect Mates he'd met had smelled this good. But then, they hadn't been *his* Perfect Mates, had they?

He almost bit her neck then remembered. Hotel. No mess. Too bad. He'd probably not get this chance again. Just as well. He kissed her lips instead and then plunged inside her.

She was wet and tight. He wouldn't last long.

She ran her hands up and down his back. Cupped his butt. Her eyes were closed, but her mouth was opened slightly. She licked her lips.

Damn, she was beautiful. He could stare at her forever.

No, no he couldn't. What was he thinking? She was a fuck. A good fuck. And they were pretending. That was all.

He pounded into her. Looking for his release. She came a second time and he lost it. She milked him but good.

He collapsed on top of her. Not once during the whole time had he caught even a whisper of a thought. Everything he had heard from her had come from that luscious mouth of hers.

If this was supposed to be pretend, what did it mean when she was the best ever? Ever!

Mandy palmed his face and kissed his lips. *"Remember, we're acting."* "I love you so much, Perry."

Thank the Great One she mentioned the disclaimer first. Yes, acting. This was all an act. "I love you too, Beautiful."

Problem was, maybe he kind of did. A little. Shit.

* * * *

Dimitri shoved the chair away from his desk and stood. He had to give it to those two, they were very convincing. But what vampire didn't like to fuck? It meant nothing.

They would be here soon. He'd hoped by giving them time that they'd slip up. Say something incriminating. But nothing so far. Not even in Natasha's shop, which unfortunately did not have microphones. Something he would have to remedy. They didn't talk to each other in the store all that much anyway, probably keeping all their secret details between them telepathically. They did touch a lot. And kiss a lot. But it was a cover. He was sure of it.

The woman even resembled Barnet. Who was she? Dimitri had tried to glean that information from Barnet, but he was strong and Dimitri couldn't get past the barrier. He shouldn't be surprised. The US vampires certainly wouldn't have voted in a weakling as their head, now would they?

"I love you so much, Perry," said the woman on the screen. Amanda Groves. Daughter? Granddaughter?

"Who is she to you, Barnet?"

"I love you, too, Beautiful," said the man on the screen. Perry Davenport. Occasional helper of the US Committee. He wasn't a warrior, but wouldn't that be the best person to send? Someone so obviously unqualified to fight?

"Let's go take a shower," she said.

They climbed off the bed and headed for the bathroom. They'd probably fuck in there, too. No cameras were installed, but the sound would be recorded. Unfortunately, Dimitri couldn't stay and listen. Not right now.

Right now he had to go find someone to fuck. Good thing there were workers on the fourth floor. Man, woman, didn't matter. He'd take whoever groveled at his feet first.

Chapter 7

Perry leaned back against the seat in the limo and held Mandy's hand. He probably didn't need to, but for some reason it just felt right. And he was playing a part. He should play it all the time just in case. Right?

Had he ever taken a shower like the one he'd taken with Mandy? No, he couldn't say he had. Most of the mortal women he'd been with never offered to blow him and he refused to ever put that thought into their heads, so when Mandy took him into her mouth, he'd been surprised. No, shocked. He hadn't even gotten a hint that she had planned on doing it. And man, if that wasn't the best thing ever.

Mandy was fun. He'd never had so much fun with one person. How could he hope to remain friends with her after all this? Especially after he met his Perfect Mate? There was pretend and then there was pretend-which-wasn't-so-pretend and he was falling into the latter category.

Besides, he wasn't here for fun. He was here on a mission. The Committee depended on him. Barnet depended on him.

Perry's nerves returned. He couldn't fail. He just couldn't.

Mandy squeezed his hand and smiled. *"Relax. You're supposed to want to be here."*

Damn. What would he have done without her? She became his voice of reason and he'd surely fail without her help.

The vehicle stopped, but Mr. Chauffeur Guy stayed behind the wheel. Another male opened Mandy's door. "This way, please."

Perry grabbed their belongings and followed Mandy out of the car. The building before him not only covered a lot of acreage, it took up part of the sky, too. Five or six stories, depending on how high the ceilings were. It sat on a small hill with the city lit up below. "This is Headquarters? You're kind of out in the open, aren't you?"

The stranger smiled. "It is. Is also one of largest tourist spots in area during daylight hours."

"Are you one of the Committee members?" Mandy asked.

"*Nyet*. No. I work here. Only Dimitri here. The other four not here."

"Are they expected to return?"

"They live elsewhere. Not live here."

Perry rolled his eyes. Well that answered nothing. "Will they be here for our visit?"

"I do not know. My job is to take you to Dimitri. Now, please. Follow me."

"This is quite a set-up," Mandy said as they strolled through the museum, following their guide. "I wonder how they swung ownership. The UK Committee had to create a business, similar to the one the US Committee created. Who came up with VAMPS, anyway? Oh, I'm sorry. I mean Vantage Accounting and Management Personnel Services. Very clever."

"Clever, huh? Well, you're looking at him."

She laughed. "I should have known it was you. You're a devil, aren't you?"

"That's me. Devilishly handsome." Always a bonus when he could steal a Richard Castle line. Perry loved that show. If only it hadn't ended.

"Do you quote television shows often?"

"You know the show?"

"*Castle* is one of my favorites. I own all the DVDs."

Now why'd she have to go say a thing like that? How was he ever going to leave her? And he would have to leave her one day. The day he found his Perfect Mate. It only made sense. "Cool. We'll have to binge them some day. As for quoting, only when it suits my needs."

"I learn something new about you every day."

They reached the back of the building to a door with a keypad mounted on the wall beside it. Their guide punched in a code that Perry memorized. Never could be too careful.

The door opened to a stairwell. They only descended one flight to another door and another keypad. Their guide punched in the same code.

"I'm surprised you don't use key cards," Mandy said.

"Too many vampires lose cards. Besides, these only to keep out mortals. All vampires welcome here."

Explained why the guide hadn't bothered being discreet. Still, he hadn't told them the number, either.

The door opened to a foyer. Hallways branched to the right and left. Two doors lined each side of the foyer and a huge picture of a man wearing some twelfth-century get up hung on the far wall. Inky black hair and striking eyebrows dominated his facial features. Perry pointed at the portrait. "Who is that?"

"That is our leader. Dimitri."

Of course it was. Vain much?

Their escort crossed the foyer and opened the far door on the left. "Please sit. I will let Dimitri know you here."

Perry guessed their esteemed leader already knew of their arrival, what with cameras situated in almost every corner. Well, in every corner except Dimitri's office.

"Thank you." Mandy sat on the leather couch that lined the wall and patted the spot next to her.

Fancy lamps—Tiffany maybe?—lit the area. The ornate desk took up half the room. Compensating for something?

He placed their backpacks and coats on an empty table and sat beside her. "Don't you think it's strange the rest of the Committee isn't here?"

"I think this whole place is strange. You sure you want to live here?"

His question was for real, but hers wasn't. He really needed to keep his head in the game. The room was most likely bugged—for Dimitri's ears only, of course. "It's a beautiful country."

"You've hardly seen any of it."

He flattened his lips at her. "You just don't like the language barrier. I'm sure you can learn Russian easy enough."

The door opened and a large man with the same features as the portrait entered. "He is right. We even offer classes to learn our language for new members."

Perry stood. "See? We can take the class together. I'm Perry and this is my lovely Amanda. You must be Dimitri. Striking portrait you have out there."

"Thank you." Dimitri motioned for him to sit as he sat across from them. "Interesting combination of shirts you are wearing. Is that not the Union Jack under your Polynesian shirt?"

"It's an Hawaiian shirt, but yeah, Union Jack. Gotta support the future missus, right?" He one-armed hugged Mandy.

"Why not wear Russian flag on shirt instead?"

"Maybe I will. If we choose to live here."

"Yes. About that. Why do you wish to live here?"

And let the game continue. Oh Great One, please let their contact succeed.

* * * *

Barnet studied the door to his cell. And the man beyond it. Even if he could manage to escape the cell, Yevgeni would be impossible to pass.

The door at the top of the stairs opened. Someone whispered in Russian. Yevgeni turned. Their conversation went on for a bit. Yevgeni growled and stormed up the stairs.

A few moments later a blonde woman wearing blue coveralls descended the stairs. "Barnet?"

"Yes."

"You are older than I thought." She opened the cell door using a key. "We must hurry. Your associates are keeping Dimitri busy so I can get you out of here."

Was that the plan? "He suspects they're here to rescue me. I don't need you to get in trouble, too."

"But they are not here for that. I am. As long as he is with your comrades, he will feel confident that you are safe down here. Plus, his eyes will not be on the monitors. We must go. Now."

Barnet followed the woman upstairs. A cleaning cart stood off to the side. She motioned for him to be quiet and get into the trash bin.

His clothes were already a mess, what was a little more trash? She lifted a bag and he climbed inside. She placed the bag on top. Okay, wasn't as bad as he thought it'd be. He blanked out and froze. No breathing. He even slowed his heart rate. Only a vampire purposely looking for him would notice the sound.

The cart moved. Someone called out, "Katya!" The cart stopped. Katya and a male spoke in Russian for several moments. No yelling or screaming. More intimate. Like they were friends, or maybe lovers.

They kissed. Yeah, more likely lovers.

The cart moved once again. Stopped. Elevator doors opened. Cart moved into the enclosure. Elevator doors closed. They went up. The lid to the bin opened. She lifted the bag.

"Out. Go up there." Katya motioned to the hatch above. She linked her hands together to give him a boost.

She didn't have to tell him twice. He stepped into her linked hands and she lifted him up. While she held him, he opened the hatch. He gripped the sides and hoisted himself through the opening. Once he was situated, he closed the hatch.

"Wait until I return. Make no noise." She replaced the bag and closed the lid.

The hatch door was more mesh than solid and Barnet could see through it. As long as no one looked up and truly examined the ceiling, he should be safe. When the elevator stopped on the first floor, she exited the car with the trash bin. Barnet waited.

A shower. That was the first thing he was going to do once he got out of this mess.

An alarm went off. Barnet covered his ears. Had Yevgeni returned to his post or was this part of the plan?

* * * *

Mandy never realized how boring logistics could be. Why couldn't it be simple to move from one country to another? They were vampires, not mortals. They had different rules. Not that she wanted to move to Russia. Hell, she couldn't understand why anyone would stay.

Well, except for the scenery. It was a beautiful country, what little she'd seen of it so far. And she couldn't fault them on their stores, either. It was a shopper's paradise and she'd only been able to window shop. It'd been kind of fun using her Russian to read and listen in on conversations, too. Not that Perry or the US Committee knew she understood the language. She felt it would be better if no one knew. So much easier to listen in when the speakers thought she didn't know the language. She figured it would come in handy during this mission. A mission that was going positively sluggishly. She'd thought for sure the alarm would sound by now. Just how long did it take to rescue her father from his cell?

Perry was on his game, though. Or he really was interested in what Russia had to offer. He seemed enraptured through the whole process. Or maybe he was just curious. Hadn't he said he'd never left the States?

An alarm blared outside the office. Finally! Mandy jumped to her feet. "What's that?"

Dimitri rose. "I am sure it is nothing that my people cannot take care of." The alarm cut off. "See? Please. Sit."

It was the plan for her to be concerned, but they couldn't leave right away. It would only look suspicious. She settled back beside Perry. "Sorry. It startled me, is all. Do they go off a lot?"

"Unfortunately, that has been the case recently. We have many workers in the building and they keep hitting fire alarm. I assure you, you are safe. I would have been called if it was an actual emergency."

Ahhh, so that was how their contact did it. Created a problematic issue and used that as a signal. Brilliant.

Perry patted Mandy's thighs. "Now that we don't have to worry about burning up, I got some more questions. How often do your vampires have to check in?"

Dimitri interlocked his fingers in front of his chest. "We no longer have scheduled check ins."

Perry sat up straight and grinned. "Really? Vampires don't have to account for their whereabouts?"

Mandy couldn't believe that was true. Even the UK vampires had to check in once a year, as did the US vampires.

"No, you misunderstand," Dimitri said without moving a beat. "Vampires are called to come in. It is random. Spontaneous."

Perry scrunched his forehead in that cute way he did whenever she'd seen him confused. "Called? Like with a cellphone?"

"Yes. Exactly that."

How the Russian vampires hadn't revolted by now was a mystery to Mandy. "What if they're away at the time?" She glanced at Perry. "Or their phone broke? Or the battery died?"

Dimitri turned that fake smile Mandy was getting sick of her way. "We allow for travel time, certainly. And a broken phone or dead battery is not a valid excuse. We expect our citizens to be prepared for a call at any time. It is better this way. Similar to jury duty in your country, Mr. Davenport. No one knows when or if they are going to be called. Am I right?"

Perry chuckled. "I guess so. I've never actually served because I'm not registered to vote anywhere. But I believe jury summons are mailed."

"Mail is not safe. It never has been. We have embraced technology. Hiding among the public has never been easier."

"I guess you would know." Perry took Mandy's hand as he stood. "Your country is very interesting and I appreciate you taking the time to talk with us. I'm very impressed, but we do need to get going. I promised Amanda we'd check out other destinations before we make a decision."

She gripped his arm and snuggled in close. There would be a time she wouldn't be able to do that, but now was not that time and she took advantage. "No offense, but I'm hoping he likes Australia better. I hear there are penguins there. I so much want to live where the penguins are."

Perry chuckled and patted her hand. "She just wants to go someplace she doesn't have to learn another language."

"That's not true. Why do you always say that? I came here, didn't I?"

He rolled his eyes. "Not now, Amanda."

"It's always not now, isn't it?" She broke away and placed her hands on her hips. "You have no intention of voting for any of the places I picked, do you?"

Dimitri clapped "Brava."

Bloody hell. Had they been compromised? How? "Excuse me? Oh, I get it. You're on his side, aren't you? You men always stick together."

"You can cut the horse manure, Miss Groves. I know why you are here."

Or he was guessing. She bet he was only trying to trip them up. "Of course you know. We told you." She turned toward Perry. "I don't like it here. Can we go home?"

"You, too, Mr. Davenport. I have to say, you two have been very entertaining. But the show is over. And if you ever wish to see your homes again, you better hope your esteemed leader takes my deal."

The only leader this pretend Mandy Groves knew lived in London. "Deal? What deal? Michael Kingston doesn't even know I'm considering moving."

"Yeah, neither does Barnet," Perry said. "I wasn't going to say anything until we made a decision. What deal are you talking about?"

"Please. I am not stupid. The jig is up. Is that not what they say?" Dimitri never moved from his seat. He sat with a calm demeanor. Then again, he could jump them at any second. "And if Michael knows better, he'll stay in UK where it is safe. If you wish things to remain as they have been, I suggest you sit down."

What the hell had gotten Dimitri so riled to kidnap her father and threaten the UK Committee Head? What could they have possibly done to Dimitri? Alexi Popolov wrote a stupid story and now the Head of the Russian Committee wanted to start a war?

"We're not sitting. We're leaving." Perry picked up their belongings. "Come on, sweetheart."

"Enough of this!" Dimitri yelled. "You think I believe your arrival here now is a coincidence?"

Well he certainly couldn't accuse them of any wrong-doing. They'd been with him the whole time. But somehow she didn't think that mattered to Dimitri.

Someone knocked on the door.

Dimitri zipped to the door and yanked it open. "What is it, Yevgeni?" he asked in Russian.

Yevgeni was one bruiser of a guy. He responded in Russian. "We have a problem."

"Outside." Dimitri turned toward them and spoke in English. "You might as well make yourself comfortable. You won't be going anywhere for a while." He left the room and closed the door behind him. A mechanical sound came from the door.

"Did he just lock us in?" Perry asked.

She placed her finger against her lips and went to the door. Perry in all his wisdom actually saw fit to keep quiet. She could kiss him for that, but then she'd probably kiss him some more, and what was she doing? Oh yeah. Listening in.

The door was at least two inches thick, but luckily the two men only walked a few steps away and continued to speak in Russian. Now she was more than pleased they didn't know she knew the language or else they would have walked far enough away not to be overheard by her vampire ears.

"What kind of problem?" Dimitri asked.

"Barnet is missing."

"What?" Something hit the wall with a thump. Or maybe someone. "How? I told you to watch him."

"I had to step away," Yevgeni said with a rasp, as if he was being choked. "When I returned he was gone. As I went searching for him, the alarm sounded on the loading dock."

"Who pulled you away? Who?" Dimitri screamed.

"My sister. Kriztina. I'm sorry, sir."

Colorful swear words echoed in the foyer. Mandy couldn't catch them all as they came fast and furious. Dimitri was one pissed off vampire. "How did he get out of his cell?"

"Someone had to have let him out. Door is undamaged." Yevgeni was speaking more clearly, so Dimitri must have released the man. "I wasn't gone that long."

"Who else is here?"

"There are at least a dozen workers on the fifth floor. They're working on the exhibit."

"Did you check the video?"

"No, sir. I thought it best to come here first."

If their contact was successful, there wouldn't be any video. Another reason she and Perry had to distract Dimitri. That man was into everything.

"Lock the place down. He has to be somewhere. Meet me in the video room." Their footsteps faded.

Mandy waited a bit then tried the door. Locked solid. Not even a little wiggle. She pulled out her mobile. "No signal. Of course. I don't think they're going to let us go any time soon. Barnet is missing, but I don't know if he escaped or not. He could still be in the building and they put us in lockdown."

"You know Russian?"

"I do."

"Well, hot damn!" Perry grinned as he punched the air. "Your talent never ceases to amaze me. So what do we do? Stake Dimitri and his goon? There's enough wood in here to stake a bazillion vampires."

"That wouldn't make us look guilty, now would it?"

"Hate to break it to you, but Dimitri could easily read our minds if that portrait is any indication of his age."

Dimitri did seem rather ancient. "Age doesn't always guarantee strength. And we're not exactly newbies, are we? I was turned in 1509. How about you?"

"1656."

"See? You're not so young. Remember, if he tries to read our minds, it would open a path to his own. I'm guessing he wouldn't want to take that risk. And as long as we stay in character, he'll question his info before he tries to read us. He was with us when Barnet went missing, so he can't charge us with anything."

"Yeah, because he seems like such a stand-up guy." Perry went over to the desk. "No phone here. Who doesn't have a phone on their desk when you can't get a signal?"

"It's probably stashed in the desk."

He tugged at every drawer handle. "All locked. Too bad I don't have my lock picks. I don't want to be buried alive again."

Again? She would have to ask about that story at a later time. "You know how to pick locks?"

"Doesn't everyone?"

"No. What do you need?"

"I'd ask for hairpins, but women don't seem to use those anymore. Plus, your hair is down. Although…" He came around the desk and stared at her breasts. "You're wearing an underwire bra."

"So? It's not like I need one. They just come this way." When he raised an eyebrow at her, she got the implication. "Oh." Her bra. Her pretty bra.

"We don't have to use it. I'm sure there's something else in here we could use."

"Don't be silly. I can buy another." She yanked her blouse from the skirt and reached around back to unhook the bra. Pulled the straps down her arms—thank goodness the sleeves were billowy. One tug later, she freed the bra from underneath her blouse.

"Awww. And here I thought I was going to get a peep show."

"Not my fault if you didn't get your fill." She tossed him the bra.

When he ripped the fabric away from the underwire, she almost sobbed. He better not have ruined it for nothing.

* * * *

Barnet stretched out as best he could on top of the elevator, making sure he didn't lose sight of any occupants in the car below. After the short alarm, two male workers entered the elevator on the first floor, each of their carts filled with crates. The one closest to the panel pushed the button for the fifth floor. They departed quite nosily and all was quiet for about five minutes. The doors opened. Same workers but now their carts were empty. They returned to the first floor.

When the elevator's doors opened, the first man exited and the second pushed his cart out, but held the door open. A large crate was being wheeled in by none other than Barnet's savior. Someone in the distance shouted. Katya held the door open.

Yevgeni entered the elevator and the doors closed, but they didn't move. He said something in Russian and pointed at the crate. Katya put her hands on hips and spoke in a scolding manner. Yevgeni bowed his head and mentioned Dimitri's name. She puffed out a breath and yanked the lid off. A statue lay inside, all covered in wrap and packing material. Yevgeni seemed to apologize, but wasn't through with his questions. Katya continued to answer. This went on for several moments. Finally, Yevgeni pushed the button for the fifth floor. The elevator ascended.

Whoever she was, she apparently outranked Yevgeni. Or maybe they were related.

When the doors opened, he held them open for her. She wheeled out the cart. He followed her. The doors closed.

The elevator didn't move. Several minutes later, the door opened. Katya had returned with the cart and five crates. She pushed the button for the first floor.

As soon as the doors closed she said, "Get ready to come down."

He opened the hatch and stuck his legs through the opening.

She lifted two crates from a third. "Get inside."

The box was barely large enough for a kid. This would take some doing. As quickly and quietly as he could, he lowered himself, using the box beside it as a step. He crawled inside. Or rather, turned into a pretzel.

Good thing he didn't need to breathe. Wasn't sure he could take a breath all twisted like this.

She placed the other crates on top with no time to spare. The doors opened and she wheeled him out of the elevator.

The air quality changed as he was wheeled over a bump. They were outdoors. Exhaust fumes filled the air. Music played in the distance and men laughed. The cart stopped.

Katya spoke to someone in Russian. Lots of feet shuffled in the area, indicating more people. Someone lifted Barnet's crate. Carried him a few steps. Placed him on a vibrating surface. An engine was running. He must be inside a van. Sounds of wood scraping and the jostling of his crate indicated more items were loaded inside. He waited. Figured he'd be told when he could leave. Or were they just going to put him in a dump to find his own way out? Anything was possible.

Doors to the back of the van slammed shut. A door up front opened and closed. The vehicle took off.

After about ten or fifteen minutes of driving, the driver spoke. "You can get out of box now. Is safe."

Barnet elbowed the lid off, crawled out and over to the front, and got the shock of his life as he stared at his former prisoner-mate. "Mikhail? What are you doing here?"

He was looking a lot healthier, too. Amazing what a good feeding could do for a vampire.

"I am helping you escape, what it look like? When Dimitri let me go, I went home. But Maria, my wife, she not there. Instead, I find Katya. I was surprised."

"Why? Who is Katya?"

"You are joking, right? Or maybe you only know her by her given name. Yekaterina Volkova."

Holy shit. Their contact was a member of the Russian Committee? "I don't understand. Why did she help me escape?"

"She is trying to make things better for us. Or so she told me. Dimitri has been working behind the members. They had no idea you were brought over here. She only knew because she has been snooping Dimitri."

"Why didn't she tell us that? We could help."

"She does not want outside help. She wants our people to help. To overthrow Dimitri. But to do that, she must be sneaky. To catch him off guard."

"I suppose he's off guard now, huh? I'm sure he's looking for me."

"Yes, now would be good time. I hope so. I no like Dimitri so much. But other vampires do like him, so I doubt overthrow happens today. Katya must change their minds first."

"But he's been your Head for centuries. Why the overthrow? Why not just vote him out?"

"You joke, right? No voting for the Head here. We only have members because it is expected of Russia to do so."

Barnet shook his head. Maybe it was time the Committee Heads got together. If they had been meeting regularly, Dimitri might not have been an issue. "Why do you stay here, Mikhail? Why not just leave?"

"I would get marked as rogue, as Alexi Popolov has. And if they don't find me for five years, descendents from my brothers and sisters families will all be killed. All my bloodlines, gone. I guess Alexi doesn't have any bloodlines, probably why he run away."

"He didn't run away. He was buried. Alive. By Dimitri. Do you think Katya could help us find him?"

"Katya wants you out of the country. Maybe when we get a new leader, you can find and talk to Alexi then."

Barnet leaned back against the side panel. Mikhail was right. Now was not the time. But could Katya overthrow Dimitri without undue attention? Or would it cause a war and be the catalyst to out vampires to the mortal world? Barnet hoped it would not come to that.

Chapter 8

Perry inserted the wires into the lock. The chamber clicked. Ahhh, freedom. Well, freedom from the room in any case. "What next, Beautiful?"

He couldn't believe she knew Russian and hadn't told him. Was she afraid he'd spill the beans, was that it? She might have had a need for that concern with the old Perry, but the new and improved Perry was much better at keeping secrets.

"You opened it?" She ran into his arms and kissed his mouth. "Brilliant. You are a dear, aren't you?"

"I try." Damn, his lips still tingled from that kiss. What was it about her? Was it because she was older? No, he'd met older ones. Victoria was older than him. Not by much, but he'd never ever been interested in her. Not even after her first husband died.

Mandy placed her ear against the door. Vampires really didn't need to go to such lengths to hear, but the wood was thick so she probably did it to hear farther. "It's quiet. Shall we?"

He shrugged into his jacket. "It's quiet because no one is out there or it's quiet because a vampire isn't making noise?" Because vampires could be quiet even to other vampires if they so desired.

"Guess we'll find out, huh?" She slipped on her coat and backpack, opened the door, and stuck her head out. Motioned for him to follow. She headed right, toward the stairwell.

Perry hooked his backpack over one shoulder, followed her, and whispered, "Do you think it's safe to leave? If he's still here…"

"I'm sure whoever sprung him is getting him out. Our job is done. Remember the alarm?"

"Right." That was supposed to be their signal. But everything else was screwed up, why wouldn't that be screwed up, too. He'd feel better once he spotted Barnet. Hell, he might even hug the guy.

Mandy reached the hallway just as the door to the stairwell opened.

"No, no, no," the petite blonde in coveralls said as she stuck out her hands. "You must go back."

"Like bloody hell we will. Get out of our way or get hurt."

Man, the forcefulness of Mandy's voice was a total turn-on. He really needed to get a grip on his libido.

"No, you don't understand. I'm here to get you out. The right way. You must go back. Trust me. Please."

Perry had no reason not to trust her. And if she was their ticket out, he was grabbing it. He took Mandy's hand and pulled her along.

They all piled back into the office and the woman shut the door. She whispered, "He is out."

Well at least they got some good news. Hopefully the day would end that way, with them in the air on their way back to London.

Mandy put a finger to her lips. Pointed at the door. Footsteps were headed their way. She hugged the woman. "Thank God you're here. That awful man locked us in. I thought we were stuck here forever."

"What? Who are you? Why are you here?" The woman smiled and nodded. Apparently fine with fooling Dimitri, if indeed those were his footsteps.

Perry could get in on the game, too. "We're here as potential citizens. Is this how you treat visitors?"

The office door opened and Dimitri entered. "Katya. What are you doing here?"

The blonde turned around. "I was helping with the exhibit when Yevgeni stopped me in the elevator. He was acting strange, looking for something or...someone. I came here to ask what is going on and found your guests locked in the office. What does he mean 'potential citizens'? I thought they were due here tomorrow."

Dimitri waved his hand dismissively. "I told you the date. You must have written it down wrong. And they are not potential citizens. They are spies. I was in process of questioning them when the alarm went off. Yevgeni was only making sure no one entered illegally."

"Spies?" Katya turned to Mandy and Perry. "Why are you visiting our country?"

"We are not spies. Dimitri is full of it." Mandy buried her head in Perry's shoulder. "I don't want to live here. I just want to go home."

Perry wrapped his arm around her in a soothing way. Yeah, they were still playing a part, but she felt good there all the same. "It's okay, Beautiful. I don't know where he got his information, but he certainly got us wrong. And you can forget about us asking for citizenship if this is the way you treat your people."

"Dimitri? What proof do you have they are not here for what they say?"

"Yeah," Perry added. "Why else would we be here?"

Dimitri's eyes widened. Ah-ha! Seemed the rest of the Committee did not know of Barnet's kidnapping. "I have no idea why they would be here. I was going to inform the other members once I verified their story."

"And that's why you locked them in the office? Dimitri, this is not the way." Katya gestured toward the door. "Come with me. I'll show you the way out."

"Katya, I know you have a soft heart, but you cannot let them go. They are our enemies."

"And just how are they our enemies? What have they done to us?" When Dimitri didn't answer, Katya snorted. "Just what I thought. We will discuss this later. With the rest of the Committee."

Katya led them outdoors, around the building to a small car. Discreetly pointed out the cameras with a nod toward one and a glance toward another. "I will drive you to your hotel. Where are you staying?"

"We already checked out," Perry said. "Our plans were to head out after this interview anyway. So if you could just take us to the airport," so they could fly on out of here and reconnect with Barnet, "that would be great."

"I wish you'd reconsider. I am very sorry for the way you were treated. Once we get the whole Committee together, you'll see it's not so different here."

Ahhh, so they were most likely being recorded, too. "Yeah, why weren't they here?"

"I'm sure I wrote the wrong date. As Dimitri said. Please. Give us another try."

"Maybe another day. After we've checked other locations." He squeezed Mandy, who hadn't let him go since they left the building. "You ready to go home, Beautiful?"

"More than ready. This whole thing has been stressful. I wish we'd never come. I'm sorry, baby. I know you wanted to try—"

"Shhh. We'll talk about it later. Inside you go, now." He opened the back door and she climbed in. After she settled in, he entered from the other side.

As Katya settled behind the steering wheel, Perry continued with the soothing suitor role and wrapped his arm around Mandy's shoulders. She felt good beside him, almost like she fit. He'd be sad when this job ended and she went back home. Then again, she could reconcile with Barnet and might stick around awhile. That would be nice. Perry wasn't ready to say goodbye to Mandy yet.

* * * *

Mandy continued to rest her head on Perry's shoulder, even when they'd entered the highway and it was highly unlikely—okay, impossible—for Dimitri to see them any longer. And the reason had nothing to do with the parts they were playing. Nope. She rested her head on his shoulder because it just felt right. He felt right. Which was crazy talk. She wasn't looking for a mate and he wasn't looking for a vampire.

But maybe Dimitri couldn't see them, but he could probably hear everything. "I see you have a dash cam in the car. Is it really necessary?"

"Wait. Dash cam? Where?" Perry asked.

Katya pointed to the device attached to the rearview mirror. "It films everything in front of the vehicle. Most vehicles have one. To not have one would draw attention. But do not worry. Sound has been muted. You are free to talk."

Mandy took that opportunity to break away from Perry and lean back in her seat. "Bloody hell. I thought for sure he was going to throw us down to *podzemel'ye*."

"He would have, too, if I hadn't intervened. Good thing I not listen to Dimitri, no? He always gives us wrong dates for events."

Perry leaned forward. "If he gave you the wrong date of our arrival, how did you know we were here today?"

"Because I get info from your Committee. I am your contact."

"Holy shit!"

Holy shit, indeed. Their intel had come from someone deeper than Mandy had even thought possible. "Why is he still in power?"

"Grigorii and I try so hard to change things, but we are always out voted. Or rather, Felicks talks Sergei into voting Dimitri's way. I swear, he's just as bad as Dimitri. But we hope to change that soon. Before Dimitri goes too far."

"What? Kidnapping Barnet wasn't going too far?" Perry asked.

"It was, but at least we were able to release him before our people found out he was taken."

"Why is that?" Mandy asked. "Wouldn't it have made Dimitri look foolish if he'd been caught kidnapping a Committee Head?"

"Oh no. There are still many people who believe Dimitri's way is the only way. We need to convince them first before we can succeed in overthrowing Dimitri. Still, I find it strange that Dimitri didn't go public with Barnet. He could have used Barnet to his advantage. So it makes me wonder why?"

"Besides having to explain himself to his own Committee?" Perry leaned forward. "I'm thinking it has to do with Alexi Popolov. Or the discovery of Perfect Mates. Take your pick."

And why either of those should matter still baffled Mandy. Maybe Dimitri was just crazy.

"Perfect Mates? From the stories?"

"Yeah. We've found some. I'm hoping to find one for myself some day." Perry smiled and flashed his eyebrows.

Mandy snorted. Bloody hell. Apparently that bout of love making had been totally pretend on his end. And he'd said he couldn't lie well. News flash! The man lied about not being able to lie. And she'd fallen for it.

Katya glanced in the rearview mirror. "You are talking about people who cannot be controlled. Correct?"

Perry nodded. "That's what they seem like at first, but when bonded with a vampire, they're so much more. Their blood can even make it possible for their mate to tolerate the sun."

"Is that why you want one?" Mandy asked. "So you can go out in the sun?" She didn't miss the sun so much. With the sun came people. And there were just too many of them out during the day. The nights were so much more relaxed.

"Well, no. Not the only reason. I hear the sex is really good, too."

Better than with her? Mandy shook her head. "You are impossible."

"I can see why Dimitri over reacted," Katya said. "He doesn't call them Perfect Mates. He calls them freaks. As for Alexi. He's been missing for almost five years. I assume he died."

"Not dead," Perry said. "Buried. Alive. You know nothing of that?"

Katya shook her head. "Dimitri?"

"That's what we've been told. It was witnessed."

"Who witnessed it?"

"Natasha Bychkova. She's afraid to do anything because the area is under surveillance and if she says something, she's afraid the same will happen to her."

"And she is not wrong. Did she tell you this in the store?"

Mandy straightened. "What store?"

"She owns the shop where you purchased that outfit. Nice choice, by the way. I'm tempted to get that skirt myself."

Mandy smiled. She knew it was a good choice when she spotted it. "You should. It's very comfortable. But no, she didn't tell us there. The US Committee was calling everyone associated with Alexi to find out where he might have gone."

"I see. Natasha's late husband and Alexi were friends. I suppose this means that Dimitri has already gone too far if he's buried Alexi alive. Poor Natasha. I shall have a talk with her. But right now? Alexi may be safest right where he is. At least until we can take care of Dimitri."

Perry leaned forward. "Safe? Are you shitting me? Do you know what it feels like to be buried alive?"

"No. I have not had that experience, but I have been told what it is like. Used to be the way we punished vampires until we created the jail. I had hoped we would no longer resort to such punishment, but that is me being naïve. I do know it is better than being dead. And Dimitri could very well have had him killed. I wouldn't be surprised if that is his final plan with Alexi anyway. Make him suffer before ending his life."

They were approaching the airport. The wrong one. Mandy leaned forward. "Where are you taking us? Our plane is no longer in the hangar."

"I am aware, but I must take you there if you want your cover story to be believed. And yes, we have cameras at the airport. After I drop you off, go inside your hangar and then proceed to terminal four. Since your plane isn't in the hangar, it won't look suspicious. Once inside the terminal, look for a man standing by the doorway wearing black coveralls and a red baseball cap. He will get you out of the airport safely and take you to Barnet and your airplane."

"And this mystery man's name?" Perry asked. "You know, in case there are more than one of them."

Katya laughed. "His name is Dima Rodchenko. Don't worry. He speaks English. His mate is from America and she taught him well."

If a vampire could turn paler, Perry was that vampire.

"Are you okay?"

"Peachy." He smiled, but it faded fast.

Katya drove up to a gate. She must have made some mental suggestion because the guard never asked for any ID. Instead, he just opened the gate for them. She drove on to the hangar.

"Are you going to need our help with Dimitri?" Mandy asked. "If not the US Committee, I could see if the UK Committee could get involved. It's to all our best interests that your overthrow goes smoothly."

"If I thought it would help, I'd ask for it. But I'm afraid any outside assistance will look suspicious to my people. Like a takeover. It is best if we can handle this ourselves. Without a lot of publicity. But I thank you for the offer. Please, tell Barnet to stop asking about Alexi. Once it is safe, I will take care of it and contact him. Until then, we must be covert. I hope he understands." Katya stopped at the hangar.

Perry grabbed the backpacks and exited the car. Offered a hand to Mandy and she took it.

Katya rolled down her window and smiled. "Safe travels."

Mandy waited until the car drove out of sight. Free. They were almost free. "Almost" being the operative word. She held her hand out. "I can carry my own backpack."

Perry slipped her bag over one shoulder and his on the other. "So can I. Hey, since you seem to know Russian, what does *kozel* mean?"

"You have people cussing at you in Russian already? What did you do?" Except they hadn't been apart since arriving, so it must have been something not so recent.

"Why do people always assume I did something?"

"Because you do?"

"Well, maybe. In the past. But I'm different now. And yet I still get the assumptions."

"I'm sure once people realize you've changed, they'll change, too. Takes time. As for *kozel*, it technically means goat."

"Goat? That's not so bad. How is that a cuss word?"

She grabbed his arm and led him to the hangar. "Because to a Russian it's like calling you an asshole. How did you happen to hear that word?"

He shrugged. "I don't know. Probably from a movie. It's always bugged me not knowing what it meant. And since I now know you know Russian, figured you could put my brain at rest. So thank you."

He was so full of it. Could his interest in the word have something to do with him being buried alive? Seemed to be a Russian thing of the past. Well, they did have a long trip ahead of them. Lots of time for talking.

Perry rubbed his hands together. "You ready to meet your dear ol' dad?"

That man knew how to change subjects. Would her father talk to her? Probably not. Five hundred years was a long time to hold a grudge. Yet, he most likely still held it. Otherwise, he'd have answered her letters.

* * * *

Perry was ready to blow this pop stand.

All the male names were starting to sound the same. How popular was the name Dimitri? Or even Rodchenko? Was it like calling someone John Smith? Because most vampires used a common name. Harder to trace. That's if it was the same here as it was back home.

Home. Perry had been excited to take this trip. Now, he couldn't return soon enough, where it was safe from vampires who liked to bury their victims alive. Figured it was a Russian thing. He never wanted to step foot in this country again.

Mandy opened the door to the hangar.

Perry held back and whispered, "You think it's safe to talk in there now?"

"Probably not. Want to hold hands?" She held out her hand.

He wanted to hold it more than anything, which he shouldn't. But if they wanted to talk freely, and they were still being observed, maybe they should be holding hands.

He passed a sign in Russian. Or Cyrillic. Or whatever the heck their alphabet was. *"Can you read that sign?"* he asked through their linked hands.

"Yes. It says we are to proceed to terminal four if no one is here to meet us. Just like Katya said."

She was so smart, whereas he was…not exactly stupid, but nowhere near as smart. Would his Perfect Mate care? Probably. Which meant that he should become smarter, or at least become more knowledgeable so he looked smarter. Hopefully that wouldn't be too hard to do.

He laughed. *"Well, that makes sense. I guess we should head to terminal four."* As soon as they left the hangar, he broke their link and spoke aloud. "What made you learn the language?"

"How else do you expect to control someone in a foreign country if you don't know their language?"

"But it's not like Russia is a neighbor to England. I only got as far as learning a little Spanish and French. You know, for those times I visited Mexico and Canada. Because they're neighbors. But this is my first time across the pond, as you put it, so I never saw a need to learn. Think you can teach me?" He'd get around to learning more Spanish and French, too. That would surely impress his Perfect Mate.

"You think I'm sticking around, is that it?"

"Well sure. This is your chance to mend fences. You do want to reconcile with your father, don't you?"

She nodded. "I do. But I'm nervous. I'll be surprised if he even lets me on the plane."

"Of course he'll let you on. You're his daughter."

"That's just a title. I haven't been his daughter in a long time. I'm beginning to think it was a mistake coming here."

"Hey, I'm glad you came. I wouldn't have been able to do all this without you. Hell, I probably would have ended up in that podzeemee-thingy. Or worse. Buried alive."

"Yeah?" She smiled and his heart melted a little. Why did she have to have a great smile?

Now was not the time to worry about why she turned him on. She was worried Barnet would reject her and frankly, he didn't believe that would happen. The man never held a grudge. She was just overreacting. And nervous, like she'd said. "Don't you worry about your father. It'll be fine. Trust me."

She squeezed his hand. "You are a dear."

And her hand felt much too nice. It shouldn't feel nice. He shouldn't feel anything romantic about her. She was a friend. Just a friend. And a vampire. A vampire. A vampire. He released her hand. "Lookee there. I think that's our terminal."

At least the numbers looked the same in Russian as they did in English. A big red 4 was painted on the side of a building. And on the door.

She pulled out her cellphone. "Hey, my mobile is working now. Thank God Dimitri didn't confiscate it."

"Who you gonna call?"

They looked at each other and shouted, "Ghostbusters!"

Wow. Of all the times he'd lead with that, she was the first to finish it with him. He was going to like being her friend.

She laughed. "Actually, I thought I'd text Oscar the Grouch that we're on our way."

"Don't text him until we see Dima in the red cap. It might be hours before we leave. What kind of name is Dima anyway?"

"It's short. A nickname. For Dimitri."

"What?" No, no, no. It couldn't be. Frantically, he scanned the area. Oh shit. Red ballcap. And a face he'd hoped to never see again. Before he could grab Mandy and hide, he'd been spotted.

"*Kozel!*"

When a vampire lived as long as Perry and faced death, it could take awhile for their life to pass before their eyes. So as Dima Rodchenko pointed an accusatory finger, Perry stood there, frozen. Should he run? What good would that do? He knew no one here. And he had to consider Mandy. She could still go home.

So he played it cool. "Hey, Roddy, my man. Bet you're surprised to see me."

"You know him?" Mandy looked over at the beast as he approached. "Of course you do. That's how you know that word. Bloody hell. Are we ever going to get out of here?"

"Sure. Have a little faith." Because he had all the faith in the world that she would go home. Whereas, he might get buried again. If not staked for the sunrise. At least Roddy wouldn't do anything in public. Perry had that going for him.

The man hadn't changed one iota since that unfortunate incident back in Wyoming, but then why would he? Vampires didn't change. Roddy still towered over Perry a good three to four inches and looked intimidating as hell as he placed his hands on his hips. "How the fucking hell did you get free?"

His English had gotten better, though.

Perry gave his good-natured laugh, hoping like hell he could lighten the mood. "Funny story, there. Apparently you bragged to the wrong person about what you did."

Roddy grabbed Perry around the neck and slammed him against the ground. "I told no one."

So much for lightening the mood. Perry winced as pain spread across his backside and wrenched free the finger blocking his airway. "Well then, one of your buddies did. If I recall, you weren't alone."

Mandy grabbed Roddy's arm. "I don't know what he did, but we're out in public. Can we do this somewhere else?"

"I knew I should have left you in the sun to burn." Roddy tightened his hold momentarily before releasing Perry.

Perry jumped up and brushed off his jacket and pants, trying to pretend his back wasn't complaining with the movement. Hopefully nothing was broken and the pain would dissipate in a few minutes. That man was strong. "And you don't know how happy I am that you didn't. I swear, I didn't know she was with you. I thought she was one of those ladies of the night. Honest."

"You calling her a whore now?"

"No, no, no." Although technically, the woman had been a whore, but why mention that? Perry didn't wish to be ground into burger meat. "Mistaken identity. I mistook her for someone else. But man, that was centuries ago. Can't we just forgive and forget?"

"It is not me who needs to forgive." Roddy stormed off.

Not him? Who then?

"What did you do?" Mandy asked.

The accusation stung. It always came down to what he'd done. Not to what other people had done. Perry ignored her question, took her hand, and kept pace with the angry Russian, who led them through the underworld of the airport.

"Did you have some fun with his food and he took offense?"

If he didn't answer, she'd probably keep at it. *"Sort of. But in my defense, I didn't know she belonged to him. Yes, I fed from her. Yes, we had sex. But I didn't coerce her. She came on to me. And it was so long ago. Over two hundred years. Why is he still mad?"*

"Because you have, or rather had that effect on people?"

That she corrected herself made the sting go away. She didn't seem to think he was that way now, and he wasn't. But back then? Hell, even a year ago he had that effect on people. Still, two hundred years? That was a long time to hold a grudge. Especially over a mortal who died long ago.

They emerged from the building to a parking lot. A blonde woman wearing jeans and a winter coat was leaning against an SUV, her arms crossed over her chest. Roddy's American wife? Perry skidded to a stop.

Okay. Not so dead.

Chapter 9

Mandy shook her head. What man never had his dick in the wrong woman? But Perry was single and he didn't seem like the kind to force himself on anyone, so wouldn't the woman be a little bit responsible? Dima seemed to think it was all Perry's fault, or maybe he was led to believe that. Did seem rather silly to be mad over something that happened two hundred years ago to someone no longer alive.

Oh, what was she thinking? Her father had Dima beat by three hundred years.

"Holy shit, he turned her," Perry muttered. He then waved and smiled. "Hey, Hannah Banana." He might have been going for confident, but the waiver in his voice gave him away.

Turned her? Now it was starting to make sense. They were still holding hands, so Mandy continued speaking to him through their link. *"I take it she's the woman you were with?"*

He nodded.

Hannah straightened; her eyes wide. "Will Robinson?"

"You had the same name as a character on Lost in Space*?"*

"Actually, I was born with that name, so more like the other way around. He was named after me. I'll tell you the story if I live through this."

Live through this? Well, that couldn't be good.

"Why is he not dead?" Hannah yelled at Dima. "You told me you killed him."

Dima was a large man, but as he held his hands out to his wife he seemed to shrink a few inches. "Now, sweetheart, I was going to go back and do that, after he suffered in the ground. But after your turning, we had to leave so I just told you I had. I'm sorry."

Something must have gone terribly wrong with Hannah's turning. Her eyes became huge circles and her head bobbed slightly in what Mandy could only assume was a nod.

Perry smiled, squeezed Mandy's hand and spoke internally. *"I know I asked for you to do all the talking, but I got this."* Out loud he said, "Can I just apologize and we forget about this whole thing? Roddy, my man, I have no designs on your wife. I have no designs on any woman. After my rescue, I felt reborn. Realized I was gay and changed my name to Perry Davenport."

"Gay! What the hell are you doing?" Didn't he know this was probably one of the worst places to admit to such a thing?

Perry continued smiling. *"Trying to get you out of here?"*

What? Why'd he say "you" instead of "us"? Bloody hell, he was going to get himself buried alive again. If not killed.

Dima turned and marched toward Perry. "Are you saying my Hannah turned you into a faggot?"

"Now, now, now. Is that anyway to talk? I'm gay. And a person can't be turned into anything. Well, except a vampire, but I digress. I was born this way. Back then, I was ashamed. Thought there was something wrong with me. So I kept trying. Please forgive me, Hannah Ba—Hannah. I shouldn't have coerced you."

"If you are gay as you say, then why are you two holding hands as if you are lovers?"

Perry released Mandy's hand. "Habit. We're only here on a mission. That was our cover."

Dima stepped closer, brought his face within inches of Perry's, and scowled. "You don't sound gay."

"It's not nice to stereotype people."

"I don't think you are gay." Dima grabbed Perry around the neck.

Oh bollocks! Dima was going to rip Perry's head off and then she would have to face her father alone and explain. Like he'd believe anything she had to say. This was so not happening on her watch. She wedged between the two and punched Dima in the balls. Even vampire men were weak there. Yowling, Dima clutched his groin and dropped to his knees. Perry staggered back a few steps, rubbing his neck.

Hannah rushed to her husband and glared at Mandy. "What'd you do that for?"

"To keep him from killing my friend. Can we go to our plane now? Or do we need to contact Katya?" Not that Mandy knew how, but they probably didn't know that.

"Get in the back seat." Hannah helped Dima to his feet, but he continued to moan and hold his groin.

Perry took Mandy's hand as they walked to the SUV. "*I don't mean to be a Debbie Downer, and I'm thankful you got him off me before he discovered my lie, but is this a good idea? I mean, they could still take us out somewhere to be buried.*"

Lie? Had Perry thought he was just being probed? Maybe it was best to let him believe that. "*If we don't go with them and Dimitri sees us on foot, he may do the same thing. Hell, he might be here now looking for us. I say if Katya trusts them, we must trust them.*"

Mandy inspected the back-door locks. No child-proofing here. So if they had to make a quick getaway, they could do it. She climbed onto the backseat, scooted to the driver's side and removed her coat. Perry tossed their backpacks inside the car and climbed in after her.

After Hannah assisted Dima onto the passenger seat, she got behind the wheel. "Where am I taking you?"

Mandy opened the map on her phone and showed it to Hannah. "Here."

"That's over thirty kilometers away."

"Katya assured us you'd take us there."

Hannah barely glanced at Perry. Almost as if she were afraid to look at him. Could she be feeling guilty because she'd led Dima to believe one thing and Perry covered her ass? And the fact Dima had never bothered to read his wife's mind said a lot about him. Mandy could respect him for that alone.

Hannah started the engine, backed out of the space, and headed for the exit.

Movement to Mandy's left caught her attention. A black SUV with no lights and a grill meant for demolition came at them fast.

"Hannah! Floor it!"

But Hannah's attention had been in front, not to the side and Mandy's shout only caused the woman to jump in her seat.

The SUV plowed into Mandy's door. Metal screeched. Windows exploded. And Mandy's whole left side screamed in pain.

* * * *

Perry shook the glass pebbles from his head and shoulders. The SUV that plowed into them was fortified with some kind of protective barrier. Thick, metal bars criss-crossed the front. The driver—unknown to Perry—shook his head as if he miscalculated the power of the crash, but Yevgeni sat in the passenger seat staring at them. Shiiiiiit.

Mandy was in bad shape. Or rather, the left side of her was. Blood had splattered all over the inside of her door. Perry slipped both backpacks on his shoulder and grabbed Mandy's good arm. She screamed. "Sorry, Beautiful. But we have to get out of here. Now."

She nodded. He opened his door, flipped her over his shoulder in a fireman carry, and boogied back to the building.

The two vampires from the black SUV were hot on his tail. A storage truck sat idling, parked at the loading dock. No one was behind the wheel. Perry opened the door. "This is gonna hurt."

He shoved her inside and she screamed. He tossed the backpacks inside and climbed in after. "Sorry, Beautiful."

"Stop with the sorries. Just get us out of here."

"Yes, ma'am." He gunned for the exit.

Yevgeni and his buddy ran back to their vehicle.

"Which way should I go?"

"Toward the city. See if you can lose them."

That made sense. He couldn't drive to the plane. Number one, he didn't know how to get there, and number two, he'd only lead them to Barnet, and that wasn't happening. Perry wasn't all that sure he could lose them, though. Not unless he found a bunch of these trucks.

"They drive on the right side of the street, don't they?" Because heaven forbid he'd paid attention on their drive into Russian Headquarters.

"I believe so because the steering wheel is on the left. Drive on the side the signs are facing you. Or follow the traffic."

That made sense, too. God, would his brain ever work right again? He'd never been under such pressure.

"Do you need me to drive?" She grabbed the door handle and sat up with a wince. Her left arm lay limp beside her.

"No offense, but you don't look like you're in any shape to drive. Do you even have use of your left side?"

"A little, but I only need my right leg and arm to drive."

"Well, if I find a convenient stopping point, I'll hand over the wheel." He shook his head in disgust. "Sorry. The stress is bringing out my sarcastic side. Just buckle up, okay?"

She grabbed the seatbelt with her good arm and secured it. "No, you're right. I'm just making it worse. You're doing fine. Really."

Perry didn't believe that for a second, but he could get them to safety. He soon discovered the drivers in this country drove on the right side and assumed any sign with a red border meant stop or no admittance, so he avoided those. A few cars were driving up a ramp, so he followed, hoping, and hit pay dirt. A three-lane highway. Better yet, trucks!

But the early hour of the morning meant less traffic. He zoomed around the trucks, but pretty much stayed in the right lane.

"Are they still following us?" she asked.

He instinctively looked out the rearview mirror and saw a wall. Or rather the trailer he was pulling. He switched to the side mirror. "They're back there. In the left lane."

"Take this exit."

Perry yanked the wheel. Tires screeched. Horns honked. He made the exit and the black SUV had to pass by because they were in the far lane and couldn't get across.

Mandy's eyes seemed to be working just fine, as did the map on her cellphone. She kept giving directions of where to turn and Perry obeyed. No sign of the SUV could be seen, but a large gas station with several tanker trucks lit up the sky ahead. She told him to pull into there.

"Good enough place to ditch this vehicle. Let's go find a lorry to stowaway in."

"A lorry?" He loved her British accent, but the words she used might as well be Russian.

"Sorry. I guess you call them semi-trucks or eighteen-wheelers." She dropped to the ground and grunted.

He came around the truck and found her clutching her stomach with her good hand. He grabbed both backpacks from the seat. "You want to feed first?"

"Not here." She straightened and shuffled—as if she were a zombie looking for brains—to a trucker refueling. Spoke to the man in Russian. Most likely controlling him, too. Something Perry could not do. What he could do was stay alert for Dimitri's men.

She shook her head and shuffled on to the next trucker. By the third one, she gave Perry a thumbs-up with her one, good thumb.

The truck was your standard, everyday eighteen-wheeler, with a long, enclosed trailer. Why it felt strange to see something so ordinary in a foreign country baffled Perry, but maybe Russia—and other countries—weren't so different than the States. At least where vehicles and gas stations were concerned.

He opened the back and tossed their bags inside. He couldn't imagine she could get inside without inflicting more damage so he turned his back to her. "Come on. Get up."

She looked at the trailer and him and made the right choice. She wrapped her good arm around his neck. He grabbed hold of her uninjured side and carefully climbed inside, trying to ignore her breasts as they pressed against his back. Now was not the time to get a boner. Except, when did his dick ever listen to his head?

"You gonna put me down?" she asked. "Or are you planning on standing like this for the ride?"

Right. Apparently he wasn't ignoring her breasts after all. Instead he was mooning over her like a randy teenager. Gently, he released her and she slid down his back. Was it so wrong that he enjoyed every second of it? Probably. He pulled the door down, thankful for the darkness. She'd still be able to see, but now his boner wouldn't be prominent. He waved his hand toward the cab. "Lead on."

She limped forward and he followed. When the door had been open, this area was hidden in the shadows. Unless the driver came inside with a flashlight, they'd be fine.

"Why this one?" Perry asked. For a semi, it was kind of empty. Only two unmarked crates filled the front end of the trailer.

"Going in our direction. I don't want to get too far off the path or have him go out of his way. It'll look suspicious. He'll stop where we need to get off. So make yourself comfortable." She grabbed hold of the crate and slowly sat on the floor, wincing all the way.

He couldn't stand to see her in such pain, and while he could help relieve it mentally, his trick would only motivate her in the wrong direction. She needed to feed. "I know it's not perfect, but do you want some of my blood?"

She shook her head. "It's kind of you to offer, but it won't help me. I'll be fine."

He didn't think either one of them would be fine until they got on that plane.

* * * *

Barnet got up from his seat in the plane and paced the aisle. The ride to here had been okay because he'd felt like he was doing something. This sitting and waiting was doing nothing and, frankly, it was driving him a little nutty.

Oscar glanced up from his laptop. "Sir? Is there something I can do?"

Barnet hated being called "sir," but had learned a long time ago that their people felt more comfortable calling him that, so he obliged. "You haven't heard from Perry yet?"

"No, sir."

"Or anyone?" Barnet was not going to mention her name.

"No, sir."

"Is your phone charged?"

Oscar chuckled. "Yes, sir. If you'd like to watch a movie—"

Barnet waved him off. He couldn't sit back and relax knowing Perry was out there. Why hadn't he checked in when they got to the airport? Had Dimitri confiscated their phones? Barnet sat and grabbed his head. This whole thing was a mess and all because he wanted answers to Perfect Mates.

Oscar's phone chimed and Oscar pushed a button. "Perry? Where are you?"

"Technically, I have no idea. But we're on our way to you. Just might take longer than we thought. Is Barnet there?"

Barnet rushed to the phone. "I'm here. You're on the speaker. What happened?"

"Man, it sure is good to hear your voice. But don't worry. We're fine. Just on a little Dimitri detour. I don't think he likes us so much."

Barnet laughed. "Tell me about it."

Someone pounded on the door to the plane.

Oscar slid a panel beside his seat, revealing a window. "Sir?"

Barnet came around the desk and peered out the window. Two of Dimitri's guards stood outside. He slid the panel shut. "We have to get out of here. Now."

Oscar rushed to the cockpit and started the plane. "Make sure to secure all loose items."

"What's the matter?" Perry asked.

"Dimitri's men are here." Barnet shut the laptop and stored it inside the desk.

"Then go. Go to London and be safe. We'll find a place to hide."

"I'm not leaving you behind."

"But Boss, you're more important."

Never. He could never be more important than his people. "That's right. I'm your boss. And I say we're not leaving. Oscar will text you our location once we know what it is."

"Do you want to say anything to Mandy?"

"Gotta go. I'll talk to you later." Barnet disconnected the call. That was too close. Eventually he'd have to meet her, but talk? Not if he could help it.

He pocketed the phone and buckled in. Oscar took off without a hitch. Thank goodness. Barnet had no idea where they would go, but any place was better than here. He pulled out the phone and brought up the time. Two hours. If they wanted to make it to London before sunrise, they had two hours to retrieve Perry and fly out of Russia.

"Sir?" Oscar called out. "We have a problem."

Barnet unbuckled and jogged to the cockpit. "What is it? Bad weather?"

"I wish." Oscar pointed to a gauge. "We're losing fuel. They must have sabotaged the tanks. I need to land. Now."

"Is there a refueling station close by?"

Oscar laughed. "At the airport. I might make it there. But they might be waiting for us, too."

"We'll have to take that chance." Barnet sat in the seat beside Oscar and buckled up.

Could this day get any worse? Oh wait. It could. It definitely could.

Chapter 10

Mandy leaned against the wall of the lorry. With a dislocated shoulder, a broken arm, a broken leg, and a stomach cramping for blood, she'd been fairly certain she couldn't feel any worse. Boy, was she wrong. Even coming all the way out to Russia to rescue him, her father still refused to talk to her. Guess she shouldn't be all that surprised. What surprised her was the pain his rejection caused in her chest.

The cherry to top her sundae.

Perry pocketed his mobile. "I'm sure he just didn't want Oscar to know you're his daughter."

Yeah, because that's what fathers did. "It's okay. I knew it wasn't going to be a picnic. I just thought…maybe…"

"That he'd forgive you?"

"He hasn't forgiven me in five hundred years. Don't know why I thought it'd be different now."

"That just doesn't seem like the Barnet I know. What happened?"

"Don't you mean, 'What did I do'?"

He shrugged. "Takes two to tango."

What do you know? She could be surprised twice in one day. This time without the sting in her chest. She just assumed that Perry would side with her father. Or side with the man, period.

"Don't let Father hear you say that. He would definitely set you straight."

"Why don't you let me form my own opinion, huh? I am capable of doing that."

He was capable of a lot of things. He just didn't realize it. If she told him the story, his opinion of her might falter, and he liked her. Even though she wasn't a Perfect Mate. But telling it to someone, someone she was beginning to care about, might lessen the ache in her heart. Because her father was never going to forgive her.

"Sure, fine. Whatever. I guess I should start at my almost wedding."

"You were almost married?"

"Shocker, huh? Father was all about getting me married. He didn't have a dowry to offer but knew enough men who were looking for a bride, and he would invite them over for dinner. Most of them were pretty horrible. And old. But one intrigued me. His name was Frederick. Little did we all know, but he was a vampire."

"Which is why you were intrigued."

"Bingo!" She placed her right index finger to her nose. "He pretty much had us all under his thrall. But his first mistake was turning me before the wedding. He wanted me to see the real him."

"And his second mistake?"

She laughed. "He let me see the real him. He had all these powers and did nothing. Went nowhere. So I broke off the wedding. But I couldn't go home. I wouldn't have been safe there. My mistake was underestimating the man."

The lorry hit a pot hole or something and jerked them around. Mandy gritted her teeth to keep from yelling out. She really needed blood, but one, there wasn't a donor around and two, she couldn't feed in front of Perry.

He straightened. "Well that was fun…not. You okay?"

She straightened her injured leg again. It wasn't too bad so maybe it was healing some. Although, there didn't seem to be enough blood in her system to heal everything. The damage in her arm hadn't changed a bit. And if it wasn't broken in two places, she would have had Perry pop her dislocated shoulder. "I'll live."

Perry nodded and drew his knees up to his chest. "So what happened next?"

"I found other vampires. Or rather, they found me. Lived with them a bit, until I could get a handle on my own powers. Frederick would visit every month and try to win my hand, but I refused him each time. By the sixth month, I guess he'd had enough."

"Why do I have the feeling things didn't go so well."

"Probably because they didn't. In retaliation, he attacked my village. Set it on fire." She could still see the flames. Smell the burning flesh. "I rushed out there as quick as I could. Found Father first. He was hurt. Bad. I couldn't let him die, so I did what I had to."

"You turned him."

She nodded. "I knew it wouldn't take hold right away, so I searched for Mother. Found her wandering in the field. I called out to her, but she was either in a daze or couldn't hear me. I sent a command, and she still didn't stop. I rushed after her. She had a head wound and looked at me as if she didn't know me. I didn't want her to feel me bite her, so I commanded her to sleep. When she wouldn't obey, I figured it was due to her head wound. So I hugged her and bit her. Injected her. She just screamed.

"She was still awake, but weak. I laid her on the ground and told her to stay still. Brought Father to her side. I was able to get them to shelter, protect them from the sun. Father started to go through the turn but Mother was only growing weaker. I thought maybe I hadn't injected enough venom, so I injected her again."

She would have covered her ears if she had the use of her left arm. "God, I can still hear her scream."

He frowned. "The venom didn't work on her?"

"No. By the time Father came out of the turn and I explained what happened, Mother was near death. He screamed at me to fix her. To show him how to fix her. She died in his arms. She was the love of his life and I'd killed her."

"No, you didn't. Frederick did."

"But if I had handled Frederick differently…"

"Oh no. You don't get to go there. It wasn't your fault."

Yeah, tell that to her father. She could still hear him calling her a "murderer." She brought up her good leg and rested her head on her knee. "I should have been able to turn her. Maybe I was too young. Only had enough venom to turn one person."

"That has nothing to do with it and you know it."

She did, but what else could she think?

"I can't believe it." Perry leaned his head back against the wall of the lorry. "Barnet was married to a Perfect Mate."

"What is it with you and Perfect Mates?" Mandy shook her head. "This was in 1510. There were no Perfect Mates."

"You sure of that? You couldn't control her. You couldn't turn her. Those are two very distinct attributes of a Perfect Mate. And then there's Barnet's reaction to her."

"Of course he had a reaction to her. He was married to her. He loved her. He was ready to die with her, but I wouldn't let him. I couldn't let him. I didn't want to be alone."

"And yet, you are. Aren't you?"

"I thought after time… He's a stubborn man."

Perry laughed. "That does not sound like the Barnet I know."

"Think again. Who got all obsessive about finding the vampire responsible for writing the story about Perfect Mates?"

"Okay, yeah. I guess he is a little stubborn. But he's also the most forgiving man I know. I'm sure once he realizes what his late wife was, he'll know there wasn't anything you could have done."

Her father would have to listen for that to happen, and she wasn't so sure he would do that.

* * * *

Dimitri stood in front of his portrait. He'd been running things here for centuries, doing things his way, and now one pipsqueak member was going to usurp his authority? He knew adding Katya to the Committee would eventually bite him in the ass, but she'd been voted in.

Voted in. Another stupid rule that Dimitri was forced to follow. Committees and votes. What happened to having one leader? What happened to challenges? Letting the strongest rule?

The world was shrinking, they said. Their existence could be revealed. So what? Weren't they the stronger species? Shouldn't they be running this world anyway? But he'd been out voted by the other Committee Heads on that issue.

Out. Voted. No challenges. Just votes. What was this world coming to?

The phone in his desk rang. Dimitri opened the drawer and lifted the receiver. "This better be news of their capture."

"Sir, they took off in the plane."

Dimitri palmed his face. "You were supposed to drain their tanks first."

"We did. They can't get far, but they're flying under radar. We have no way of tracking them."

First Yevgeni lost the two foreigners, now these two imbeciles lost Barnet, because Dimitri was sure Barnet was on that plane. Most likely waiting until he could collect his two comrades. It was a miracle Dimitri found the plane in the first place. Now he might not get so lucky.

"Send someone to every fuel station. They'll need more fuel, if they don't crash first." Dimitri could only hope that they would crash. Then Barnet would no longer be an issue.

* * * *

Perry leaned back against the wall of the trailer, facing the most beautiful woman in the world. Would that mean his Perfect Mate would be even more beautiful? Of course, she'd have to be, wouldn't she?

Mandy's eyes were closed. Not that she was sleeping—vampires didn't do that. Most likely she was concentrating on healing. Or just trying to breathe through the pain. Whether the pain was brought on by the accident or her father's rejection, Perry wasn't going to ask. No need to poke the wound. Neither one.

He'd thought about sitting beside her, but one, her good side was leaning against a crate, and two, made it hard to stare. Because no matter what, he liked what he saw. A smart, sexy…vampire. Even hurt, she could still think fast.

"You gonna tell me about Will Robinson now?" she asked.

"Technically, we're not out of here alive…yet."

"Humor me, then."

"Sure. No problem. It's not much of a story, though. I was living in the Los Angeles area at the time. Happened to stop at a drinking hole frequented by the Hollywood types. Someone was talking about creating a sci-fi show, about a family who crashes on another planet like the Swiss Family Robinson, but in space. And that they'd have a robot. And well, me, thinking about this, decided to walk up to them all stiff-like, waving my arms, and said, 'Danger, Will Robinson!' You should have seen their faces."

She chuckled. "So you put it in their heads to do that? To name the character Will and have the robot say that?"

"No. That's just it. I didn't add or wipe their memories. There wasn't anything to wipe. I was just having fun. Two years later, *Lost in Space* debuted. I watched every episode."

"Me, too. That was a fun show. So why'd you really change your name? I'm sure it had nothing to do with Hannah."

"When a person is reborn, and that's how I felt when I was rescued, they tend to make changes. I decided to change my name."

"But not your ways?"

"Well… Nobody's perfect." His phone vibrated and he chuckled. Cheap thrill! If he'd known it had done that when he'd been given the phone years ago, he'd have kept it charged. Not that many people called him. Usually just the Committee. Thus, he never charged it.

But he was a new vampire now. One that would be respected. And that meant keeping the stupid phone charged. And it had nothing to do with the fact he was stuck in a country he desperately wanted out of.

He stared at the screen and answered the phone, being super careful not to use the nickname he'd given the man. Groucho might not be able to put him in the slammer, but he could certainly leave him behind. "Hey Oscar, you got a new destination for us?"

"We're in trouble," Barnet said. "Dimitri's men found us and sabotaged the plane. We're basically out of fuel sitting at an abandoned airfield, stuck in the snow. Oscar was able to fix the leak and we'll be able to clear the runway, but you're going to have to bring us fuel before we can fly again."

"Oh shit. How are we going to do that?" Perry couldn't imagine jet fuel was sold on the corner. Not even in Russia.

"Oscar says that there are fuel trucks at the airport. You need to go back there and get one."

Perry looked at Mandy. Mandy, who only had the use of one side of her body. And him, who knew absolutely no Russian to save his life. He mouthed, "Can we do that?" and she nodded. Actually nodded. Good enough for him. "Sure, Boss. No problem. Text me your coordinates so we know where to go."

Perry almost laughed. He sounded so *Star Trek*.

"Thanks, Perry. I knew I could count on you. Let us know when you're on your way."

"Will do." Perry disconnected the call. No one had ever counted on him before. At least not in a life-and-death matter. And if this wasn't life-and-death, what was? But then, was Barnet really counting on Perry? Because Perry was counting on Mandy to get them through this.

"We'll get them the fuel," she said.

"Yeah, sure. Piece of cake." And that was no lie. Cake was not easy for a vampire to keep down. But to come across weak in front of her, he wasn't doing that. Because he wasn't weak, damn it. He *could* do this.

A moment later he got the text. "Do you know where this is?"

Mandy pulled out her own cellphone and did her thing—one handed. "They didn't go far. Pretty smart on Oscar's part. Abandoned means no fuel. Dimitri's men will never think to look there. Once the lorry stops, we'll find a way back to the airport."

Perry wasn't so sure Mandy could go much further without blood. Her left arm lay limp by her side and she hadn't moved her left leg in the past twenty minutes. "When we stop, you need to feed. Tell me what to say to get the driver back here."

"We won't have the time. It can wait."

"You can barely walk."

"I can walk. And I can still use my right arm." She lifted it and flexed her fingers, bent her elbow. "See? I'll be fine."

"God. You know who's stubborn? You are. What's the big deal? You feed and heal."

She lowered her head. "It doesn't work that way for me. Okay? I'll be fine."

"What do you mean it doesn't work that way for you? You're a vampire, aren't you?"

The truck stopped.

"I think this is our stop." But Mandy didn't even try to stand. Perry wasn't sure she could.

The back door rolled open. The driver stood there waiting for a command. A command from Mandy.

Damn it. Perry hoped the driver knew English. "*Come inside the trailer.*"

The driver climbed inside. Hot damn!

"What are you doing?" Mandy asked.

"Getting you fed."

"You can't make me feed from him."

"What is your problem? Is it privacy you need? Fine, I'll give you privacy. But we're not going anywhere until you can use your arm and leg. Do you hear me?"

"But it'll take too long. We don't have that kind of time."

Now that he thought about it, she had taken more time to feed than he had back at the London airport. "You a slow feeder? Is that it?"

The driver jumped out of the trailer. Shut the door.

Perry dashed to the exit. Pulled up on the handle, but the door wouldn't budge. "What the hell! What are you doing?"

"I told him to lock the door and go to the airport."

Perry returned to his spot in the trailer before movement forced him on his ass. "I thought you were afraid it would look suspicious if he veered from his route."

"We really don't have much choice here, do we? And did you see any SUVs out there? No one's following us. They'd have no reason to believe we'd head back to the airport."

"Except Dimitri knows the plane needs fuel."

"Then I guess we'll have to be extra careful."

"And how do you propose to do that when you can barely walk?"

She didn't answer him, but then why should she? They were stuck inside the trailer until they got back to the airport and there wasn't a damn thing he could do about it.

Chapter 11

When Mandy refused to answer any more of Perry's questions, he finally settled on his side of the lorry. Frowning, he hugged his knees to his chest. Was he pouting or plotting his next move? With him it was hard to tell. He seemed to have the same mannerisms for both.

She stretched her bad leg. Lifted it slightly. Pain, but not unbearable. His main concern seemed to be her ability to walk. She was fairly certain she could do that. But run? Probably not so much.

Her left arm was still useless. Until the bones healed, she daren't try to pop the shoulder in place. But she didn't really need her left arm. Her dominate arm still worked normally. Well, as normally as it would work when she was down a quart or two. The stomach cramps weren't helping, either.

But feeding in front of Perry was a big no-no. One look at her allergy and he'd report her first chance he got. Anything to impress his future Perfect Mate. And she went ahead and actually told him she'd help him find one. Maybe she should have her head examined.

Whoever bonded with him would be one lucky woman. To have those emerald green eyes gazing upon her in love could be some heady stuff. And the woman would be able to loosen his hair and run her fingers through it. And after some mind-blowing sex, she'd be able to play around with him. Do fun stuff. Like they had done in the hotel shower.

Ahhh, good times.

If there was ever a perfect vampire for Mandy, Perry would be it. But he was unavailable. Out of reach. Just as well. She was defective. A vampire who should have been put down five hundred years ago. And while Perry would probably be a great friend, she didn't want another friend. She wanted more.

Bloody hell. She wanted Perry.

"Are you going to feed when we get to the airport?" he asked.

Ahhh. Not pouting. Plotting.

"We won't have time if we want to get the fuel to the plane and leave this place before sunrise."

He glared at her and damn, that lit her body right up. "Then we'll bring someone with us and you can feed on the way."

That might work. If Perry concentrated on driving and she put the donor between them, Perry wouldn't be able to see her. Better yet, she could use the excuse that no mortal should catch her feeding, crawl in the footwell, and feed from the donor's leg.

"I can do that. We have to bring the driver anyway, so he can return the tanker."

Perry smiled. Another thing his Perfect Mate would enjoy. That smile. It sure set Mandy's insides on fire. Too bad she couldn't take his blood. She almost had back in the limo, and in the hotel as they'd made love in the shower, but she wasn't lying when she said his blood wouldn't help. If anything, it would make things worse.

Sometimes life was so cruel.

The lorry stopped. Less than a minute later, the back opened.

She looped her backpack on her good shoulder and, using the box beside her for leverage, stood.

"Nice to see you can stand, Igor. But can you walk?"

"Igor? I don't have a bloody hunchback!" Of all the nicknames he could use, he came up with that? She'd show him. Her leg didn't buckle under her weight. The knee even worked. She walked over to the opening, turned her head around, and stuck her tongue out at him.

He laughed that crazy, wonderful laugh. Damn. How many more things was his Perfect Mate going to enjoy on a daily basis?

Mandy sat and lowered herself to the ground. She wasn't about to chance a jump and an I-told-you-so look from Perry.

The driver had dropped them off on the outskirts of the airport. Perfect. She grabbed five American twenties from her bag, since that was all she had, and shoved them into his pants pocket. Using her vampire manipulation, she placed a memory in his head that he'd found them on the ground earlier in the day.

"What's that for?" Perry asked as he smoothly jumped to the ground. Show off.

"Petrol. I feel bad having used so much on this trip. I'll send him back to the station we found him at. When he gets there, he'll think he just refueled and then he can go on his way, as if we never bothered him."

"Except you can't mentally explain how he lost all that time."

"Yeah, well, no plan is perfect."

Perry closed the trailer door. "Have him fall asleep."

"Where? Here?"

"No. At the fuel station. Have him pull in and then fall asleep. When he wakes up he'll think he slept all that time."

"Brilliant!" She only wished she'd thought of it first. Maybe her injuries were worse than she'd thought, which meant maybe her manipulation skills weren't at their peak. She grabbed the driver's hand to solidify their link and sent the instructions that way.

After the truck drove off, Perry pointed at the chain-link fence. Or rather, what was beyond the fence. "Are those tanks our destination?"

At least he knew his fuel. She hobbled through a pile of snow to the fence. Chain-link was the easiest of all fences to climb, but in her condition it would take a while.

Perry, though, had no issues. He scaled the fence as if he were a monkey and mumbled, "Should have fed from the driver." At the top he dropped their bags to the ground and lowered his hand. "Come on, Igor."

"Will you stop calling me that?"

"I'll stop calling you that after you feed."

Damn man. She was beginning to see how he frustrated people. She slapped her good hand against his and he lifted her. When she reached the top, she planted her good leg on a wire and swung her damaged one over the fence. Once he lowered her to the ground, he jumped down beside her.

Perry kicked at the snow. "Kind of glad I got these boots, now. But if Dimitri's men are looking, we'll be leaving a nice trail for them to follow."

Pristine snow covered the ground between the fence and their target. Yeah, their footsteps would definitely be noticed, if anyone cared to look.

"All the more reason to hurry, right?"

"Says the person who can barely walk. Get on my back. We'll get there faster with you on me."

He'd get no argument from her. After he picked up their bags, she wrapped her good arm around his shoulders and hefted herself up. Damn, he still smelled good. His vanilla scent teased her nose and other parts of her body just like they had when he'd carried her into the lorry. Another thing his Perfect Mate would enjoy.

Unlike the last time she climbed up on his back, he looped his arms around both her legs. She gritted her teeth at the pain it caused. Ahhh, but it wasn't as bad as it could have been if she'd been forced to walk. And then he'd call her Igor.

Damn man.

Perry kept to the fence line until they were closer to the first tank, then he made a dash for it. He stopped, probably listening for someone. "There's some activity farther in."

There was? Oh great, her hearing was starting to act wonky now.

Slowly, he walked around the tank. The area was deserted. He jogged toward the other tank and found the source of the activity. A man was filling up his tanker. No one else was in sight.

"Hold still. Let me take care of him." She sent a command for the driver to sit in the passenger seat after filling his tanker and await his next command.

And sure enough, after he disconnected the line and secured the tank, he climbed inside the passenger seat.

"Do you hear anyone else?" Apparently she couldn't trust her hearing. Thank God her command had worked.

Perry shook his head. "We're clear here, but that doesn't mean vampires aren't watching us from afar."

So true. "If they are, hopefully we'll be long gone before they reach us."

He headed for the tanker. The driver was sitting as in a trance. Perry lowered her to the ground. She opened the passenger door, placed their bags on the driver, and climbed into the footwell. So far so good.

* * * *

Perry shook his head. The woman was clearly deranged, or maybe just lacking blood. "What are you doing down there? There's plenty of room on the seat."

"Don't need anyone witnessing my feeding, now do we?"

Anyone, meaning him. What was it with her and privacy? Oh yeah, sure, the general public shouldn't see a vampire chowing down, but in the middle of the night, who the hell would notice? Even if they could see through the window, it would just look like she was nuzzling his neck.

"How are you going to tell me which way to drive if you can't even see the road?"

She huffed. "Fine. Then I'll wait until you're on the highway to feed."

He slammed the door in her face. No woman had ever irritated him as much as her. No woman had ever turned him on more, either. What the hell?

He stormed around the tanker truck and climbed behind the wheel. She had climbed out of the footwell and sat in the seat, beside the door, leaving Mr. Driver between them.

Probably just as well she used him as a barrier. When she'd climbed on Perry's back earlier, her jasmine scent nearly undid him. She wasn't a Perfect Mate, so why'd she smell like them? The Great One was teasing him. What else could it be?

Right now, he needed to get their asses out of the airport and on the road before being spotted. And as a precaution, he found the switch controlling the dashboard lights and turned them off. He didn't need to help his enemies recognize his face.

At least the tanker didn't have a dash cam to worry about. Probably never left the airport.

Mandy pulled out her phone and directed him toward the highway. He should probably have one of those map things on his own phone. Hell, maybe he already did. It's not like he ever looked. Once he'd found the game apps, he'd stopped exploring.

Driving this tanker truck was exactly like Perry thought it would be like: driving a tanker truck. The thing was heavy with fuel and not all that easy to get up to speed. He considered it a miracle he made it up the ramp to the highway.

"In a little more than sixteen kilometers, you will need to exit this highway."

He calculated what the odometer would be at in sixteen kilometers, since there was no way he would be able to read which exit sign to take. "You have about ten to fifteen minutes to feed. Get to it."

"Bossy much?"

He wanted to laugh that she'd thrown his phrase at him. When had he ever been bossy? Never. Because he was usually given orders, not giving them. Huh.

She removed the driver's parka and placed it in the driver's lap. She grunted, groaned, and spit out a few curse words as she scooted into the footwell. Took the parka and placed it over her head. All because she didn't want Perry to watch? What was the big deal about that?

"You gonna feed from his leg?" Blech. Why bother with hair when there were plenty of non-hairy places to feed from?

"You just keep your eyes on the road and don't worry about me."

"Yeah, yeah, yeah."

Mumbled curses came from under the parka. The driver was wearing boots. Probably wore long underwear. It wouldn't be easy to reach his skin.

Perry checked the left side mirror. No flashing lights, so the airport hadn't sent anyone. If they were being followed by vampires, they would be more discreet. Probably wouldn't even turn on their headlights. Perry was tempted to turn off the truck's lights, but why risk being pulled over? He stayed in the right lane and stuck to the speed limit, if the sign with the big 8-0 on it could be trusted to indicate maximum speed.

The few cars on the highway passed him as if he were standing still, though.

The radio squawked. The speaker on the other end spoke Russian. Of course. Probably looking for Mr. Driver. Perry pushed a button and turned the sucker off.

For the next ten minutes he drove in silence. How long did it take for her to feed? Two minutes was all he needed. Of course, if she didn't find a large enough vein, it would take a while. But ten minutes?

"Are you almost done?"

"Yeah."

So why was she still down there? Did feeding turn her on, was that it? He'd think after five hundred years she'd be able to control that part of her body. But, whatever.

"You need to take the next exit, but don't turn. Not yet," she said from underneath the driver's parka.

Thank goodness for GPS. But... "Hey. They can't track us with our phones, can they?"

"They'd have no idea what my number is. Same with Oscar. They wouldn't know he was coming, right? But you? Would my father have your number on his mobile?"

"Barnet didn't keep any numbers. They're stored in his head. Even after he called someone, he would delete the record. So Dimitri wouldn't have gotten mine that way. Makes sense they would have Barnet's number, since he'd called Dimitri. But mine, or anyone else's? Not likely."

"Unless you have a mole."

"Yeah. Unless that." But Perry doubted that. Safety was their number one priority. That meant not only against mortals, but foreign vampires, too. Perry attended every meeting. Not because he had to, but because he wanted to. He'd met every vampire. He knew their faces. Maybe that was why Barnet had picked him to be the tie-breaking vote in his absence.

He took the next exit. Stopped at the road. Paid attention to the rear.

"Anyone following us?" she asked.

"Not that I can tell. But I'm sure I'm lit up like a Christmas tree and they wouldn't have to be all that close to see me."

"Turn off the lights."

He turned the knob. "If they followed us, won't they know we're headed to an airfield?"

"Yeah. That's why we took this exit. There's an airfield to the left. The one we want is another five kilometers ahead."

"So I turn left? Or go straight?"

"Left. Then find the first building where you can pull in around back."

And that didn't have feet of snow covering it, either. No easy feat, there. Perry turned left and after a quarter-mile found a warehouse of some sort. Lots of tire tracks, too. He pulled in and drove around back.

The passenger door opened and Mandy jumped out. "Come on, let's see if anyone followed."

Well, at least the feeding had healed her enough to make her mobile. Perry followed Mandy to the side of the building where they wouldn't be spotted by Dimitri's men. If indeed they were following. "You're looking much better."

She gave him the evil eye.

"What? You liked being crippled?"

She rolled her eyes and focused on the highway exit. Five minutes later a black SUV with its headlights off came zooming from the highway and passed them.

"Holy shit. It worked." He hugged Mandy. "You're a genius, Einstein." He kissed her. Meant for it just to be a little peck, but then her scent came alive and he deepened it. Used his tongue to get a better taste and instantly got hard. Damn. What the hell was he doing? And why was she kissing him back? He broke the kiss and backed away. "Sorry about that. Guess I was still playing the part."

"No worries. I'm having a hard time separating the real me from the fake me, too. So I'm Einstein now? Not Igor?"

At least she hadn't slapped him. He certainly deserved it. "I said I'd stop calling you that after you fed. That SUV must be a tank. There was hardly any damage to the front end."

"Yeah. And they still had the power to drive quickly. Let's go before they realize we tricked them."

Perry was starting to get a good feeling that they might actually get to leave this country alive.

* * * *

Barnet borrowed Oscar's phone—since his own had been demolished soon after the abduction—and exited the plane. They'd done a decent job of clearing the runway. He'd have never thought to bring snow shovels on a plane, but there they were, stored in the back.

The man deserved a bonus.

It seemed to be taking forever for Perry to get here with the fuel truck. As for Perry's companion… Barnet seethed.

He called the one person responsible for that.

Victoria answered the phone. "Oscar? Is something wrong?"

"It's not Oscar. It's Barnet."

"Barnet! You're safe? Oh thank goodness. Is everything okay? Are you on your way home?"

"Not quite. We had plane troubles by the name of Dimitri. We're hoping we can refuel within the hour. Why did you send her, Victoria? Why?"

"I didn't. I contacted her like your letter requested. She came here of her own free will and insisted on going there. I didn't ask."

It figured she'd opened the wrong damn letter. "That shouldn't matter. She's not one of us."

"She's your daughter."

"Please. Don't call her that."

"You might not want me to call her that, but that doesn't make it untrue."

"Just don't expect to see her when we return."

"You're not leaving her in Russia, are you?"

"Don't be ridiculous. Oscar says we will stop in London to refuel. We'll leave her there."

"I'm sorry about whatever it is that's between you two. She seems like a nice woman. And I never would have opened the letter if we knew where you were."

"Yeah, next time you might want to wait until you know I'm dead before you go opening the letter marked in case of my death." Not that it mattered anymore. The cat, as they said, was out of the bag.

"I didn't open that letter. I opened the other one. For emergencies."

He palmed his forehead and could only laugh. "I mixed up the damn letters."

"Should I open the other one?"

"Not necessary now. But if something should happen, if you don't hear from me by three a.m. your time, contact Yekaterina Volkova. She goes by the name Katya."

"She's one of the Russian Committee Members."

"Yes. But she's an ally and is trying to oust Dimitri. In fact, I believe she's our contact."

"*Scheisse*. She never said."

"And don't go broadcasting this information, either. You can tell our Committee Members, but no one else. And they aren't to tell anyone else, either. Not even family members. If you don't hear from me in an hour, Katya's our best bet to find us. If we're not dead."

"Don't go borrowing trouble, Barnet."

"I don't need to borrow it. I seem to have a good collection."

The worst one being a woman he refused to acknowledge.

Chapter 12

Mandy drummed her fingers on the window ledge of the tanker. Soon they'd arrive at the airfield. Soon she'd have to face her father.

Soon she'd find out if she was flying out of here.

She didn't expect her father to greet her with open arms, but would he acknowledge her? Or even look at her? A simple hello would be more than she dreamed. A smile, a miracle.

Which shouldn't even be forefront on her mind. Getting to the plane, getting it refueled, those were more important.

Eventually Dimitri's men would discover their ruse. And then start checking other airfields. They didn't have the luxury of time and Perry was driving like an old man.

"Can't you make this thing go any faster?" She should have taken over driving. They would have been there by now. But Perry had gotten behind the wheel and she'd let him. Hadn't thought it would matter. Boy, was she wrong.

"I'm already doing one-ten. It's not like driving a Lamborghini. And if you didn't notice, there's snow on the road."

Excuses, excuses. "Turn left in three hundred meters."

He slowed the tanker.

"I said three hundred meters. Not here."

"It doesn't exactly stop on a dime. And why are you in such a cranky mood? We ditched them. We're good."

"We're not good. It'll probably take fifteen or thirty minutes to refuel the plane."

Perry's eyebrows shot up. "That long?"

"Yeah. That long." She should have driven. She was all healed and raring to go. This sitting as a useless passenger frustrated her more than being injured had. She pointed ahead. "There's your road."

Although, by the looks of it, no one had used the road since the first snow stuck. No ruts of any kind.

"Where? I don't see a road."

"On the left. To the right of that street sign. It just hasn't been plowed."

"Oh Great One, I hope we don't get stuck." He took the turn. The tanker slid a little, and he slowed a lot, but he kept it moving in the right direction. "They'll certainly know we came this way."

"If they know the airfield is here, it won't matter. Go faster." She knew he couldn't. But it sure felt better to say it.

Perry shook his head. A building appeared ahead. And then the plane came into view.

Oscar and her father had done a decent job of clearing the runway. Vampire strength and speed to thank for that. Oh, and Oscar's snow shovels. The man knew how to be prepared.

Oscar descended the steps and motioned where Perry should go. No sign of her father. Just as she suspected. She drummed her fingers faster.

"Are you starting up a band? 'Cause I can play the keyboard."

"Clever." She stilled her fingers. Riding roller coasters, beating the sun, those things brought on adrenaline and were fun. This? This was just torture.

"Are you going to be this nervous on the plane, too?"

"No." But then she probably wouldn't be on it.

Perry stopped the tanker and cut the engine. He opened his door. "You getting out?"

She still had control of the driver. "I'll just wait here until the jet's filled. Then I'll send the driver on his way."

Perry smirked. "Chicken."

Yeah, maybe. "You gonna call me that now?"

"You'd rather I call you Igor?"

"I'd rather you not call me any of those names."

He laughed that ridiculous laugh of his. Why'd he have to be so charming? And why'd he have to kiss her earlier and then be all apologetic? Couldn't he tell she'd liked it? Couldn't he tell she liked him? No, of course not. He still wanted that Perfect Mate.

After Oscar started refueling the plane, he came over to Perry. "Were you followed?"

Perry waffled his hand back and forth. "Yes and no. We were being followed, but averted them. But once they realize we led them to the wrong airfield, it's possible they'll come here next."

"That's if all the airfields aren't being checked out to begin with," Mandy added. "Especially now that they know we stole the tanker. They won't limit their search to just airfields with fuel."

"Our only luck is that Dimitri doesn't have that many men looking. He's acting against his Committee. I'll sure be happy to get back into the air."

"Don't get too happy right away," Oscar said. "The patch might not hold."

Perry's eyes widened. "You don't know if the patch will hold?"

"How was I supposed to test it? It's not leaking, so hopefully it'll be good."

"What happens if it leaks?"

"Then we make another emergency landing. Hopefully outside of Russia."

That was a lot of hopefullys for Mandy's taste. "Are you filling the tanks completely?"

"No. Just enough to get us to London. But even that will take fifteen minutes. I'm not liking the odds."

She wasn't either.

If Dimitri's men found them before they finished refueling, Oscar would need time to disconnect the hose. "What you need is a lookout," she said as she climbed out of the cab. "I'll call when I spot them. Or you call when you're done. I'll take care of the driver when I return."

Anything not to have to face her father until necessary. She'd like to make it difficult for him to throw her off the plane.

Oscar nodded. "Yeah, that would probably be best."

"I'll go with you," Perry said.

"You don't have to."

"You're not doing this alone. Come on."

She ran toward the road. She wasn't a hundred percent well yet, but so much better than she had been. Once they landed in London, she'd have time to find that hunky athlete and enjoy the feed as well as she could enjoy it. And then she'd put them all behind her. Her father. Perry. His Perfect Mate. All of it.

She could go back to living her lonely life. It'd been fine for five hundred years. It would work for another five hundred.

Perry stopped at the intersection. "There's nothing to hide behind out here."

"There's that snow bank over there. Does it matter? Like you said, they'll see the tracks we made. We just need to listen." Right now the only thing making any noise was the wind.

"How cold do you think it is out here?"

Mandy hadn't thought about that. They might not be able to feel the cold, but their skin could still freeze. Wouldn't be a death sentence, but if their skin froze and cracked, their body would heal and use blood they couldn't afford to lose. At least, she couldn't afford to lose. Even if she had her coat—which had been left behind in the crash—wearing it would have been useless. Wearing gloves, the same. Vampires didn't generate heat like mortals did.

She pulled out her mobile and opened the weather app. But it didn't seem to work in Russia. She Googled it instead. "It's ten below Celsius in Moscow right now."

"Ten below? Shit. I bet you're rethinking that skirt now, huh?"

"This skirt protects me just as much as your cargo pants do." Besides, she'd seen the way he'd looked at her when she tried it on. It was the only reason she'd bought it. The boots were just a bonus. Hopefully the blood would come out. She really liked this outfit. "We won't be out here long enough to do any damage."

"Right. Right." He still shoved his hands inside the pockets of his jacket, as if that would help keep them from freezing.

Standing here doing nothing was crazy. And then she'd run back if, or when, they arrived only to be kicked out of the plane? She should fight them. Yeah, that's what she should do. That would show her father that she wasn't useless. That she was worth something. And Dimitri's men would slow for the turn, just like Perry had.

"We can take them out." The good adrenaline was already rushing through her.

"Dimitri's men? Are you shitting me?"

"Yes, Dimitri's men, and no, I'm not shitting you. We need to start taking the offensive." She could already picture it. Attacking them unaware. Snapping their necks.

Perry put his hands on his hips. "With what weapons? They probably have stun guns. Stakes. What do we have? Hmmm?"

"Stop being a Negative Nelly." She laughed. "Oh look, I came up with a name for you."

"I'm not being negative. I'm being reasonable."

"Reasonable? Then look around you. We can make stakes from those trees across the street. We can hide behind that snowbank."

"That snowbank?" He pointed across the street. "It's not even high enough to hide a raccoon!"

"On the other side of the road. They won't be looking there." She dashed across the street, climbed the chain-link fence and jumped on a tree. She broke off several branches. "They wouldn't dream we'd fight back. Or that we'd even be out here waiting to ambush them. We'll have the upper hand." She dropped to the ground and made a pile of the branches. "We can do this."

"What is wrong with you? You'd rather die than see your father? Is that it?"

"I don't plan on dying. I'm trying to give us time to escape."

Or at least give her enough time to find a place to hide. Because she had to face it. Her father was not going to let her on that plane.

* * * *

Perry picked up one of the branches Mandy had broken off the tree. She expected him to make a stake? From this wimpy branch?

"Did something happen to your brain between the airport and here?" Because she was not acting like the smart vampire he knew.

"Nothing's wrong with my brain. If you don't like my idea, then go wait back in the plane with my father. I'm sure he won't mind your company."

Perry gritted his teeth. He knew she'd act all weird when Barnet hadn't left the plane. He just didn't think she'd go coo-coo. "I can't leave you alone. You're gonna get yourself killed."

"And you think my father will care." She chuckled, although there was no joy behind it. "Think again. He didn't even bother to leave the plane when we arrived. He doesn't even want to look at me."

"You ever think that maybe he's just as scared as you are?"

"Who said I was scared? I'm willing to fight these wankers. If anyone's scared, it's you!"

No denying that. This was far from being in anyone's comfort zone. But there was scared and there was reasonable. "Fine. You

125

want to fight, then we should take the fight to the plane, where we have Barnet and Oscar. We'll outnumber them."

"They'll expect a fight there. We need to surprise them and fight them here. That's the only way this will work."

Could she be right? Disabling Dimitri's men would certainly give them the time they needed to leave this place. Maybe his fear held him back.

He kicked the pile of branches. "We need better sticks than these."

"No time. They're coming. Bollocks. We have to fight now. Oscar needs more time."

Perry spun around. Couldn't see anything yet, but yep, sure enough, the sound of an engine came their way. Shit. He texted Oscar and hoped to hell they weren't making a huge mistake.

"Get down."

Yeah, right. He zipped to the snowbank, where Mandy was working with a piece of fence wire.

"What's that for?"

"They'll have to slow down like you did. I'm going to flatten their tire with this. When they come out of the car to investigate, then we'll attack."

Sounded easy enough. But the branches? He pulled out his knife and quickly whittled points on the best of the bunch. When he finished, he handed over the knife. "Here, use this instead of the wire. I sure hope these sticks are strong enough."

"Only takes a splinter, right?"

Yeah, but they still had to be stiff enough to penetrate. "You sure you want to do this? We still have time to make it to the plane."

"And if the plane doesn't have enough fuel? This is the best thing we could do. And they'll never expect it. Trust me."

"I do trust you. You're smarter at this stuff than I am. Just tell me what to do."

At least he didn't have to worry about being buried alive. Oh no. These guys would probably just outright kill him.

* * * *

Barnet paced inside the plane. He'd heard voices outside earlier, but now it was strangely quiet. And no one came inside the plane. He poked his head out the door. Oscar was leaning against the tanker. "Where did they go?"

Oscar came over to the steps. "Back to the road. To be lookouts. They'll call if they spot Dimitri's men or I'll call when we're finished fueling. Frankly, I hope I get to call first. Can you help me?"

Barnet descended. "They brought the driver with them? I didn't know Perry knew Russian."

"He doesn't. That has to be Mandy's work. She seems like a smart one. Find it strange someone from England is on this mission, though." Oscar raised an eyebrow.

Barnet shrugged. Eventually everyone would learn he had a daughter. Why had he bothered listing her in his in-case-of-death letter? Which he ended up sticking in his in-case-I'm-missing envelope. It was his own damn fault she was even here. "What do you need?"

"To drive this over to the other wing." Oscar removed the hose from the plane and held it out of the way while Barnet moved the tanker truck to where he needed it.

The driver sat in a trance. Kind of freaked Barnet out, but he had no way of making the guy sleep. And if the driver came out of it? He'd probably have to knock him out the old fashioned way and hope to hell he didn't kill him.

Barnet climbed out of the cab. He'd be sitting in the plane for several hours so he took advantage of the fresh air. Of the scenery. Of the stars. Russia was beautiful. Too bad Dimitri was the leader here. Katya would make a better Head, but Barnet had no say in that. He could only hope the vampires here were conducive to change. Dimitri had led for far too many centuries.

Oscar pulled out his phone. "Oh shit."

"What?"

"Perry just texted. Dimitri's men are on their way and he and Mandy are staying to fight them."

"He's what? Tell him to come back here."

"But we don't have enough fuel, sir. And I need to balance the weight. If they can delay them for just ten minutes…"

"You stay here, I'm not letting him fight them alone."

"But sir. He's not alone. He has Mandy. You can't go."

"Like hell I can't." Barnet didn't trust that woman to do the right thing. "Is there a stun gun in the plane?"

Oscar nodded. "In the cockpit."

Barnet dashed inside, found the weapon, and sprinted for the road.

Chapter 13

Mandy hunched behind the snowbank, the knife held tight in her fist. At least she had a knife now. That fence wire was iffy at best, but she couldn't admit that to Perry. No. He would have used that as another excuse to run away. And she wasn't running away. Not if she could stop these wankers.

The SUV approached at full speed, the lights off.

When they were within a couple hundred meters of the road, they slowed. The SUV slid sideways. If only she could throw the knife at the tires. But if she missed, she'd not only lose the knife, they'd be discovered. And she wasn't about to ruin the surprise.

"Be ready."

Perry held onto a whittled branch and handed another over to her. "You want?"

She took it and bent it easily with her fingers. Why hadn't she noticed that when she ripped them from the tree? She couldn't worry about that now. Surprise was on their side. Surprise would work.

The SUV started to make the turn. Mandy jumped up and rammed the knife into the rear tire. Air hissed out as it continued to roll forward, with the knife still stuck inside.

Damn it. She reached for the moving knife when the vehicle stopped and the passenger door opened. Yevgeni, Dimitri's goon, climbed out. No time to get the knife, Mandy grabbed him from behind and threw him to the ground. Perry pounced and went to stake the man, but the branch only bent against Yevgeni's coat.

Perry tossed the stick aside. The two men fought in the snow. She turned to get the knife for the driver, but ran into a hard body.

"Look what I found."

The words were spoken in Russian. Oh shit. The driver. His stake looked much sturdier than hers.

"I think first I stake you, then I fuck you. I bet you make a good fuck."

Not if she could help it. But her whittled branch was useless and she tossed it away. What she needed was his stake. She dove for his legs and knocked him over. He landed against the vehicle with a thud. As she reached for the stake, he spun, pinning her to the vehicle. He plunged the stake into her heart.

Noooo! This wasn't supposed to happen. They had the upper hand.

Her legs gave out and she crumpled to the snow.

The driver reached inside the SUV, pulled out another stake, and headed toward the fight. She called out Perry's name. "Watch out!"

He looked up. At her, not at the driver. But it didn't matter. Yevgeni snapped Perry's neck. He collapsed as if Yevgeni had stripped him of his bones.

"Noooo!" This was her fault. Again. And Perry had paid the price.

The driver approached her. Tossed the stake to the ground. Opened his coat and proceeded to undo his belt. "You want her after me?"

He was still speaking in Russian. Because he didn't want her to understand—although who wouldn't understand the removal of a belt—or because one or both didn't speak English?

"We don't have time for this, Ivan. We have to get Barnet off that plane."

Her only solace: knowing that she had detained these two goons. Oscar and her father should be able to get away.

"Ahh, Geno. There is always time for fucking. You need to loosen up. They won't leave without these two." He lowered his pants, got on his knees and shoved her skirt up.

Oh, bollocks. Her father wouldn't have any issue leaving her behind, but Perry? Why didn't she think about that? She closed her eyes and would have cried if her tear ducts worked.

Something sizzled and Yevgeni spasmed. Fell to the ground.

Father? Her eyes must be deceiving her. But there he was, holding a stun gun.

Ivan turned just as her father shot him in the arse. Ivan spasmed and collapsed on top of her.

She'd like to think her father came to save her. But she knew better. She always knew better.

He turned away from her and went to Perry. Straightened his head and palmed his face. They were most likely talking telepathically. That would be the only way Perry could communicate for awhile. And it'd be hours before he could feed and walk again. All because she wanted to stay and fight.

She should have listened to Perry. Taken the fight to the plane, where Dimitri's men would have been outnumbered and where they had at least one weapon. But no. She wanted to do this on her own. And why? To prove to her father that she was good? If anything, she'd only made herself look more foolish in his eyes.

Father stood. He found the discarded stake and drove it into Yevgeni's heart. Kicked Ivan off her body. Yanked the stake free from her chest. She screamed from the pain. Her heart, however, was confused. Was he actually going to save her?

He drove the stake into Ivan's heart.

No, not save her. Disable the other goon. She didn't even know what she could say that would make any of this better, but she had to try. "Father—"

"Shut up." He returned to Perry. Lifted him with care.

It would take her several minutes, if not an hour, before her strength returned enough to even stand. Would her father return for her next?

He glared at her with hatred in his eyes. "Find your own way back."

And then took off.

Was she supposed to find her way back to the plane? Or to London? Guess she would find out soon.

* * * *

As Perry was carried to the plane—loose as a partially filled sack of sand, no less—he went through the list of near deaths he'd experienced.

Staked? Check.

Buried alive? Check.

Almost decapitated? Check.

Broken neck? Check.

Those were a lot of near deaths. Would the next one succeed? He wasn't placing any bets that that wouldn't occur on this trip.

His fingers and toes tingled. And he could wiggle them…barely. But without a fresh supply of blood, it could be hours before he was strong enough to stand. And since Mandy had fed on the tanker driver already, he wouldn't even try and feed from him. Which meant London. He'd be like this until London.

Barnet ascended the steps into the plane—turning so Perry didn't smack his head or his legs on the entrance—and placed him on a seat. Problem with putting a partially filled sack of sand on the seat, though: it didn't like to stay upright. As Perry tilted to the side, Barnet grabbed the seatbelt and strapped him in, turning him so he leaned against the wall of the plane.

One down, one to go. By the time Barnet retrieved Mandy, they should be fueled up and ready to go.

Barnet sat in the seat across the aisle from him.

"What are you doing?" Thankfully, Perry's voice worked. It wasn't the prettiest of sounds, but at least air could get to his vocal chords now that they weren't all twisted out of shape. "You didn't really intend for her to walk back on her own, did you?"

Barnet didn't answer. Just leaned his head back and closed his eyes.

"Boss?" No answer. "You have to go back and get her."

"I don't have to do any such thing."

"She can't possibly walk here so soon after being staked."

"That is not my problem."

Perry hadn't believed Mandy. Had been sure she'd been exaggerating. Seemed he was wrong. "But she's your daughter!"

"She stopped being my daughter the day she turned me."

"She did that to save your life." Damn. He never would have guessed that Barnet could be so cold. Because Barnet just didn't do that kind of thing.

Barnet glared at Perry. "What do you know about it?"

"I know a lot more than you, apparently. She came out here to help you. And this is how you treat her?"

"She killed my wife. She's lucky I let her live."

"Boss, do you really think she'd kill her own mother? She tried to save her. You want to blame someone, blame Frederick. But don't blame Mandy. It's not her fault your wife was a Perfect Mate."

Barnet narrowed his eyes. "A Perfect Mate? What garbage has she fed you? They didn't exist then. And for your information, Rachel was not her mother. Her mother died in child birth. Rachel was her step-mother. I always knew she was jealous and she hated that I was making her get married. Her refusal to turn Rachel and to… This was her way of getting even."

"You're wrong. Mandy couldn't control her. She couldn't turn her. Think about it, Barnet. I get that if she had brain damage that Mandy might not be able to control her. But turn her? Even the brain damaged can be turned. Only Perfect Mates can't."

"Stop with the Perfect Mate thing. She lied to you, Perry. She would say anything to make herself look good."

"I don't believe that."

"How can you side with her after what she's done to you?"

"She did nothing to me. That was Yevgeni. You can't leave her out there. You can't leave her behind."

"She knew the risks involved."

Perry's heart ached. "Where is Barnet? You are not the man I know."

"You rest. I'll see how Oscar is doing." Barnet left the plane.

Perry stared at the door. How was this even happening? To leave another vampire behind—a stranger, even—was against everything Barnet had ever stood for.

Perry moved his hand to the buckle on the seatbelt. With some jerky movements, he was able to lift the clasp and uncouple the belt. He willed his legs to move. They didn't listen so well. Would he be able to stand or would he have to crawl? Maybe he should try sitting up first.

As he straightened from the wall, he continued to fall forward and landed on the floor. Guess he'd crawl after all.

"Perry, what the hell are you doing?" Barnet lifted Perry and placed him back on the seat.

"Stop it. Let me go." But his pleas were ignored. Barnet buckled him back in and then knotted the belt. "I can't believe you're doing this to her."

Groucho boarded the plane. "We're all set. Where's Mandy?"

"Please, Oscar. You have to go get her. She's hurt, back on the road."

Groucho looked at Barnet. "You didn't bring her back? Why?"

"Oh, for Pete's sake," Barnet said. "I'll go get her."

"No. I don't trust you." Perry gave his best sad look to Groucho. "Please get her."

Groucho's phone rang. "It's Mandy." He answered it. "I was just coming to get you."

"Don't bother. I'm not there."

"What do you mean you're not there?" Perry yelled. Well, as loud as his voice allowed anyway.

"I'm going to find Alexi Popolov. To find out if it's possible Mother was a Perfect Mate. I unstaked Dimitri's men and will let the Committee know where to find them before sunrise. And I'll take care of the tanker driver. So you all go on back to London. I'll be fine."

The woman was crazy. Crazy hurt, for sure. "No. You come back to the plane. It's not safe."

"Yeah, it's not safe on the plane either. I'll talk to you later."

"Mandy! No!"

Groucho looked at the screen. "She disconnected the call."

Perry glared at Barnet. "This is your fault. She's going to get herself killed because you won't talk to your own daughter."

"What?" Groucho's eyebrows shot up. "Mandy is your daughter?"

Barnet crossed his arms. "I'm not going to discuss this. Get us out of here. I want to go home."

"You can't do this, Barnet. We can't leave her."

"You heard her. She wants us to leave."

She didn't want that and Barnet damn well knew it. What Mandy wanted was to be loved, but how could Perry convince Barnet of that?

* * * *

Mandy slipped the mobile back into her pocket. Would they believe she left? Or rather, would Perry believe it? Frankly, she surprised herself when she'd sat up. Once the plane took off, she would feed off these two. Their blood would make death a blessing, but it was necessary and would give her some strength. Hopefully enough strength to load them into the SUV and drive somewhere where people were. Somewhere she could feed properly. And then? Go back to Natasha's store. Find out exactly where Alexi Popolov was buried. If she could unearth him, maybe then her father would forgive her.

Rachel might not have given birth to Mandy, but she was her mother all the same. And if Rachel had been a Perfect Mate, Alexi would be the proof Mandy needed.

Why hadn't the plane left yet? They'd had enough time to refuel. The SUV was still running, but she'd be able to hear the sound of a jet plane over that.

Oscar came around the SUV. "There you are. Guess Perry was right."

"Bloody hell." She'd have to cross off that dream of being an actor. Because she apparently sucked at it.

He crawled inside the SUV and shut off the engine. Pointed at the two staked vampires. "Unstaked them, huh? Did you call the Russian Committee about them already?"

"No. I was going to take them with me."

Oscar's eyebrows shot upward. She had to laugh. Not because he looked silly, because he did, but because of the absurdity of her statement. Truth was, she wasn't completely sure her plan would have worked. Now she'd never know.

He lifted her and headed toward the plane. "Maybe you can call them after we're in the air."

"I like that idea, but..." And it was a big but: her father. She just wasn't sure how to go about saying it.

"I know Barnet's your father. I'm sorry he left you behind like this. I almost didn't believe it, but...here you are."

Oh? He had to have learned that from Perry. Her father would certainly never admit to such a thing. "Then you know he's not going to want me on that plane."

"Well, see, he doesn't have much say so in that. I'm the pilot. That makes me in charge."

"Even over the Head of the Committee?"

"Even over. You don't think I took this job if I didn't have that authority, do you?"

She wasn't prepared for that bit of kindness and her eyes stung from unshed tears. "Thank you, Oscar."

"Thank Perry. He's the one who convinced me that you were lying."

When Oscar reached the plane, she tugged on his collar. "Stop. Let me take care of the driver."

"No need. He'll leave as soon as the plane does."

Sure enough, the driver was sitting behind the wheel and the engine was running.

"You know Russian?"

"No. I used Google Translate. Should have seen Perry's face when I told him that. Barnet's for that matter, too. I swear, I don't think they realize how powerful their phones can be."

Oscar might as well put her in the same column. She'd never thought about using that app. Although understanding the language was the smarter way to go. More reliable than wireless zones and batteries, too.

He ascended the stairs, placed her in a seat, and returned to the opening to secure the door.

Perry was sitting rather crookedly across the aisle, but the seatbelt was fastened around his waist. Knotted, too. His smile worked just fine, though. He wagged his eyebrows. "Hey. You hungry or just happy to see me?"

Her fangs. They'd lowered since she'd been staked and she'd been unable to retract them. "Are you ever serious?"

"I try not to be. Although, I was afraid you'd actually left."

Okay, maybe her acting skills weren't totally sucky. "How are you feeling?"

"Oh, I'll be up doing the rumba in no time."

She glanced around as much as her head would turn. All the other seats were empty. "Where's—?"

Perry's face grew serious. "In the cockpit."

Right. That made sense. No inadvertent glances her way, then. He could just pretend she wasn't on the plane.

Oscar closed the door and rubbed his hands together. "We all set? Oh, your belt." He strapped her in. "Fingers crossed we get out of here."

The engine started. The plane turned around and they took off.

"Think he'll turn off the seat belt sign?" Perry asked. "This belt is cutting into me."

"That belt is keeping you off the floor."

"I suppose it is. You know, if Groucho didn't want the weight distributed evenly, I'd sit with you."

"And that's the only thing keeping you over there? It has nothing to do with the fact you can't move."

"Hey, I can move. See?" He lifted his arm about an inch from his leg for a whole second. "I'll hold it longer in another hour. Higher, too."

She almost laughed. But she had done that to him. "I'm so very sorry, Perry."

"What are you sorry about? We won."

"Won? What fight were you in?"

"We're on this plane aren't we? I call that winning." Perry leaned his head back against the wall of the plane. "Were you really going to find Alexi Popolov on your own?"

"Why not? If what you believe is true, that my mother was a Perfect Mate, he's the proof I need."

"I know she wasn't your real mother, your birth mother. Barnet told me."

Mandy shook her head. Her father probably told Perry a lot of things. Oh, they were things Father believed, she'd give him that. They just weren't accurate. "True, she didn't give birth to me, but she *was* my real mother. The only one I ever knew. She raised me. She loved me. Did we always get along? No, but I still loved her. Maybe not as much as I loved Father, but there was no way I would hurt him like that. No way."

Oscar cursed from the cockpit.

"Everything okay?" She grimaced. Why would he cuss if it were?

"The patch isn't holding. We're losing fuel. I have to go back."

"No," her father said. "Find another airport. Something closer to the border."

"Oscar's right. We should go back. There's a car back there. The SUV. It's our best shot at—"

"Don't listen to her. Find another airport."

Why did she ever think he'd come around? The hatred in his voice squeezed her heart. She couldn't be mad at him, though. She'd just hoped that after five hundred years, he'd stopped grieving.

"I'm sorry he's being an ass," Perry whispered. "I wish I could do something to help."

"You've done enough. I'm here, aren't I?"

"Mandy, did you call the Russian Committee yet?" Oscar asked.

"No." She hadn't even pulled out her mobile.

"Then she's right. There is a vehicle we can use. And right now, I'm not so sure I can land at another airport without Dimitri getting word of it. I'm sorry, Barnet, but we have to go back."

Mandy smiled. Oscar wasn't kidding when he said he had last word.

"One good thing," Oscar said. "This landing should be easier than the last one. Runway's clear."

The landing was fairly smooth. Too bad the trip out to the SUV wouldn't be as smooth. Mandy could move her arms and legs, but she wasn't strong enough to walk. Neither was Perry. She didn't need to guess who would carry who.

Oscar emerged from the cockpit and smiled at her. She would never call him Oscar the Grouch again. The man was far from being grouchy and he had every reason to be on this mission. A mission that wasn't over by a long-shot.

"I'm so sorry about your plane."

He shrugged as he stowed his laptop into a backpack. "It's just a machine. I can always get another."

"Get another?" Perry said. "Man, you do have deep pockets, don't you?"

She unbuckled her belt. Oscar had slipped his backpack over his shoulders and held hers out to her. She stared at her bag a moment before taking it. That had to be Perry's doing. She'd completely forgotten it was inside the tanker cab. "Thank you."

Just as she suspected, her father carried Perry with his bag and Oscar carried her with hers. The tanker was gone, and most likely headed back to the airport from where it came.

The SUV was still parked in the middle of the road. The two vampires still lying in the snow beside it.

"You put her in the front with you," her father said to Oscar. "After I change the tire, I'll sit in the back with Perry."

"Guess I'm driving," Oscar muttered.

"Don't worry. I'll help navigate. First we have to figure out where we're going."

"Hey, Boss," Perry said. "Since we're stuck in Russia, you want to go find Alexi Popolov?"

Mandy turned and faced Perry, who sat behind the driver. Mouthed, "What are you doing?"

He grinned and shrugged.

"Why don't we concentrate on getting you fed first?"

Mandy hadn't missed that barb.

"You mean us, right? Mandy and me. Getting us fed?"

Her father only climbed into the vehicle. Behind her. So he didn't have to see her.

"What about Dimitri's men?" she asked.

No reaction from her father. As if he didn't even hear her.

"I thought you were going to call the Russian Committee," Oscar said.

"I can, but when? They'll know we took their vehicle. If I call now and they're found before we're able to dump this vehicle, Dimitri might be able to track us. And if I call later, they might not be found in time. Are we willing to let them die in the sun?"

"Wouldn't Dimitri just love that," Perry said. "You willing to risk his wrath, Boss?"

Her father opened his door. "No. Come on, Oscar."

The back opened. Oscar shoved in Yevgeni. Her father held Ivan. The guy's pants were hanging off his knees. Her father hadn't even bothered to pull them up.

"Why is he half naked?" Perry stared at her.

Damn it. She really didn't want to get into this with Perry. He hadn't been able to see what Ivan attempted to do and certainly didn't understand Russian. But before she could make up some excuse her father spoke.

"It's what men do when they get ready to rape someone."

Perry's eyes widened. "He what now?"

"He's no threat to me now."

"He tried to rape you? Throw his ass out. Let him burn."

"You're willing to risk Dimitri's wrath for her? I'm not." Her father shoved Ivan in the back. "I'll let the Committee know where to find them after we've secured a getaway. Which means, we can't talk freely in their presence."

Right. Because no matter whether or not these two understood English, they would still record everything they saw and heard mentally and report it to Dimitri, who did understand English. The perks of being a vampire.

"But you stopped him, Boss? You kept him from raping her?"

"I disabled the enemy. That is all I did."

At least he hadn't labeled her an enemy. Or maybe she was the lesser of two evils? If there had been a spare stake around, would he have even bothered removing hers? And here she'd thought that maybe he still had some love left inside him when he'd kept Ivan from raping her. Boy, was she delusional.

As the three men discussed where they would find the most people, she didn't bother to pipe in. Didn't think her father would go for anything she suggested anyway.

Her father passed Oscar's mobile to Perry. He read the message, nodded, and handed it to Oscar. Oscar glanced at the phone. When he went to hand it off to Mandy, Barnet snatched it back.

Okay, then.

Perry held his hand out to her. She took it. He spoke through the link. "*Barnet texted Vic about our situation. She's getting us a plane tomorrow evening.*"

Seemed they were stuck in Russia another day. Or at least the guys were. She wasn't sure about herself.

Chapter 14

The two staked vampires behind Perry seemed to be having an argument, and the way the words were batted back and forth he'd bet swear words were involved.

Yevgeni was definitely mad. Was he mad at the other guy because he'd almost raped Mandy? Or was it worse? Had the other guy raped Mandy and was finishing when Barnet disabled him?

The not knowing, along with a heavy dose of guilt, gnawed at Perry's gut. Between the two, he wouldn't have a stomach left.

He'd failed her. When she depended on him the most, he'd failed her. Oh sure, he still thought they'd won—they were still alive—but that was all Barnet's doing.

And now Barnet was acting like an ass. First he'd been willing to leave her behind, and now with him not giving Mandy the phone to read Vic's text? Did he honestly think she wasn't coming with them? Did he honestly think Perry would even allow that to happen?

Groucho pulled into the parking lot of a hospital. When Barnet had suggested they find one, Mandy had opened her map and gave Groucho directions.

"Go around the back so we're not exposed," Barnet said.

The late night/early morning crowd was thin at worst. Not many cars were parked in the lot and no one stood outside smoking. The frigid temperature might be responsible for that, but when smokers wanted a smoke, the weather usually didn't deter them.

"Park in the last row." Barnet patted Perry's leg. "You should be safe to feed over there behind those dumpsters."

Again, Perry got the inclination that Barnet used the singular you. But it didn't matter. Groucho would take care of Mandy. "How are you going to get someone over to us?"

Oh shit. Could he take those words back? Those bozos didn't need to know that Mandy knew Russian.

She pointed to Groucho's phone. "You have a translation app, right?"

And she apparently didn't want them to know, either. Why couldn't he be smart like her? He knew about the stupid app and couldn't blame his loss of blood on forgetting. She'd lost blood, too, and remembered.

Groucho nodded and held up his cellphone. "We tell them to follow us. Or rather, we say, 'follow me.'" He tapped the screen a few times.

Perry had been impressed with that translation app. Man, he really should see what else his phone could do. And once he had the ability to do more than turn his head and lift his arm, he'd get right on that.

A robotic-like voice said, "*Podpisyvaytes' na menya.*"

"All that means 'follow me'?" And he thought German was bad. Not that he knew much of that language. Only the few words Vic used when she cussed.

Groucho chuckled. "I hope so. Barnet, do you need to hear it again?"

"I'm good. Let's go." Barnet came around the vehicle and opened Perry's door.

He really hated not being able to walk. He wasn't a damn baby. If he were back home, he'd just control someone to help him to a private place, feed on them, and send them on their way.

Here? He couldn't imagine a translator app would be much help. What if he didn't have a signal? Or his phone wasn't charged? Or worse, he was so incapacitated he couldn't use his phone? Yeah, learning the language was certainly more reliable.

Barnet pulled out the stun gun.

"What, I'm not crippled enough for you?"

Barnet reached over Perry's seat and zapped both staked vampires.

Perry jumped. "Why'd you do that? It's not like they're going to walk out of here."

Barnet raised an eyebrow and leveled an are-you-for-real look. "So they don't cry out for help."

Oh… Right. He chuckled. "This lack of blood to the head isn't helping me think straight." Maybe he was a baby. He couldn't walk and, apparently, he couldn't think, either.

Barnet lifted him and jogged to the dumpsters. At least the cold temperature kept the scent of leftover food and soiled whatever to a minimum. Wasn't great, but on a hot day it would be almost unbearable. Barnet lowered Perry to the snow-covered ground and propped him against the building. Groucho did the same to Mandy.

It really was the perfect spot, as long as no one needed to dump any trash. They couldn't be seen from the parking lot so no passersby would notice they weren't exactly dressed for the weather.

Perry itched to hold her hand, but if he even tried, Barnet would probably separate them. He'd rather stay close, even if he couldn't touch her. Instead he offered his best grin to her. "We gotta stop meeting like this."

She didn't laugh. Not even a twitch of her lips. She just stared at her lap. How could he fix the rift between her and Barnet? Was it fixable?

"So, was the app correct?" Groucho asked.

Mandy raised her head. "Surprisingly so. Just make sure you pronounce it the same as the app does."

"We'll be right back." Barnet turned and walked away. Groucho, who wasn't being so grouchy considering the circumstances, smiled and then followed.

Mandy leaned her head back. "God, he really hates me."

It did appear that way, but Perry wasn't going to let her get depressed or think she wasn't valuable. Because she was valuable. To him. "He doesn't hate you. And once he knows the whole truth, he'll come around."

She chuffed. "Yeah? Do you believe Doctor Who is real, too?"

He widened his eyes. "He's not real? You mean those aren't documentaries?"

Finally, laughter. And it was such a lovely sound. "You're impossible."

"I've been told that before. Also, unreliable. I'm so sorry I let Yevgeni get the upper hand. I didn't even think that you might have been at risk. That they would have…" Damn. He couldn't even say the word. "Did he save you in time? Or did he get there too late?"

She placed her hand over his. "Ivan did not rape me."

"Oh, thank the Great One. Is that what those two were arguing about? Because they didn't get to finish the job?"

Mandy shook her head. "No. Yevgeni is pissed at Ivan. Said his dick would always get them in trouble. He's also afraid Dimitri will punish them for failing. Blames Ivan for that, too."

"Maybe they can be convinced to change sides, then. I can't imagine Katya being so strict."

"I don't think Ivan can be convinced of anything. Yevgeni might, though. He's just following orders."

Groucho and Barnet returned with two men wearing scrubs, following like sheep.

Groucho looked at Mandy. "Can you take over?"

She nodded. "I've got them."

One man settled in beside Perry and the other sat beside Mandy. Barnet slipped out of sight.

"Perry, you need to feed first," Groucho said. "Then you and I will go look for another car."

"Wait, what now? What about Mandy?"

"Barnet will stay with her while she feeds."

After the way Barnet had treated her, Perry didn't trust the man. "Boss!"

Barnet came around the fence. "Will you keep your voice down?"

Voice down? That was a joke, right? Perry could barely talk. "What are you planning?"

"I'm not planning anything. You're better at breaking into cars than either one of us."

Well, that much was true. He did have a knack for that. Still… "You're not going to leave her behind."

Barnet lowered his head, muttered softly, and ran his hand through his hair. "I give you my word. That will not happen."

He sounded sincere, but why wouldn't he look Perry in the eye?

Mandy placed her hand over his. "It's okay, Perry. Go on. I'll keep control of him while you feed."

With everyone staring, Perry went for the jugular. It would take the least amount of time and besides, he was famished. He stopped once he'd taken enough from the man. It wasn't near enough to be at a hundred percent, but he wouldn't risk this man's life to get that way. Not when he could just find someone else to feed from. He licked the area clean and healed the holes.

Barnet grabbed Perry's arm. Helped him stand. "You good?"

Perry wiggled one leg, then the other. "Good enough to walk, but don't ask me to run the marathon. I hate not winning." He turned toward Mandy. He couldn't leave her. Not with Barnet. Plus, she liked her privacy.

She offered him a smile. "Go on, now. Find us a good car."

Right. A good car. Perry nodded and turned to Barnet. "She prefers to feed in private."

"Is that so? All the more reason for you to leave then. Right?"

Oh crap. Had he just made things worse?

"Come on, Perry." Groucho tapped his shoulder.

Right. He had a car to procure. He followed Groucho, walking slow, but walking. Every step away from her was pure agony and it had nothing to do with his legs. *Oh Great One, please look after her.*

* * * *

Mandy sent Perry's donor back to the hospital, but hadn't reached for her own. She couldn't imagine why her father had sent Perry off unless he knew. But why would he care about that?

"I'll do my best to give you your ten minutes, so I suggest you hurry."

Damn it. He *did* know. And he was protecting her…why? She could ask later. Now she needed to feed and start the clock.

She latched onto the neck and bit. So much better than the last two times. No perfume to deal with. No hairy leg. When she got her fill—and she took a little extra—she healed the holes and sent the donor on his way, with instructions to drink some juice and have a snack.

She leaned her head back as the fiery pain surged through her body. Made it hard to speak but she wasn't wasting this time. "How did you know?"

"You don't think I would find out why I'm allergic to blood?"

"You? How are you allergic?" Unless she transferred it. "Bloody hell. I did that to you?"

He folded his arms across his chest. "Like you didn't know."

"I didn't! No one told me."

"Lies. I went to Frederick when I realized what he was. He told you not to turn anyone. Was pretty pissed you'd turned me."

"No, no, no. That is *not* what he said."

"Lies. Do you even know how to tell the truth?"

"I am telling the truth. You just don't want to believe it."

"Lies. I read his memories just before I killed him. You knew you would pass on the affliction because he told you."

"Then you were reading some other memory, because that's not what he said to *me*. He threatened to report me if I turned someone to mate with, because I refused to mate with him. Not once did he mention I would pass on the affliction. Don't you think I would have told you, warned you, if I had known?"

"Lies. I am so sick of your lies. Once this mission is over, I never want to see you again. Do you understand?" He turned and faced the parking lot.

He might be finished with their conversation, but she certainly wasn't. "It doesn't matter what I say to you, you're going to believe what you want. But I didn't kill Mother. As for the allergy, I'd do it again in a heartbeat. I couldn't just watch you die. And I wish so much that Mother could have survived."

"Stop it. You've made it abundantly clear in the past that Rachel was not your mother."

"When I was twelve! If anything, I was madder at you than her when you sent me off to Frederick's."

"Is that why you filled Perry's head with this atrocious idea that Rachel was a Perfect Mate? To have me believe you didn't kill her?"

"I didn't fill his head with anything. That was all him. But you have to admit, it's a plausible explanation."

"No, it's not. You don't think I checked her for bites? She had none. Which means you didn't try to turn her."

Oh bollocks. How stupid had she been? If she had left the bite marks, would he have believed her all this time?

After she had injected her father with venom, she'd licked the site, as if she'd fed. Then she searched for Mother. Had done the same to her. It hadn't been until Mandy moved them to safety that she'd noticed her father's marks hadn't healed, but her mother's marks had. But telling her father that wouldn't matter. He'd never believe her. "If you hate what I've done to you, how come you never ended your life? How come you just didn't kill me?"

Because he certainly had his chances in the past, as he did today. Yet…she was still breathing.

* * * *

Barnet leaned against the dumpster. A long time ago he'd read somewhere that the dead were not dead as long as they lived in the hearts they left behind. That was why Barnet never committed suicide, even though he'd been tempted all those centuries ago. If he died, there wouldn't be anyone left to remember Rachel and he wouldn't have her memory shortened.

So he honored her every day. Hung her likeness in his office. Never forgot her. He lived for both of them.

But to think she could have been a Perfect Mate? That was ludicrous. And it would throw all his theories out the window. Although… It kind of made sense, if what Amanda said was true. And he could confirm her story easily enough. So why didn't he? Didn't Martha's daughter deserve that much?

Martha. She'd been a good wife. Dutiful. But there was no love between them. Their marriage had been arranged. When she and their second child had died during childbirth, he'd been forced to be both mother and father to Amanda. He'd been hard on her. Disciplined. Hell, he treated his vampires better than he'd treated Amanda. But she had never complained. Not until Rachel.

Maybe part of that was his fault. He'd never been in love before and he'd been head over heels with Rachel. So much so, that he might have ignored Amanda some in the beginning. Rachel had always treated Amanda as her own, especially when it turned out she was barren. Amanda would be the only child he would ever have. But by then, the rift had already begun.

Did he want her dead? No. She was Martha's child. But he'd hated that she wasn't Rachel's child. And she never would be.

* * * *

Perry found a van in the back of the lot, covered in snow. "When do you think it snowed here last?"

Groucho shrugged. "Not since we arrived for sure. Does it matter?"

"Just looking for a car that won't be reported stolen right away."

"So we should take one that isn't covered in snow?"

Should they? Damn, he still wasn't thinking clearly. Barnet had messed with his brain somehow. Why did Barnet want to stay back with Mandy? He said he wouldn't leave her behind, but would he hurt her?

"You okay, Perry?"

"Yeah. Just thinking." Which, hey, really wasn't his specialty. At least he had Groucho on his side when it came to Mandy. And Barnet wouldn't dare do something foolish in front of Groucho. Unless Barnet made it look like an accident.

Damn it. Perry looked back toward the dumpsters. Would he be able to hear her scream?

"You like her, don't you?"

"Well yeah. Don't you?"

Groucho chuckled. "I do, but not like you do. You like her, like her. Romantically like her."

Romantically? Just because he enjoyed being around her company and wouldn't mind repeating what they'd done back at the hotel, couldn't possibly mean anything. Groucho had to have misinterpreted their act. Because it had been an act. Perry chuffed. "No. Not at all. I have a Perfect Mate in my future. But Barnet's been acting weird. I don't want him doing anything he'll regret later."

"He is acting different, I'll give you that. So should we find a car with or without snow?"

Yeah, the car. The quicker they got a vehicle, the quicker Perry could return to Mandy. "Actually, we need an older vehicle. One I can hotwire. Might as well try this van first."

He brushed the snow away from the door. Tested the handle. Unlocked. Well, that was almost too easy. Maybe it was covered in snow because it wasn't working.

The interior lingered of smoke. Actually weed. A little smoking hideout maybe? Was marijuana legal in this country? Probably not, thus the hideout. Hmmm…would they miss this vehicle? It hadn't been opened since the last snow, so hopefully not. Perry bent under the dash, found his wires.

The engine started right up.

Groucho slapped Perry on the back. "Way to go. You clean off the van and I'll go fetch our things."

Perry wanted to fetch Mandy. Was she okay? Was Barnet letting her feed? Hell, would she feed in front of Barnet? That was the real question.

Groucho returned with the three backpacks and tossed them in the back. "I'll wait here if you want to go check on them."

Perry wiped the last of the snow from the windows. "You're a peach, Oscar. Don't let anyone tell you different."

"Oh God, don't go liking me, now."

"What's wrong with me liking you? Afraid I'll call you Peachy?"

Groucho covered his face. "Please. Just go."

This was too fun and it'd been ages since he'd had fun-fun. "I mean, you do live in Georgia. And your head resembles a peach."

"Stop." Groucho scowled.

Yeah, that was the face that earned him the name Oscar the Grouch. Not that Perry ever called him that to his face. Now would be a good time to try it, though. "Maybe I should just call you Groucho."

Instead of grumbling, Oscar lowered his hands. "You called me Groucho? As in Marx?"

"Are you kidding? Groucho Marx was funny. I called you that after Oscar the Grouch. Because you're always grouchy."

Groucho laughed a big old belly laugh. "Oscar the Grouch was my favorite Muppet. I actually took his name when I was looking for a new ID."

"You don't say." Perry couldn't help but laugh with the man.

"Go on. Get Barnet and Mandy. I'll wait here. Wait. What is that?" Groucho pointed at the windshield.

"Oh shit. The dash cam." Perry crawled inside the van and disconnected the camera from the recorder.

"A dash cam? You mean a camera?"

"Yeah. Apparently, the citizens around here don't trust their fellow drivers and need to record every second on the road."

"Why didn't you just yank it off the windshield?"

"Then it would look suspicious, now wouldn't it?" Hey lookee there. His brain was working again. He crawled out of the van. "Don't worry. I disabled it."

Perry wanted to race back to the dumpster, but that wasn't happening. Trotting was out, too. A fast walk was about all he could manage. Barnet was leaning against the fence. Mandy was standing on the other side, out of Barnet's view, looking so much better.

"Did you find a car?" Barnet asked.

"Yeah. Back corner lot." Perry pointed the way and Barnet took off without a word. Perry turned back toward Mandy. His heart ached at the pain etched across her face. "You okay?"

She nodded, but he didn't believe it for a minute. Barnet was being an ass. He had a daughter. A smart daughter. And he was just throwing that away.

Perry took her hand. "Let's go, then. Groucho already fetched our bags."

She stared at him with wide eyes. "I thought you two were getting along."

"We are. He actually likes that I call him that."

Her laughter was still the most wonderful sound to his ears. But it lived a short life. She grew serious. "I'm not going with you."

Damn that man. "Yes, you are. Barnet can't stop you."

"That's not what I mean. He just proved to me that I need to find Alexi Popolov. I'm staying behind to find him."

"That's a suicide mission!"

She just shrugged. Shrugged!

He reached out, ready to shake some sense into her, but lowered his hands and continued walking. "He'll let you on the plane. Groucho and I will make sure of it."

"Oh, I know he will. But that's not it and you know it. He'll never believe me unless I have proof. And, well, I'm really hoping Popolov is the proof I need. But if anything, he's someone my father wants. So I'm going to find him."

She made sense, in a way, and when would they have this chance again? There was no guarantee that Katya would overthrow Dimitri. "Then I'm going with you."

"You don't have to. It may seem otherwise, but I can take care of myself."

"Oh, I have no doubt that you can. But you shouldn't do this alone. Unless…" He stopped. "You don't want me around."

Not many people counted on him for anything. Why would she be any different?

She palmed his cheek. "I'd be honored to have you accompany me. But if something should happen to you, my father would only blame me."

Honored? Well, hell. "Then I guess he should come, too."

"What? No. Trust me, he'd prefer I wasn't anywhere near him."

"Won't know until we ask." And Barnet was having a hard time saying no to Perry. Had to take advantage of that.

Barnet sat up front this time. Groucho played driver again.

Perry opened the sliding door to the back and slid his butt onto the bench seat. "Hey, Boss. Remember when I asked if we should go find Alexi Popolov?"

"We don't have time to look for him."

He held his hand out to Mandy, making sure she came inside. "Sure we do. What do we have, something like twenty hours before our plane arrives? Why spend it doing nothing? Why not spend it unburying him? I mean, we know where he is."

She settled on the seat beside him and slid the door shut. Not quite in Barnet's view. Probably just as well.

"We don't know where he is." Barnet kept his attention on the windshield.

Perry snapped his fingers. "That's right. You don't know. Natasha Bychkova owns a store in Moscow. We've met her. She'll be able to show us on a map where to go."

"And you don't think Dimitri isn't watching his people?"

Mandy pulled on Perry's sleeve. "It's okay. I can do this on my own."

Barnet turned around and glared at Mandy.

Perry placed his hand on Barnet's seat, blocking his view to Mandy. "Oscar, did you ever leave the plane?"

Groucho blinked. Probably surprised he was getting involved in this conversation. "No. I stayed inside the whole time."

"See? It's highly unlikely Dimitri would recognize Oscar. If we warned Natasha of his visit, he could go into the store asking directions to someplace else and she would write down the directions to Alexi's grave. When will we ever get this opportunity again?"

Perry could almost see the thoughts spinning through their leader's head and he smiled. He must have said the right thing.

Chapter 15

Mandy sat in the backseat of the van with Perry. The van stunk of marijuana, but that was the least of her worries. The man sitting in front of her—her father—was at the other extreme.

Because he had agreed to search for Alexi Popolov.

Even Oscar was okay with the plan.

She should have never told Perry her plan. What if she was wrong again? They'd all just blame her. No. Strike that. Her father would blame her. Too late to fix that; she'd just have to live with it. Besides, if she wanted to be truthful to herself, their chances were much better with Oscar. Like Perry had said, Dimitri wouldn't recognize him. At least, not right away.

After her father agreed to this crazy stunt, he'd gone inside the hospital to call the Russian Committee about Dimitri's men. While he was there, Mandy used her cellphone and called the shop—since she had no fear they would track her phone—and spoke to Natasha. Gave her a heads up to what they wanted. She was scared, but willing to help. She just wanted her friend safe.

And if they succeeded, it meant another passenger in the plane. One her father could focus on instead of her. Alexi wouldn't be safe in Russia, especially in the condition he'd be in. It would take several feedings to get him back in action. And those first feedings would not be easy.

Best they start doing that in friendly territory. Whether they chose London or Atlanta was up to her father.

But first, they had to rescue the man.

Her father climbed back inside the van and slammed the door shut. "Let's go."

Oscar put the van into gear and drove out of the parking lot avoiding the SUV.

Perry leaned between the two front seats. "You were gone awhile. Did you talk to Katya, Boss?"

"No. Probably just as well. We don't need her involved any more than she already is. I spoke to Felicks."

"Felicks?" Perry asked as he turned toward her, concern in his eyes. Concern that had every right to be there. If what Katya had told her and Perry was true, Barnet might as well have spoken to Dimitri. "What did you tell him?"

"Pretty much the truth."

"The truth?" The words blurted out of her mouth before she could stop them.

Her father turned in his seat, fury in his eyes. "Yes, the truth. He recognized my voice. Saw I was calling from a local number. I wasn't about to lie to the man. He deserves to know what kind of leader he has."

Perry leaned back in his seat. "But Boss, what about our plan to rescue Alexi? Is that scrapped now?"

"The topic never came up. He asked me what I was doing in Russia, so I told him. That Dimitri had me kidnapped, that I was trying to get home, and where he could find their two goons." Her father chuckled. "Felicks couldn't apologize more. He even offered to fly me out of here."

"He thinks you're alone."

"He did. Doesn't anymore. I said there were three of us and that we'd find our own way home."

Mandy almost laughed. Of course three. Because he had no intention of taking her.

Perry frowned. "Why three?"

"I don't need Dimitri finding out about Oscar right away."

Okay, that made more sense. Still didn't mean he didn't want to leave her behind. And maybe he wouldn't be so cruel to do that here, but in London? Oh yeah. She could see getting kicked off the plane there. But if her father seriously thought that Dimitri didn't already know there was a pilot involved—

"But those goons will know Oscar is with us." Perry said the words she almost blurted. And because he had said them instead of her, her father's response was much…friendlier.

"Yes, I realize that. I'm hoping we get the information we need before Dimitri finds out."

Their trip to downtown was definitely shorter than anyone coming from Russian Headquarters to the hospital to rescue Dimitri's men. Provided they came from Russian Headquarters. She prayed that luck was on their side for a change. Oscar parked several blocks away from Natasha's store.

Mandy found an old hoodie in the back and handed it to him. "Cover your head. It's a cold night and you'll blend in better."

Oscar took the garment, sniffed it, and grimaced. "Now I know why the van stinks. Do I really need to wear this?"

"Yes. It'll keep people away from you, right? Just look natural or maybe a little stoned. We don't know how many cameras Dimitri has on her shop. Do you know another language?"

"French."

"Use that. She'll understand you. And remember, ask where Gorky Park is."

Oscar nodded. "Barnet, you sure my credit card will be okay to use at the ATM?" During the drive over here, the men had debated about which card to use. Oscar's won out since it was his business card.

"We have no choice. We need cash. Yours is the least likely to be recognized right away. Get the max it allows. We'll see you on the other side of the store."

When Oscar exited the vehicle, her father crawled over to the driver's seat and drove off. Perry gave instructions of where to turn and park. Mandy just sat quietly. When they got to the hotel, she'd make sure to get a room far from her father's. On a different floor.

Ten minutes later, Oscar jogged over to the van. He removed the hoodie and climbed into the passenger side. "Man, this thing is nasty. I don't ever want to wear it again."

Oscar passed the hoodie back to Mandy and she tossed it in the back of the van.

"How far away is he?" her father asked.

"About forty miles to the south. I marked the coordinates on my phone's map."

"Forty miles? That's cutting it close if we want to get him tonight."

"We probably shouldn't." Could she just take the words back? Or better yet, find some tape for her mouth?

"And why is that?" He practically spat the words, but kept his head forward.

Perry patted her hand. *"Just tell me what I should say, okay?"*

But she couldn't do that. If they were going to get through this mission, her father would just have to get used to her input. "He has cameras there. Whether or not we disable them, he's going to know what is going on. If we go in tonight, it will give Dimitri time to find us. None of you know Russian and it's highly unlikely Alexi will be able to walk. We'll draw attention and I might not be able to catch everyone who sees us. We need to stay inconspicuous when we check into our hotel. Same with checking out. I suggest we wait an hour or two before our plane arrives to rescue Alexi. We should be able to get him and fly out of here before Dimitri's men can catch us."

"That makes sense," Perry said. Oscar agreed.

Her father must have thought the same thing, but had he acknowledged that? Of course not. "We can't stay in town here, though. Oscar, find us a hotel closer to where Alexi is."

"He's kind of out in the boonies, but there are plenty of places to choose away from downtown."

They had ten hours to kill. Ten hours before the soon-to-be-rising sun would set. She had a feeling it would be the longest ten hours of her life.

* * * *

Dimitri placed his phone on the desk, using restraint. He had wanted to crumble the device in his fist, but then he'd just need another phone and wasn't about to explain why he'd broken this one.

Fucking Committee. Always wanting explanations for everything. And for what? So they could vote on it? He was surprised he'd lasted this long and should have never gone along with the other countries to begin with. Committees were a waste of time. If he had used them to capture Barnet, he'd still be waiting for transport. Hell, he'd still be arguing his case.

Going around the Committee was quicker. And he had men who followed his every command. Men like Yevgeni and Ivan.

Where were they? They should have reported in long before now. But every time Dimitri called Yevgeni's phone, he was directed to the voicemail. He'd dismissed his other group of soldiers, the ones who'd found the plane, but maybe it was time to call them back in. He lifted the handset just as Katya, Grigorii, Sergei, and Felicks entered his office.

Now what? He hung up the phone and greeted them like old friends. "This is unexpected. Is something going on?"

Felicks came forward. Dimitri kept his face neutral at this surprise. He'd been sure Katya was behind this little intervention. Bad enough he had to deal with a Committee. Adding a woman to the mix only made it more distasteful. And so illogical. Men were the warriors. And it took a warrior to do this job.

"Dimitri, I just got the most distressing phone call. May we meet in the conference room so we can discuss this?"

And have it recorded for anyone to hear? Not likely. Oh, it was to be used for Committee business only, but that was a load of bullshit. "Something wrong with my office?"

"Please, sir."

Dimitri sighed. If the conversation wasn't to his liking, he'd just have one of his men do away with the recording. It wouldn't have been the first time he'd had to resort to such tactics. "Very well, then."

At least the table in the conference room was rectangular and Dimitri still sat in the seat of honor: at the head.

Felicks sat to his right with Sergei between them. "Barnet called."

Had the man actually made it out of the country? Damn. But Dimitri couldn't let on. He laughed as that was what he did. "Again? What does that make? Fifteen?"

"From Moscow."

"Moscow? I was not aware he was in our country."

"He says you brought him here. Against his will."

"Did he now? Did he also say where I kept him?"

"In the holding cells downstairs. Where Mikhail was being held. He confirmed Barnet's story."

Mikhail? Dimitri almost swore aloud. He should have done away with that miscreant instead of freeing him.

Katya sat on his immediate left and leaned forward. "Is that who Yevgeni was looking for earlier tonight? Barnet?"

Dimitri leaned back and crossed his arms. She acted all smug, but something told him that maybe she had something to do with Barnet's disappearance. He directed his question to Felicks. "Where is he now? I assume you offered him a way home."

"I did. But he didn't accept. Said there were three of them and that they'd find their own way. He was mainly calling to let us know that Yevgeni and Ivan were staked in the back of their SUV."

"He staked our men? Why?" That explained why Dimitri couldn't get hold of his men. But three? What about the pilot? Surely, Barnet wasn't leaving him behind.

Sergei slammed his hand on the table. "We should be thankful he didn't kill them. What were you hoping to accomplish?"

"First off, I did not kidnap Barnet. I caught him in our country illegally."

"If that were the case, then why didn't you inform us?" Felicks asked.

"I would have eventually, but then his minions arrived here." Dimitri leveled his gaze at Katya. "I told you they were spies. And now they are free roaming our country. Spewing lies!"

"The only person lying is you," Sergei said.

Dimitri already knew he'd lost Katya's and Grigorii's allegiance. Seemed he'd lost Sergei's too.

Felicks placed a hand on Sergei's shoulder. "Dimitri, don't you see? Whether or not you captured Barnet here or on US soil, you've practically declared war against the US vampires. We are a Committee and should make decisions as one."

"You, too, Felicks? I thought of all the men here, you would understand the most. We are weaker with a Committee. We need to be strong. To fight for our rights."

"What rights have you lost?" Katya asked. "We have never been stronger."

"The right to tell you to shut up. To tell all women to shut up. Men are leaders. Warriors. Women are nothing more than a thing to fuck."

Sergei stood. "Dimitri, that was out of line."

If anyone was out of line, it was this fucking Committee. Dimitri grabbed the knife from his sheath and slit Sergei's throat. Blood spurt across the table and covered Katya and Grigorii. Sergei slumped to the floor.

Felicks jumped back. "Dimitri! What are you doing?"

"Dismantling the Committee. I am the true leader of the Russian vampires. What I say goes. If you are not with me, you are against me and I will have you killed."

Grigorii grabbed Katya's hand and they fled the room, like the cowards they were. Dimitri would deal with them later.

He looked at Felicks. "Are you my right hand man or not?"

Felicks bowed. "I serve at your command, sir."

As it should be. Dimitri kicked Sergei's body. The vampire wasn't dead…yet. "You are to sever his head and lay him out for the sun. Afterward, we need to find Barnet and his lackeys. We can't let them escape."

"Yes, sir. As you command, sir. What about Katya and Grigorii?"

"I will tell you when to worry about them."

But first, he must go get his men. He couldn't afford to lose anyone else in the fight to preserve his kingdom.

Chapter 16

From his position behind the driver, Perry glanced over at Mandy. She'd been quiet on the drive. He'd love nothing better than to pull her in close and give her a big squeeze. Just to show her that she was important, even if her father didn't think so.

But if he did that, she might get the wrong impression. Or would that be the right impression? He didn't know what to think. More and more he was drawn to her. Would love to protect her and defend her, but something told him she'd kick his ass if he did. Maybe that's what he liked best about her.

Barnet parked the van on the street a few blocks from the hotel they chose and the silence was now broken. "Oscar, get one room with one key. We need to avoid detection and hopefully this will make it difficult."

Mandy straightened. "You want to spend all day in one room with me?"

While the thought of spending an entire day in one room didn't sound pleasing to Perry, it might be the one thing to bring Mandy and her father together. That, or someone was going to die.

Barnet stared at his hands. "I can set aside our differences for one day."

"Differences?" She snorted. "You can't even stand to look at me."

She had a point, there. Barnet had probably looked at her three times, and every time it was more like a glare than a glance. Glares that had brought her pain. But separate rooms would not bring them together.

Perry leaned between the seats. "How about a suite? Think they might have one of those?"

"I'll get the biggest room I can." Oscar climbed out and slung his backpack over his shoulder. "There should be an entrance from the parking lot. I'll meet you there."

Once Oscar dashed out of sight, Barnet opened his door but kept his focus in front of the van. "It's best if we don't all go together."

He left quietly, but he might as well have slammed the door.

Mandy covered her face. "This is a nightmare. A living nightmare."

Again, he got the urge to hug her, but he really didn't want to be kicked. "It is not that bad. In fact, this could be the best thing to happen to you two."

She lowered her hands. "How in the world is this the best thing?"

"It'll force you two to be together. And once we get Popolov, he can confirm the Perfect Mate story and Barnet will then see you were not at fault."

She laughed, but there were sad undertones to it. "You're such a terrible liar. Or a horrible optimist. I haven't decided."

"He'll come around. He's never held a grudge like this. Not even with me. And trust me, I've given him ample opportunities."

"But he has. Against me. For five hundred years."

"See? He's due to stop holding it." He grinned, but she wasn't buying it. If anything, her scowl deepened.

"I wouldn't hold my breath if I were you." Mandy grabbed her bag, opened the side door, and exited.

Perry grabbed his own bag and followed her out. He slid the door shut. The streets were deserted—not a soul or moving car in sight. They could have all gone together, but it was clear that Barnet just didn't want to be with her. "You have to admit that being apart is not in your best interest."

"You don't think he'll just leave the room and wander the halls all day?"

"No, I don't. He knows about as much Russian as I do. He can't control anyone here unless they know English. He will not risk our detection, so he'll stay in the room."

"So instead, he'll kick me out, because I *can* cover my tracks."

"That's not what I meant, and you know it."

He followed her across the street and jumped over the pile of snow to the sidewalk. As they headed toward the hotel, out of habit he almost took her hand. Except they weren't really on the mission anymore. They didn't have to pretend anymore. So he kept his hand to himself.

Perry turned and walked backward so he could see her. "Maybe you can bond watching television."

She shook her head. "You do realize that the shows are most likely spoken in Russian."

"And you're an interpreter. See? Instant bond!"

"You mean instant death. He'd rather chop my head off than listen to me."

"You're such a kill-joy." Somehow he had to get her to lighten up. He stopped, dropped his bag to the ground, and held his hands out. "Dance with me."

She stopped, but held onto her bag. "You've gone bonkers, haven't you?"

"No, no. I must fix your kill-joyness. Otherwise, we'll never get through this day."

She placed her free hand on her hip. "Kill-joyness?"

"Yes. Come on. You're over five hundred, you should know how to dance."

"And am I supposed to pretend there's music?"

He leaned his head back. "Have you no imagination? Fine." He reached into his pocket and pulled out his phone. He'd been told there was music on this thing. Hmmm…maybe the little icon with musical notes? He pressed that. "Hey, lookee there. I have music."

And quite a list to choose from, too. He scrolled until the right song appeared, selected it, and slipped the phone back into his pocket. "No excuses now."

The Beatles' "And I Love Her" played. The sound wasn't the greatest, but it could be heard.

She raised one lovely eyebrow. "Some reason you picked that particular song?"

"You're a Brit, so I thought you'd appreciate the Beatles. And you need a real dance, not something to jump around to. Are you gonna make me come get you?"

"You want to do this out in public? For anyone to see us? How is that being discreet?"

"Do you see anyone out here? I don't."

He was ready to grab her when she dropped her bag and stepped into his personal space. Took his left hand with her right and placed her left hand on his right shoulder. Old-fashioned style.

Just those tiny touches were enough to wake up his libido. And that wasn't what he was after. His dick could just wait. But since she went old-fashioned, he would, too. He placed his right hand on her hip and led the dance. This was nice. She fit nicely in his arms. Except she was way too tense. "Will you relax and enjoy this?"

She only stiffened more. Hmmm… Maybe the old-fashioned way wasn't the best way. He placed her arms around his neck and pulled her in close. Damn, she smelled good. Felt good this way, too.

After a few moments, she loosened up, placed her head on his chest, and mumbled, "I am not a kill-joy."

"Maybe you didn't mean to be a kill-joy, but you were. We got to get you more optimistic."

"How is my being optimistic going to get my father to listen to me?"

"Oh, he won't. I get it. I don't understand it, but I get where you're coming from. So we trick him into listening instead."

"How? By talking to you?"

"Nope. Groucho."

"What could I possibly talk to Oscar about?"

"What else? Alexi Popolov."

"Does he know who that is?"

"I don't know. But if we're going to go search for the guy, we need to talk about him. Plan it out. I'm sure Groucho has questions. And Barnet did say he would set aside his differences for the day."

She snorted.

"Hey, none of that. Be optimistic."

"Can I just stay here and dance instead? This is nice."

It was nice. Better than nice. "I'd be all for that except the sun is due to rise in about an hour." He palmed her face. "Don't get discouraged. You're not alone in this fight."

"I've been alone a long time. I don't want him to shut you out, too."

"He won't. I won't let him."

She placed her hands over his. "Why are you doing this?"

"Because we're friends." Except…had he ever desired a friend like he did her?

"Just friends?"

"Friends with benefits?" Whoa. What made him say that? Except…it was true. She was a friend and the sex they'd had earlier was certainly a benefit.

She pulled away. "No, not that. I won't do that to your Perfect Mate."

"What if I said I wasn't looking anymore?"

There went that eyebrow again. "Why would you say that?"

Because he wasn't? Oh sure, the language barrier was a problem, but not once did he even think about looking for one here. Not even in London, where they spoke English!

"Listen. I think it's sweet you want to help me. But I've come to the realization that there isn't anything I can say or do to change my father's opinion of me. I doubt even Alexi Popolov can help. Let's just get through this day, find him, and go home. And then I won't be a bother to anyone again."

Not see her again? Didn't she know how much he cared about her? Maybe the dance hadn't shown her. He leaned down and kissed her.

She stiffened, but he wouldn't take that as an insult. Instead, he wrapped his arms around her and nudged her mouth open with his tongue. Her jasmine scent enhanced the air around him and her sweetness exploded in his mouth.

And she molded against his body, just the way he liked.

* * * *

Mandy sunk into Perry's arms. Kissing him was heaven. Being kissed by him, even better. But why was he doing it?

Blimey, did it really matter? She pushed him against the building and kissed him back. Rubbed against his erection. She grabbed his shirt and was ready to rip it off when a car drove by.

"*Snyat' komnatu!*"

She chuckled and backed away.

"Don't go." He grabbed her arm. "What did he say?"

"Get a room."

Perry laughed in that wonderfully, delicious way of his. "I don't think the other occupants of our room would approve."

"No, they definitely would not."

"So maybe we should find an empty one."

He couldn't be serious. "What are you talking about?"

"I'm talking about getting this crazy notion out of your head that I don't want to see you after this mission. When it couldn't be further from the truth."

"My father would not want you to see me."

"I don't know if you noticed or not, but just because I call him Boss, doesn't make him so. He has no control over who I can see. And I want to see you."

"Even though I'm not a Perfect Mate?"

"Will you stop? I wish I never told you about that."

"But it's true, isn't it? If you found one, you'd drop me like a hot potato." And why did that matter? Sex with him had been awesome. Why was she arguing with him?

"I'd like to think I'm not *that* rude."

"But you'd still drop me." It wasn't her head that said that. It was her heart. A heart that had already suffered damage from her father. She wasn't sure it could handle being damaged by Perry, too. When had he become so important to her?

"I'm not so sure about that. I've never met anyone like you before. I've never wanted to be with someone like you before. I like being with you."

"As a friend with benefits?" Before, she'd have jumped at the chance. Now? She wanted more. She wanted all of him.

He closed his eyes as if he were in pain. "I didn't mean it like that."

"Then how did you mean it?"

"I want to try being a couple. For real."

"But I'm a vampire."

"I'm very aware of that."

"You don't date vampires. You said so yourself."

"Why are you fighting me on this? Is it because you don't like me? 'Cause if it is, then just say so."

She could never say that. It would be a lie. "You scare me, Perry. Look what you did to poor Susannah."

"Susannah has…issues. A big one in that it isn't me she's interested in, it's your father. And not just as a friend. Or didn't you notice that?"

"I noticed."

"I know I'm not the greatest catch out there. I've been flakey, I admit that. But I've been trying to be better. I want to be better."

He didn't finish that sentence, so she finished it for him. "For your Perfect Mate."

"For *a* mate. I always said Perfect Mate because I never thought anyone else would want me. And maybe I wasn't wrong." The song ended. "We should get going. I'm sure Groucho is waiting for us by now." He picked up her bag and handed it to her. Picked up his own and headed toward the hotel.

"Perry, wait."

He stopped, searched the ground. "Did I forget something?"

"Yeah. Me."

His eyes widened, but he didn't say a word.

She slipped her hand in his. "I can try being a couple. For real."

The smile practically took over his whole face. He gave her a quick peck on the lips. "Thank you for trying. I'll do my best to be what you want."

"No, Perry. Just be yourself. That's all I want. Is for you to be yourself." Because that was who she liked.

* * * *

Okay, so this day was turning out way differently than Perry ever thought. He figured he'd be on his way back to Atlanta by now. That Mandy and Barnet would have come to some kind of an agreement. And that he'd go back to searching for his Perfect Mate.

Atlanta was definitely delayed. It would take an act of the Great One, or maybe Alexi Popolov, to get Barnet to even acknowledge his daughter. And that Perfect Mate?

Perry was pretty sure he'd found her.

How crazy was that? That his Perfect Mate wasn't mortal, but a vampire?

Barnet stood by the back door and eyed Perry's hand in Mandy's. Frowning, he didn't say a word. Just made finger notations to them of a three, four, and two.

Room 342.

No sooner had Perry nodded, Barnet entered the building.

"I sure hope he got a suite," she said. "Else I'm parking it in the loo."

"Come on." Perry tugged on her hand and led her through the door. Stairs were off to the right.

A door upstairs slammed shut. Probably Barnet. Perry indicated Mandy go before him and he climbed the stairs behind her, getting an eyeful of that gorgeous rump of hers. That one look and he became hard. For her. And he was okay with it. More than okay. She'd told him to be himself—shocker all in itself—so he did what his fingers had been itching to do. He grabbed her ass.

She stopped and turned around. "Did you just grab my bum?"

Oh Great One, he loved the way she talked. "You told me to be myself. I've wanted to grab your ass since I first saw it."

"Is that so?" She planted a hand on one sexy hip. "What else have you wanted to do since you…saw it?"

Was this for real? Was she actually playing along? He rubbed his crotch, his growing erection clearly evident. "What do you think?"

She palmed his cheek. "You are a bad boy, aren't you, Perry?"

He leaned into her. "Does that mean you're going to tie me up and spank me?"

Her eyes widened. Shit. Had he gone too far? But man, just the thought of her doing that only got him harder.

"You're evil. You know we're stuck in a room with my father and you do this?"

Okay, so he hadn't gone too far. She seemed into it. "And I told you, we can find an empty room. We'll just say we're going to feed. It wouldn't be a lie if we feed after."

Her eyes widened even more at that.

How was it she was okay with some kinky sex, but when it came to feeding she slammed on the brakes. "Don't tell me you want your damn privacy. We're a couple now, right? And what's the big deal? You let Barnet see."

"I didn't let my father do anything. After he yelled at me, he pretty much ignored me."

There was more to it. She just wasn't sharing. It stung that she couldn't—wouldn't—say more. "I thought you wanted to be a couple."

"I do."

"Couples don't keep secrets. Or at least they shouldn't. Not if they want to stay a couple."

She sat on a step. "You're right."

Those were words he never thought he'd hear directed at himself. But he fought the grin that threatened to take over his face. "So what's the big secret?"

"If I tell you, you can't tell anyone."

She was acting all serious. How bad could it be? Unless…no. If she lost control, he would have noticed in the truck. Hell, the driver would have been dead. Perry sat beside her. "I believe what's said between couples stays between couples. But why would you think I'd tell anyone?"

"Because. You might feel the need to turn me in."

"Turn you in? For what?"

"For being an abomination." She covered her face. "I'm allergic, okay?"

Of all the things she could have said, that was not even on his list. He'd never heard of a vampire being allergic to anything. "To what? Blood?"

"What else would I be allergic to?"

Okay, maybe that was a stupid question. "Why would I turn you in for that?"

She blinked several times as if she couldn't believe he'd ask such a question. "Because I'm a freak and should be destroyed."

"Who told you that? Oh, wait. Frederick? And you believed him?"

"I had no reason not to. Do you know of any vampire who is allergic to blood?"

"No, but that doesn't mean anything. How allergic?"

"Enough for someone to wonder if I have the plague. It's not pretty."

It did explain why it took her so long to feed. "And it takes you, what, ten to fifteen minutes to heal?"

She wagged her head side to side. "Something like that."

For that amount of time, how did she hide it earlier from Barnet? Unless… "Barnet knew. Before today."

She nodded.

"He was protecting you."

She rolled her eyes. "Don't. It's not like that."

"Seems like it to me." Perry grabbed her shoulders. This was the best news yet. "Mandy, he cares about you."

"No, he doesn't. Please. Will you drop it?"

He placed his arm across her shoulders. Nuzzled her neck. "Your secret is safe with me. Although, I can't believe you ever believed you would be destroyed for such a thing. Now, if you could pass that on…"

He'd only been joking, but she tensed in his arms.

Of all the ding dong days. "You *can* pass it on. That's it, isn't it? Barnet is allergic, too, isn't he?"

"You can't tell—"

"Do you distrust me that much that you have to even say it?"

"I'm sorry. I didn't mean it like that. It's just that he already hates me because of Mother. Add in the allergy and, well…"

"Yeah. I get it. It does explain a lot, though."

"What do you mean?"

"Why he stayed with you when you fed. Why he's always been a loner. Why he never talked about his past. I just figured it was because of his position with the Committee. But surely he knows no one will even suggest he be destroyed. That's crazy talk."

"It's not crazy if you don't know for a fact. And it's not like we would ever bring up the subject."

She had a point. Why bring up something that didn't matter, unless it mattered? He never asked anyone else if they had special talents because they'd only want to know what his special talent was. "Was Frederick allergic?"

She shook her head. "I saw him feed. Never got a reaction. It's why I never even dreamed that I could pass it on. That I *had* passed it on."

"You just found out today?"

"Yeah."

"So how would you have gotten allergic if it wasn't passed on to you?"

She shrugged. "How would the first allergic vampire get allergic? Maybe I'm ground zero. I'm just so glad that I never got around to turning anyone else."

"You were never tempted?"

"Nope. How about you?"

He laughed. "Up until last year, I figured I was a bachelor forever. Women didn't seem to like the real me."

"Did you let them see the real you, though?"

Had he? Probably not. There was something about feeling important. Another finding out it was just an illusion.

Chapter 17

Barnet paced the hotel room. Unfortunately, Oscar couldn't get a suite, because they apparently didn't exist in this hotel. This one only had two rooms: two beds and a desk in the big one and a bathroom in the other. That was it.

He'd said he could lay aside their differences for one day. Differences. Yeah, that was a joke. There was no difference. There was her version and there was the truth. But in order to keep the team in peace, to keep conflict at bay, he would just have to be a leader and keep the conflict at a minimum.

That might mean sitting in the bathroom all day. He could lie and say he needed to reflect. Oscar might believe it. Perry? Probably not. And he really didn't care what *she* thought. Eventually she'd go back to London and he'd never have to see her again. And then life would go back to normal.

Oscar had set his laptop on the desk unit. He didn't have any extra clothes, but he had his computer. "I'd have thought they'd be here by now. Maybe they found an empty room."

"An empty room?" Barnet stopped his pacing. It sickened him to think that Perry was interested in that woman.

"Yeah. To feed. I'm sure both of them could use a top-off. Hell, it's been awhile for me, too. How about you? You were in that prison for a long time."

"I'm fine. Dimitri actually fed me."

Feeding? Could that be it? Would she expose their secret to Perry? Not that Perry would ever turn them in. He wasn't that type.

And not that being allergic was actually a death sentence. Barnet had believed it back when Frederick told him, but since then hadn't seen any proof. Only what he'd seen from Frederick's memories. Too bad he couldn't glean what had cured him, though. Because Frederick had been allergic. Had been close to being destroyed when he claimed a witch had cured him.

A cure that apparently wasn't passed down to any vampire he turned or any vampire they turned. It was the only reason he'd never turned anyone. He wouldn't put another person through what he went through during feeding. And the fact that she hadn't cared said a lot about her.

Unfortunately for Barnet, he hadn't been able to find this witch in Frederick's memories. He'd caused too much damage and the vampire had perished. It was then that Barnet realized his anger would not benefit him. And he'd been calm and reasonable since.

Mainly because he'd left England, and her, and never returned. Never wanted to return.

A knock sounded on the door. Barnet looked through the peep hole. About damned time. He yanked the door open.

"Hey, Boss," Perry said. He still held onto her hand and pulled her into the room. Tossed their bags onto the closest bed. "Mandy and I were talking. Out in the stairwell. It might be a good time to feed."

Feed or do more? God, not the more. Why else hold hands? "Now is not a good time."

"Why is that?"

Oscar's phone went off. He frowned as he stared at the screen. Pushed a button. "Hello?"

"Is this Oscar?" When he confirmed, she continued. "I'm Katya. With the Russian Committee. I need to speak with Barnet. Is he there?"

Barnet walked over to the phone. "I'm here, we're all here, what's the matter?"

"We have a problem. After you called Felicks, he called a Committee meeting to confront Dimitri."

Barnet could only chuckle. "That couldn't have gone well."

"It did not. Sergei became outraged at Dimitri's cavalier demeanor so Dimitri killed Sergei and dismantled the Committee. Said he was now the true ruler of the Russian vampires. I am sure he will come for Gregorii and me. After he finds you."

Why did that news not surprise him? Of the few times Barnet had communicated with the Russian Head, the man had seemed to thirst for power. Doing away with the Committee would certainly give him that if he had the manpower to back it up. "What about Felicks?"

"I do not know. He stayed behind. Whether it was out of fear or he believes Dimitri, I am not sure. I just know we cannot count on him."

Perry came over. "I guess you could say he's gone too far now, right?"

"Yes, you could say that."

"What do you need from us," Barnet asked.

"Nothing. I only called to inform you. This is our problem. We are handling it."

"The hell it is! If he's disbanded your Committee, it's all our problems. Do you know he wants every Perfect Mate destroyed?"

Perry jerked his head up. "He does?"

Katya continued, "I am unaware of there being any Perfect Mates. Perry had mentioned it, but it was the first I heard they actually existed. That is why you have been trying to reach Dimitri, is it not?"

"Yes, but I could never get past Felicks." Barnet resumed his pacing, hoping it would relieve his itch to hit something. "He's going to start a war, Katya. You know this, don't you?"

"Not if we can help it. Gregorii and I are forming another Committee. If you want to help, you need to leave Russia as soon as you can and get the other Committees to recognize our new one."

"You can't do this alone."

"We must. Our people will not take kindly to outside assistance. They will follow Dimitri before they follow a foreigner. Let us handle this, please."

She had a point and he had to respect her wishes. "I'll promise not to interfere if you and Gregorii remain alive. If Dimitri kills either one of you, I will consider that an act of war and will advise the other Committees accordingly."

"I understand. Thank you, Barnet."

Barnet smiled. Maybe there was a way to help after all. "I may be able to assist you indirectly, though. Would you be okay with that?"

"Indirectly? How?"

"By distracting Dimitri."

"Do not put your life in danger. Your death would not be beneficial."

"I don't plan on dying."

"What is your plan?"

"It's best you don't know. Just be prepared. He's going to be angry tonight, I've no doubt about that. And if I've learned anything, I've learned a person makes mistakes when they're angry."

* * * *

Could a woman go stir-crazy in a hotel room with three men in just one day? Mandy would soon find out. She'd been stuck in this room for five hours. While Perry and she wanted to go out and "feed," her father had suggested—to everyone's agreement—that they wait until the hotel became less busy, between check out and check in.

So for five hours she spent the time teaching these three men Russian. Whether or not her father was paying attention, she didn't know and didn't care. He'd spent most of the time in the loo.

Which was kind of funny. Hadn't she planned on doing the same?

At least she'd been able to take a shower and change her clothes before the lessons. While she hoped her skirt and duster could be salvaged—blood could come out sometimes—her blouse was ruined, what with the hole from being staked. Sadly, she had tossed it in the trash bin.

By one p.m., not too many people remained on their floor. The cleaning woman had already tried to clean their room, but Mandy had sent her away.

"I think we're pretty safe to venture out of the room," Perry said from the bed, where he'd been lying for most of the day. "The windows in the hallway are sufficiently covered and no vampire has stormed in and subdued us."

"You think they would do that?" Oscar said. "It's daylight out there for them, too."

"Right. Which means they're not in this hotel or they would have done that. I think we're in the clear."

"I agree," her father said. Those were the first words he'd uttered since that phone call with Katya. A phone call that ended on a strange note.

Mandy had almost laughed during that call. Did he not realize he was angry with her? That it was likely he would make mistakes because of that? He was such a hypocrite.

"In that case," Oscar said as he stood, "I'm going to try using my new-found language. I really appreciate you teaching us, Mandy. I don't feel quite as lost now."

"I'm glad I could help." Teaching vampires was a breeze. They remembered so much better than mortals. Another reason she was surprised none of them knew the language. Knew no other language besides Spanish and French, if that. It certainly would have been easy enough for them to learn. Guess being Americans might have had something to do with that.

When Oscar departed, Perry leaped off the bed. "How about you, Boss? You going out now or waiting until someone gets back?"

"I can wait to feed."

"Great." Perry grabbed her hand. "Let's go, Beautiful."

He'd gone back to his original nickname for her. While her insides were beaming, she kept her face neutral. No use giving her father ammunition.

Although, maybe the hand-holding was enough ammunition. Before Perry could open the door to freedom, her father blocked their way.

"Why her, Perry?"

"I like her."

"But she's not a Perfect Mate."

She could almost hear what he hadn't spoken aloud. That she was nothing.

Perry one-armed her across the shoulder and pulled her in close. "You worried about her? Is that it? Don't think I'm good enough for her?"

What the hell was Perry doing? Deliberately egging her father on or being completely dense?

"I'm worried about you. Why do you believe her and not me?"

"Come on, Perry. This is useless." She tugged on Perry's arm to release her, but he budged as well as a cement pole.

"Hold on a minute." Perry squeezed her shoulder, so she stopped. He then turned his attention back to her father. "I believe her because she's telling the truth. Question is, why don't you believe her? Have you ever *tried* reading her memories of that day to see if she lied to you? I know you haven't, or you would know the truth by now. But here's some truth for you. She's a good person. She'll do anything for family. You raised her, Boss. You know what she's capable of."

"I know very well what she's capable of. I saw it firsthand."

She was grateful that Perry had stood up for her, but this wasn't his fight. It was hers. "You saw nothing. You only assume. You were still in the throes of turning. And you were grieving. I get that. But if someone would have told me that you'd still be angry at me five hundred years later, I don't know if I would have turned you. Maybe I should have stayed away that day. I'd have gotten over the pain by now. Instead I was stupid enough to think you'd want to be with me. But you don't have to worry. After this mission, you won't ever have to deal with me again."

Without a word, her father moved from the door. She didn't wait for Perry and opened the door to freedom.

A weight was lifted. She'd said her piece. If he couldn't believe her, it was his own bloody problem. She knew the truth.

Perry quietly shut the door behind him, took her hand, and led her to the stairwell. "You okay?"

"You didn't read my memories." She'd never dropped the wall to give him access.

"Didn't have to. I believe you. He's wrong, okay? And I think he knows it."

"I don't think he knows any such thing." But it didn't matter. She was through with her father. If he wanted a relationship with her, he'd have to initiate it. "But thanks for trying. You ready to go pick out some donors?"

"Yep. And then I'll get to see how much you exaggerated about being allergic."

"I wasn't exaggerating. I *can* see myself in a mirror. Can't you?"

Perry laughed as he opened the door to the stairs. "I can't wait to talk to Alexi. Just to see if he was the one who told Bram Stoker to write such a thing."

It was a good idea if he had. Light sensitivity could be explained eventually, but being invisible in a mirror? Brilliant. "He might not be alert enough to tell you any stories for a while."

"Oh, he's alert. Trust me on that. He's very alert."

As they headed downstairs, Oscar appeared on the landing. "You just now leaving?"

"Yeah. I'm surprised you're done so quick," Perry said.

So was she. "Did it go okay?"

"Yeah. Got a little scare. Thought maybe I did it wrong. It was like the first lady didn't hear me at all, so maybe she didn't know Russian or English. But when I tried it on someone else, my words worked."

Perry scrunched his forehead. "You tried to control a woman and it didn't work? Where?"

"At the indoor pool. Why does it matter?"

"Were you close to her? Get a sniff?"

"No, I didn't get close to her. And all I smelled was chlorine. I still don't see why that matters."

"Groucho, my man, you might have just found your Perfect Mate."

Bloody hell. How could it be that she'd never found one before—hadn't even believed they existed—and now she was tripping over them? And if there was one in this hotel, did that mean her time with Perry was over, or was he seriously letting Oscar have this one?

Oscar shook his head. "She wouldn't be my Perfect Mate."

"How can you say that? You weren't close enough to know."

"I know because she's a she."

That news wasn't good. Not good at all. If Oscar wasn't interested, that meant the Perfect Mate was free for Perry to pursue.

Perry blinked until recognition dawned on him. "Ohhh. My bad."

Oscar chuckled. "It's okay, Perry. Not a lot of people know. She's wearing a blue swimsuit. Here." He grabbed Perry's hand for a few moments. "Good?"

Perry nodded, but no smile lit up his face. She assumed Oscar had sent Perry a visual of the woman. Shouldn't that make him happy?

"I'll see you guys later. Have fun." Oscar climbed the stairs. The closing of the door echoed in the stairwell.

"Shall we?" Perry indicated Mandy go before him.

To the pool or not to the pool? No way did she want to witness his involvement with a Perfect Mate. Her heart couldn't take that kind of pain right now.

But wouldn't it be better to get it over with quickly than to let anything else happen between them? No matter what he said earlier, if that woman at the pool was a Perfect Mate, he would drop Mandy like a hot potato. She had no doubt about that.

* * * *

Perry had met two female Perfect Mates. Knew the differences between the two. One—Sarah—could have been his if he'd met her first and he had been a better person than he was then. The other—Janie—would never have been his even if he'd met her first. Oh sure, he got a shot of warmth after he'd touched her, but it hadn't lasted long.

That was when he discovered that one Perfect Mate wasn't exactly perfect for just any vampire. And while his friend Sammy tried to convince him that it was more than a first meet, Perry still didn't believe that. Look at poor Barnet. He'd touched Janie and was instantly turned on. Just like Sammy had been. But Sammy had found Janie first. Had met Janie first. Therefore, Barnet lost out. Just like Perry had lost out on Sarah, because she'd met Johnny first.

Now there was a possible Perfect Mate in this hotel. A Perfect Mate who had most likely been untouched by another vampire. Not even a week ago he would have been ecstatic that Oscar wasn't interested. Would have swooped in and claimed his prize. Provided there was a connection.

So what was stopping him? He made it no further than the exit to the lobby. Stood in the stairwell like some kind of idiot.

"Perry? If you're going to the pool, it's out that way."

What was stopping him? Mandy was. If he took even one little step toward that pool, he'd lose any chance of getting to know her better. Of being in her life, even. "I don't want to go to the pool."

"Why not? I thought it was your mission to discover all the Perfect Mates."

"That would be Barnet's mission. Maybe I should tell him." Yeah, that was it. He'd march back upstairs and let Barnet get a shot first.

She grabbed his arm. "Perry. You're not going to hurt my feelings if you go check her out. What if she's yours?"

But he would hurt her feelings. More than her feelings. He would hurt her. And he didn't want to do that. As for the Perfect Mate…he couldn't imagine anyone being more perfect than Mandy. She was smart, beautiful, and just the right amount of crazy to make life interesting. "I told you I wanted to be a couple."

"Yeah, but that was before—"

"No. No stipulations."

"But—"

"No buts, either."

She placed her hands on her hips. "Aren't you even curious?"

"No." That answer even shocked himself, especially since he hadn't hesitated. He wasn't curious. Not in the least. Not as long as he had her.

"You hardly know me."

"So? I know enough to want to know more." He palmed her face and urged her against the wall. Stared into those electric blue eyes of hers. All he wanted to do was kiss her. So he did.

She opened for him and he dove in for a taste. So sweet. So sexy. While he plundered her mouth, he ran his hands down her neck, along her shoulders, and thumbed the sides of her breasts. Her nipples were evident even through the bra she wore. She was hard. For him. Just like he was hard. For her. They really needed to go find a room.

He nuzzled her neck and took in that sweet jasmine scent. "Can we feed later? I want in you so bad."

She wrapped her arms around his neck. "Yes, please. And I feel the same." She gave him a quick peck on the lips. "Wait here. I'll go manipulate someone and get a key."

He didn't have to wait long. When she returned, she practically launched herself at him. Wrapped her legs around his waist. "Second floor. 211."

"Yes, ma'am." He hightailed it to the second floor.

Best decision ever.

Chapter 18

Mandy twisted in Perry's arms and inserted the key card inside the lock. Turned the handle. Perry pushed the door open with his foot and carried her inside the room. The door shut on its own.

When she'd manipulated the clerk from guest services, she'd requested a small room and boy, did she get it. They didn't need more than one bed anyway.

Well, that and a shower. Oh yeah. The shower.

She couldn't believe they were actually doing this. That he didn't go rushing off to find that Perfect Mate. This was going to be the best day ever.

He practically threw her on the bed and proceeded to remove his Hawaiian shirt in a slow-mo stripper way. "You like what you see?"

She propped up on her elbows. "I do. You got some stripper music on that mobile of yours?"

"Oooh. I like the way you think."

He'd talked about kinky sex. Was he for real or all talk? Guess she'd find out today.

He chuckled as he searched his mobile. "Will this do?"

"The Stripper" by David Rose played from his speakers. "You have actual stripper music?"

"Yeah. Who knew, huh?" He slipped his shirt off and twirled it around his head, swaying his hips to the music. On a drum beat he tossed it in the air. Off went the Union Jack shirt. More twirling.

More tossing. He unbuttoned his cargo pants and slowly lowered the zipper.

She got on her knees and moved closer. He stepped back and turned around. Cheeky bastard.

Oh, but maybe this view wasn't half-bad. He lowered his pants—uncovering the best bum she'd ever laid eyes on—and twerked to the music. Some day she was going to bite that bum. Maybe today.

What was she doing with her clothes still on? She fell back and removed her boots. The rest of her clothes hit the floor in record time. By the time he turned back around, she was lying naked on the bed, waiting for him.

His eyebrows nearly shot up to the ceiling. "Anxious much?"

He should talk. His erection practically pointed upward. "You wanted in me."

He crawled onto the bed, placed his knees between her spread legs. "That I did. But I think I want to taste you first."

Up went her knees. Down went his head. He tongued her clit and she nearly exploded off the bed. "You're already wet."

He sounded shocked and she had to laugh at that. "Well, duh. You're quite a kisser there, Perry. Hadn't anyone told you that before?"

He popped his head up. And then she realized. No. No one would have told him that. No other vampire, in any case. Would he have let the mortals he'd been with even remember him?

Hell, had he ever really let loose during sex? Let the vampire out? What they'd done back in Moscow had been pretty great, but they'd had to pretend it wasn't the first time. It wasn't the real him. She wanted the real him.

"You can't hurt me, Perry. And I'll give as good as I get." And boy, would she give.

One side of his mouth curled up and his eyes darkened. He rose over her. One thrust and he entered her. That one thrust nearly caused her to come. She was so damn close.

He pounded into her and she grabbed onto his shoulders. This was what she wanted. What she'd craved. "Yes!"

He latched his mouth on the spot between her neck and shoulder and bit. Not some tiny bite, either. He savaged her. She came as he sucked her blood. She came as he continued to pound into her. She came as he grabbed her breast.

God. She never thought an orgasm could last so long. And be so glorious.

As her nerve endings returned to normal, she flipped him onto his back. Now it was her turn.

* * * *

Perry licked the blood off his lips. He was still hard. If not harder than before. Her blood was an aphrodisiac. That had to be it. He'd never been so turned on before.

Beautiful straddled his body.

"You're leaking." He licked the blood trickling from the holes he'd left behind. The mark he'd left behind. Too bad it would heal. That no one else would see his declaration. That she was his. He'd never bitten anyone that hard before and it had felt…freeing to know he could do that to her and not hurt her. It also got him harder thinking she could do the same to him. That she could mark him the same way. *Oh Great One, please let her do the same to me.*

"Are you praying or talking to me?"

He smiled. "Heard that, huh?"

She palmed his face. "What is it you want me to do to you?"

"Bite me."

"Yeah?" She scooted down his body until her mouth hovered in the vicinity of his groin. "Where? Here?"

"What? No." What was that bit about her being a little crazy? Maybe she was a whole lot crazy.

"Why not?" She tipped her head to the side, like a curious cat. "Didn't like it before?"

"Ummm… No one has ever bitten me down there."

The smile took over her face and it gave him the chills. "Do you trust me?"

"You're not going to bite it off, are you?" Oh sure, it could probably be reattached, but that wasn't the point. The pain was the point. He'd admit it. He was a wuss.

She crawled back up his body. Placed her nose on his. Her blue eyes electrified more than usual. "Do. You. Trust. Me?"

Kinky sex. That had to be it. Because he wanted to trust her. In everything. "Yes."

"Good. Wait right here." She jumped off the bed and disappeared into the bathroom.

He sat up on his elbows. What the hell was she doing in there? But as quickly as she left, she returned holding some string, a washcloth, and a towel. "What are those for?"

"You. I just hope the washline is long enough."

Ahh, not string. "Long enough to…?"

"Tie you up."

Oh yeah. Kinky sex. Now she was talking. "Well, don't tie me to the bed. I might break it."

"I know." She tied one end to his right wrist. Tugged. Then disappeared under the bed only to reappear on the other side. She grabbed his left hand. "Lookee there. It's long enough."

He nearly laughed. She was mimicking him. He kind of liked it.

Perry tugged on the washline. He could easily snap it if he wanted. He just hoped he wouldn't wanna. This was supposed to be fun. Not torture. Right?

She ran a reassuring hand along his arm and smiled. "How are you feeling?"

"A little vulnerable."

"But you trust me."

"I do."

She rolled the washcloth. "Open up."

His nerves piped up again. "Why?"

"In case you scream out. Don't want to disturb the neighbors."

Scream out? As in pain or ecstasy? Oh Great One, please be the second. Please. He couldn't say he wasn't turned on. He'd always dreamed of having kinky sex. Just hadn't done it before. Yeah, he was all talk to his friends, but that was it. Talk. He wasn't about to force a mortal into doing something they weren't comfortable with and he wasn't about to hurt a mortal by accident, either. But this was different. Mandy was a vampire. And she did say she would give as good as she got. "Just so you know, I've never really had kinky sex before."

"I kind of figured."

Man, did she know everything about him? "Do I need a safe word?"

"Do you want a safe word?"

Holy shit. Hopefully he wouldn't come before the kinkiness started. He opened his mouth and she shoved in the washcloth.

"You'll still be able to communicate when we're touching and I hope to hear every nasty little curse word you know." She patted his cheek and kissed his forehead. "You okay?"

He nodded. He trusted she would give as good as she got. Hell, it was probably going to be better than she got. His boner ached to be used.

"Good." She took the towel and blind folded him.

If he thought he was vulnerable before, he was sorely mistaken. And if he thought he was turned on before, he was sorely mistaken there, too. He just hoped he didn't squirt before the fun began.

She straddled him. Palmed his pecs. Flicked his hardened nipples. Kissed her way down his stomach.

Anticipation was torture. Or maybe that was the not knowing. The not knowing what she was gonna do next. Blow job with a little nibble? He could probably handle that. Bite the inside leg, alongside his nuts? Yeah, he could probably handle that too.

She licked the underside of his dick and he arched his back. That felt sooooo good.

She took him into her mouth. All wet and wonderful. So it was going to be a blow job?

Something sharp pricked his dick and he gasped through his nose. "*Fuck!*"

"Ah, that's my boy." She licked him. Sucked him. Another sharp prick.

He tried his best to control himself. To not come right away. Because as nervous as he was, he was enjoying it. He was enjoying the anticipation.

She bit gently on his dick and he nearly lost control.

"*You want some blood from there, is that it?*" Because all his blood had certainly rushed to that one body part.

More licking. More sucking. As his balls tightened, she raised his knees. Spread his legs. Stuck a finger up his ass.

Holy shit! That was new territory for him. And damn if it didn't feel good.

She pounded away. And bit. Harder.

"*Fuck!*" He lost it. Over and over and over. And she took it all.

He'd never come so hard in his life. He'd never enjoyed sex so much in his life. He never enjoyed being with another woman like he did with her.

Perfect Mates? A thing of the past. He'd found someone better. He'd found Mandy.

* * * *

Dimitri stopped the video and cursed the lack of microphones in Natasha's shop. But the Committee had over-ruled him on that. Had said it was too invasive. Too invasive! No more invasive than asking vampires foolish questions during their check in. In fact, it was better than the questions. It was incentive to keep his people in line. To make sure they followed the letter of the law. His law. As soon as the sun set, he would get Felicks to oversee installing microphones in all their people's businesses. Hell, maybe even their homes, if they owned one.

No one would double-cross him. No one.

He dialed the familiar number.

She answered on the first ring. Good girl. "Yes, Dimitri. How may I help you?"

"Natasha, I noticed a bald man came into the shop early this morning."

"Yes, Dimitri. I remember him."

"What did he want?"

"Directions to Gorky Park."

"At six a.m.?"

"They are open twenty-four hours. And I believe a coffee shop opens around that time."

Maybe, but he smelled deceit. "He was American?"

"No. He was French. I don't even think he was a vampire. Just a lost tourist." She chuckled. "Who'd been smoking."

"Smoking?"

"His clothes reeked of marijuana."

A ruse. No one in their right mind would walk around Moscow advertising that. "You didn't think that was suspicious?"

"No. Not everyone who comes into the shop is a vampire, Dimitri. We get lots of lost tourists since we're the only shop open all night in the area."

"Did you catch his name?"

"Told me his name is Oscar. Did I do something wrong?"

Oh she did plenty wrong. Her worst offense: being friends with Popolov. It was why he watched her more than others. He didn't trust her. Not one bit. "You did nothing wrong. It has come to my

183

attention that some American vampires have entered our country illegally. I am helping in the search as best I can."

"An American man came into the shop yesterday. With an English woman. They were both vampires."

Very good, Natasha. Of course she knew about them, and the only reason she mentioned it now was because they'd come over legally. "Yes, I am aware of them. This Oscar, he was from France you say?"

"He spoke French. Didn't say where he was from. Only knew a few words of Russian that was translated on his cellphone and was very pleased I understood French."

Or this Oscar spoke a language no other helper at the store would understand. "You are the only one in the store who knows all the languages, don't you, Natasha?"

"Yes, sir. It is hard to find mortals who know languages to work in the store and I need mortals here during the day. I cannot run the shop by myself. We get a lot of tourists."

"A lot of vampires, too?"

"At night, yes. It's one of the few places open after eight where they can try on clothes before they purchase them. Do you think these illegal Americans will come here?"

He was fairly certain they already had. Or at least one of them. The only one Dimitri didn't know about: the pilot. "If you are the only store open, it is possible."

"Then I will keep an eye out for them, Dimitri. It is my honor to help the Committee."

He disconnected the call. Help the Committee. What a joke. He was the Committee from now on. And once the sun set, she'd know it, too.

Now to go find that pilot's name.

Chapter 19

Mandy towel-dried her hair. Sex with Perry was just what she needed. She hadn't felt this relaxed in years.

Too bad the relaxation would be short lived. She shouldn't let her father affect her so; she'd done all she could to convince him of her innocence. Well, short of tying him up and forcing her thoughts into his head. She wasn't even sure she could do that. In vampire years they were pretty much equals—only a year apart. Still, if Alexi Popolov wasn't able to corroborate Perry's theories, then she would grant her father's wish: to stay out of his life forever. But first they had to get out of Russia alive.

Perry yanked the towel from her hands and pulled her in for a kiss. A thorough kiss that made her toes curl. Having his naked body against hers didn't hurt any either.

"Mmmm… You taste good. But I'm a little disappointed that you never took my blood. Not even when you bit…down there."

She chuckled against his lips while his hands massaged her bum. "I didn't break the skin, Perry." She hadn't even used her fangs, even though she'd been tempted to bite the inside of his thigh. Way tempted.

"I know that *now*. Didn't feel like it *then*. But why didn't you take my blood?"

She'd disappointed him. Would probably always disappoint him in that regard. It was probably just as well he would eventually find that Perfect Mate. She was certainly not perfect for him. "I told you. Vampire blood is worse. I only take it in an emergency."

"Because of your allergy? I would have thought it would be different."

"It is. It's worse. Okay?" She bent over and snatched the towel Perry had tossed earlier. She hated this line of questioning and wished she'd never told him the truth.

He grabbed her arm. "I'm sorry. I'm just trying to understand."

She sighed. "I know you are. It's not easy for me."

"Got it. Why don't I go get us some donors and bring them here? That way you can take your time getting dressed?" He wagged his eyebrows.

The man was a sex machine. He was nearly hard now and that was after he'd come twice in the shower. How long would his desire last once he got a look at what feeding did to her? "You think you can bring two donors here? Using Russian?"

"Okay, so I bring one donor. Then after you feed—and heal— we go out and get me one. You can be my lookout." He stepped back, took her towel, and wrapped it around his waist. "I promise I won't be long."

As much as she enjoyed the view, the guy had to be nuts. "In a towel?"

"You think I can go without?" He opened it up and swung his hips back and forth, slapping his semi-hard penis against his thighs.

The man was impossible. And so much fun to be around. Still… "I think you should get dressed first."

He placed a hand over his heart. "That you don't think I could get away with it hurts. It really hurts."

Talk about bad acting. "Does that really work on other people?"

He dropped the towel on the floor. "Fine. I'll get dressed first. Kill-joy."

She would have argued about his new nickname for her, except he winked and smiled and that alone turned her to goo. Yeah, she had it bad for him. And he'd given up a possible Perfect Mate for her. Maybe their chemistry was stronger than she'd thought. But what would happen after this mission was over? Would he come to England with her? Because she wouldn't be able to stay in America if her father couldn't forgive her.

Perry's "dressing" only consisted of his cargo pants. He didn't even put on his shoes. He moved the security bar so the door wouldn't close.

After she finger-combed her hair, she went in search of her clothes. She'd just slipped on her panties when he returned. "That was quick."

"She was down the hall."

The she was a maid, standing and waiting for her next command.

"I'm impressed." But now Mandy would have to feed. She slipped on her bra and hooked the back.

"Thank you." He sat on the chair and crossed his arms. "Ready whenever you are."

"You're going to watch?"

"Mandy… No secrets. Remember?"

She might as well get it over with. After a nod to Perry, she took over control of the maid and stood behind her. No hair to slide away as she wore it up in a bun. Mandy licked the site. Good. No perfumes. She bit and closed her eyes. When she got her fill, she licked the site, healed the marks, and sent the maid on her way, giving her an urge to grab something to eat.

Perry latched the door. "Now that wasn't so bad, was it?"

If only that were the bad part. Mandy plopped onto the side of the bed. Her whole body was exposed. What was she thinking? She should have gotten dressed. She leaned over, grabbed her head.

He knelt in front of her and caressed her cheek. "Does it hurt?"

She yanked her head away. "Please. Just go."

Red splotches broke out on her legs. Her arms. She lay back and curled into a ball as the pain burned through her. Bloody hell, she hated feeding.

"It *does* hurt." He sat beside her and placed his hands alongside her head.

"What are you doing?"

"Letting you in on one of my secrets. And helping. I hope."

His touch was very nice, but how was that— Ohhh. The burn. It subsided. She took a cleansing breath.

"Is it working?"

Her body was still covered in splotches, but the pain was gone. "What did you do?"

He released her head. "Suppressed the pain. I went in that pretty brain of yours and sort of pinched the pain receptors."

"Vampires can do that?" And how come she'd never noticed before.

"Well, no. Not all vampires. Apparently I was blessed with the gift. Why me? Who knows?"

A gift. As if he were made for her? Fate sure had a funny way with things. Maybe if she'd followed her father to the States she'd have met Perry sooner. "You can do that to yourself, too?"

"Unfortunately not. When I'm in pain, it's hard to focus. And I'm usually too weak. I knew it worked on mortals, wasn't sure about vampires. And it only works for about an hour, but I figure you'll be healed before it wears off."

"You never tried it on vampires before?"

"Never wanted to. People get used for unusual crap. Just because we're vampires, we still started out as people-people. I don't want to risk being a thing. But I can't stand seeing you in pain. So please. Keep the secret between us, okay?"

"I wouldn't dream of telling anyone else."

He smiled. "Glad I could help." He rubbed his hand on her arm. "Too bad I can't fix the allergy."

"Don't worry about that. You did more than enough." If she had working tear ducts, she'd be crying. "Thank you."

"You're welcome." His grin was infectious and she grinned with him. What a gift to have.

A gift he could have used on her earlier. "Wait a minute. Why didn't you help me when I broke my arm and leg?"

"Are you kidding? I wanted you to feed. Pain is a good motivating factor. And I didn't know it hurt you to feed, too." He studied her body, got up, and returned with a pen.

"What are you doing?"

"I want to connect the dots. I think I see a dog on your arm."

She shoved him away. "Will you stop?"

He climbed on top of her and kissed her. "Never. Now, if there was only something we could do to pass the time."

Indeed. Maybe feeding wouldn't be such a chore with Perry around. Hell, it could be fun if she got to kiss him like this afterward.

He licked her neck. "I know what you can do now. You can bite me."

"I told you, I don't take vampire blood."

"Because it hurts, right? Shouldn't hurt now."

"What if it does?"

"Then I'll pinch those pain receptors again. Come on. Just a little taste. Aren't you even curious?"

She was a lot curious and had been soooo tempted to bite him earlier. Oh, not on his penis, that was just a tease. But his thigh would have been good. "I don't know."

"Sure you do. You put your mouth on my neck and insert fangs." He tilted his neck, giving her easy access.

"Your finger. I'll bite your finger."

He slouched and sighed. "My finger isn't very sexy."

"It is when it's in me." His fingers were very talented indeed.

"Well, yeah, but…"

"You just want to get off again, don't you?"

"I'd be lying if I said no. But if my finger will prove it won't hurt now, then here. Take a bite." He placed his index finger against her lips.

She lowered her fangs and bit him. Surprise! He tasted great, not bitter like Frederick's. And her stomach didn't even get queasy.

"So?"

"It's lovely." She covered his finger with her mouth and pulled it out like a sucker. He closed his eyes and groaned. She laughed. "You get off on the strangest things."

"Your mouth is not strange. It's sexy. Very sexy. And you seem to be faring well."

"I am. Color me shocked. You seem to be good for me. The next time we make love, do that thing with my pain receptors." Then she'd be able to give him the pleasure he'd so badly wanted earlier.

He brushed his lips lightly against hers. "If only we didn't have to go back now."

And if they weren't in Russia, she would have been more than happy to stay.

* * * *

Disappointment clouded the general giddy feeling Perry had been feeling since Mandy had taken his blood. Now that she was healed, it was time for him to feed and time for them to head back to the other room. Thank the Great One they only had an hour before sunset.

Perry helped Mandy make the bed. "Do you think anyone will notice it's been used?"

"We only used the top. The sheets are still clean."

"But the towels?"

"We'll toss them in the hallway. The maid will collect them and if someone rents the room out, they can ask for fresh towels." She giggled. "And soap. And shampoo."

He'd never been so happy. Here he was in a foreign country, might not even get out alive, and he was happy. Because of her. "Let's blow this pop stand, get me fed, and head back to the gang. We should be able to leave soon."

"Listen, Perry. I know you mean well, but please, don't try to force my father to have a relationship with me. Okay?"

"You don't want a relationship with him?"

"I do, but that's not the point. If after today he still hasn't come around, I'm fine with it. Truly. I don't want to hurt him and seeing me hurts him."

"He's being an ass."

"He's in pain. I won't make it worse for him."

"So what does that mean? You're going back to England?"

"It's my home. You're more than welcome to join me there. In fact, I wish you would."

Him. In England. With all the Brits. He'd miss his friends, but he'd miss her more. He pulled her into his arms. "You got some more kinky tricks to show me?"

"Oh, most definitely. With toys, too."

"Toys?" Damn it, he was getting hard again. "You sold me." He gathered the towels before he did something stupid, like throw her on the bed and ravish her body.

Toys. He could only imagine what kind of toys she had. But wait. "Who'd you use the toys on?"

"I haven't bought them yet, you ninny."

Oooh. Even better. They could pick them out together. He opened the door and tossed the towels on the ground just as someone passed by. "Excuse me. *Izvinite.*" Hey, look at that. He used Russian. And hopefully it was the correct word. He turned around and it was her. The woman from the pool Oscar had shown him. Wearing the same blue swimsuit but with a flowery skirt knotted around her slender hips.

Mandy bumped into him. He held his arms out to keep from falling, and Pool Woman grabbed his arm.

A glorious heat rushed through him, straight to his heart. The scent of jasmine filled the air. Of all the ding dong days.

She gasped and released him. "What was that?"

Oh great. She was American. An American Perfect Mate. How the hell did she get here?

"You okay, Perry?" Mandy gripped his upper arm.

Oh, he'd be fine once he cleared the area. But she couldn't know. "Yeah. Peachy. She startled me and…" He turned back to Pool Woman and smiled. "Sorry about that. Thanks for catching me."

Her brown eyes lit up and she gazed at him as if she liked what she saw. "You're American? So are we. Where are you from?"

"We?" Well lookee there. A little person stood beside her. A boy, probably seven if that.

"I'm sorry. Where are my manners? My name is Lily DiMarco. This here is Nikolai." She patted the boy's head.

"Your son?" *Please be married. Please be married. Pleeeeeeease be married.*

"She's my nanny!" Nikolai proclaimed.

The nanny. Of course. One Perfect Mate. One kid. And neither could be controlled. He'd have to skedaddle like a human. Politely. Because he couldn't wipe their memories.

* * * *

Something was up with Perry. Was it the child? Because he'd have to be on his best behavior? Vampires couldn't control children until they reached puberty. No one knew why, but other vampires had tried. She surmised it was a safety precaution and glad vampires couldn't control children. It forced them to be good in that regard.

Or was Perry hungry? They'd had quite a workout. But whatever the reason, didn't mean he should be rude.

Mandy crouched in front of Nikolai. "Well, aren't you the sweetest? My name is Mandy. That big guy there is Perry." She straightened. "He's from Atlanta. I'm from London. Where are you from?"

Lily stared at Perry as if Mandy hadn't spoken. "Atlanta? That's not so far. We live in Charleston, South Carolina."

Okay, now who was being rude? Sure, Perry was a handsome man, but did that mean she should be ignored completely? "What brings you way out here in the winter?"

Lily still hadn't acknowledged Mandy, but Perry grabbed her arm. "Sweetheart, we don't need to detain her."

Since when was polite conversation a detainment? Not that what they were having was polite. Not in the least.

"Oh, you're not detaining me. You don't know what a relief it is to find someone who speaks English around here."

"I speak English!" Nikolai said.

"Yes, dear. I know. I meant adults." Lily sighed "It's been a long week. His father has business out here and didn't want to leave his son behind for so long. It would have been nicer if his trip was in July, though." She laughed. "I keep Nikki busy during the day with school work and the pool. His father takes over at night. But there's nothing to do here by myself. Are you free for dinner?"

Did she mean "you" in the singular or plural? If the former, she was extremely rude. If the latter, she could have at least looked Mandy's way. Mandy wrapped her arms around Perry to get the message across to Lily. "I'm afraid we're checking out soon. So sorry."

But she wasn't sorry. Not one bit.

"That's too bad." Lily looked at Perry as if she'd lost an opportunity. And not just a dinner companion.

Jealousy was an unfamiliar emotion to Mandy. But she recognized it for what it was. Perry was hers until he found his Perfect Mate. So this simple mortal could just scram. She sent a command for Lily to just walk away. Lily didn't move. Mandy tried several times and got the same reaction each time: nothing. Lily didn't react to anything.

No wonder Perry was acting strange. He'd found that Perfect Mate. A Perfect Mate he touched. His Perfect Mate? And she was American to boot. Mandy never believed in broken hearts, but what else could cause the sharp pain in her chest?

"We need to get going," he said. "Got people waiting for us."

Lily blinked. "Yeah, sure. Nice meeting you." She took Nikolai's hand and walked away. The little boy waved.

Perry ushered Mandy into the stairwell. "First floor, right?"

Mandy grabbed Perry's arm as he headed downstairs. "What are you doing?"

"Going to feed?"

"No. With her. You let her go."

"Why wouldn't I let her go?"

Was he trying to protect her? She didn't need any protection. "I know what she is, Perry."

He placed his hands on his hips. "Yeah? What is she?"

Okay, now he was just pissing her off. "Your Perfect Mate."

"And you're so sure of that, why?"

"I'm not blind. I saw you touch. I saw the way she looked at you." And only him.

"She looked at us like life-lines. English life-lines. That's all."

"Why are you arguing with me about this? It was one thing not knowing if she was one or not. Now you know. And you touched her. Isn't she what you've been dreaming about? And don't lie to me."

"No. I mean, not really."

"I said don't lie."

"I'm not lying. I thought I wanted a Perfect Mate. Then I met you."

"I am not a Perfect Mate." Hell, she wasn't even a perfect vampire.

"No. You're better."

She laughed. "You have one day of kinky sex and now I'm better than a Perfect Mate?"

He winced as if she slapped him. "You think I only like you for the sex?"

"You don't know me, Perry. What else do you have to base it on? I'd hate to see you waste this opportunity."

"And apparently you don't know me."

"I think I know you very well. You were itching to go with her. Admit it."

He backed away to the opposite wall. Folded his arms across his chest. "Why are you pushing me away?"

"I'm not. I'm pushing you to her. Your destiny. I just don't understand why you're not going." Maybe if they'd known each other months instead of days, she could believe he'd want to stay with her. He couldn't let his temporary lust for her spoil what could be a lifetime with a Perfect Mate.

"My destiny." He chuffed. "What makes you think you're not my destiny?"

If only she were because he certainly was hers. But that wasn't the point. If she had to hurt him to see reason, then she would. "I told you before I wasn't looking for a suitor and nothing's changed.

The sex was great, but that's all it was. Just sex. We both know it wasn't going to last. Better to end it now before it got messy."

"Messy." Pain flashed in his eyes and struck her heart. "Fuck you, Mandy." He charged up the stairs. The third floor door opened. Closed with a bang.

Could someone hand her a gun? She needed to shoot herself in the head.

Chapter 20

Perry didn't like being told "I told you so" by anyone. Especially Barnet. And while he hadn't said it in those exact words—hadn't said much of anything—his eyes…his eyes said it every time he looked at Perry.

After he stormed away from Mandy he'd forgotten he needed to feed. Since the pool was now clear of any Perfect Mates, he'd gone down there from the other end of the hotel. Seemed his Russian worked, much to his surprise, and he'd been able to take care of his needs.

Well, one need. All his other needs were in this annoying, sexy vampire. But she didn't want him. Probably never had. He was just sex to her.

And while that wouldn't normally bother him—sex had never bothered him—it was the lying he couldn't stand. She agreed to be a couple. Why agree if she planned on leaving at the first sign of trouble?

The sun couldn't set soon enough for him and he was thankful the van hadn't moved. Perry called driver. No way was he sitting in the back seat with Mandy. Not when it was clear she wasn't really interested in him. Hadn't really wanted to be a couple. He'd been so sure, too.

Groucho sat in the back with her. No surprise there. Barnet had no desire to sit beside her, either. But now Perry was stuck with those I-told-you-so eyes from Barnet every couple of miles. Or maybe he should get with the program and call them klicks. The odometer was in kilometers.

Perry refused to look in the rearview mirror. Did she sit behind him on purpose? If she wanted to avoid eye contact, she should have sat behind her father. Hell, Barnet would have probably preferred that.

Instead, like the traitors they were—as if Perry had no control over them—his eyes would glance at the mirror. And each time, her reflection was missing. She either sat so far over to the window or had scrunched down in her seat.

Maybe it was a good thing he'd run into that Perfect Mate now. Found out the truth before he'd given all his heart away. Except…he sort of had already.

So why hadn't he gone after Lily? Mandy practically pushed him to do it.

Maybe that was why. She was pushing him. What had he done wrong? He didn't make a move on Lily. Didn't show any interest. Did she smell great? Yeah. Was there a pull? A little. But he wasn't about to act on it. He didn't know Lily. And he still didn't.

Hell, he didn't know what he wanted anymore.

Well, that wasn't true. He still wanted Mandy. She just didn't want him.

"Turn right at the next road," Mandy said.

"Oh, so you *are* still back there," he said. She didn't answer him.

The drive hadn't been too bad. The roads were clear and paved. But they weren't so fortunate on the next road. And it kind of made sense since they were headed to a park or forest. The only way Perry could tell it was a road was by the fence—wooden poles with wires linking them—lining each side of the snow-covered path. Otherwise, they'd be in a world of hurt.

"According to Natasha, there should be a parking lot up ahead," Mandy said, sounding all business-like. Like her heart was in one piece, unlike his. "We'll have to hike from there."

Something reflected off the tree ahead. Perry slammed on the brakes. The van slid a bit, and Mandy might have hit the back of his seat, but the van stayed between the wires.

"What's the matter?" Barnet asked.

Perry pointed ahead. "Is that a camera?"

Luckily it was aimed in the other direction. As if to catch someone leaving or to capture the license plate. Mandy poked her head between the seats and stared out the windshield. "Bloody hell. Do you think there were others?"

"I didn't see any others." Perry turned off the headlights just in case the camera was motion activated. "Do you think it belongs to Dimitri? Or is this the Russian government's work?"

Barnet shook his head. "Probably not Dimitri's, but that doesn't mean he can't see what's going on around here. Could be why he picked this place."

"Hold on. Let me go check it out." Mandy climbed over Groucho and exited the vehicle. She dashed over to the tree where the camera was attached and climbed the branches like a monkey.

Perry didn't want to be impressed. He wanted to be mad at her, but he couldn't. Maybe she'd give him another chance since he didn't go after Lily DiMarco. And never would. All this time he'd thought he wanted a Perfect Mate when in reality he just wanted a mate who was perfect for him. A mate like Mandy. But how could he convince her otherwise?

Mandy jumped to the ground and returned to the van, laughing. "Definitely not Dimitri's. It's labeled camera one of five. And they seem to be motion activated. You almost tripped the sensor. Another yard and you would have."

"Wonder why Natasha didn't warn you about the cameras," Perry said.

"Maybe she doesn't know about them."

"But she was here, right?"

"What are you getting at, Perry?" Barnet said.

"That if Dimitri can hack into these, he'll know Natasha followed him." That might make their surprise visit not that much of a surprise.

Barnet unbuckled his seatbelt. "Then I guess we better hurry. Oscar, grab the equipment. Perry, turn this van around. We need to make sure we can leave this place quickly."

Yeah, unless Dimitri's men blocked the road. *Oh Great One, please don't let them block the road.*

* * * *

Yevgeni ushered Natasha into Dimitri's office. Dimitri was impressed. The woman seemed cool. Calm. As if she wasn't being sent to her death sentence.

"Thank you, Yevgeni. You know your next assignment?"

"Yes, sir."

"Report to me when you get there."

Yevgeni bowed. "My pleasure, sir."

Dimitri loved loyal employees and Yevgeni was one of the best. Did what he was told and never argued. Never questioned. Just acted.

Natasha, on the other hand, had been given so much. A shop to run. And what had she done? Stuck her nose in business that was no concern of hers. She glanced over her shoulder as the door shut. Turned and faced Dimitri. "You wanted to see me, sir?"

"Yes, I did. Explain to me again what you told Oscar." Dimitri had been told by Yevgeni and Ivan that Oscar was the pilot. They even confirmed it was him in the video.

"Oscar? The French man? I gave him directions to Gorky Park."

"Do not lie to me. He is the illegal American I'm looking for."

"He asked for directions to Gorky Park. Ask anyone in the shop."

"You mean those people who don't understand French?"

"He said Gorky Park. In Russian."

Dimitri had no doubt that Oscar had said the words. It was the only way the other employees could corroborate Natasha's story. "Do you have a mate, Natasha?"

Her face scrunched up at the change of subject. Good. Dimitri liked to keep his people guessing. Especially the disloyal ones.

"No, sir. Not since Anatoli died."

"Ah yes, the man who turned you. Was he not friends with Alexi Popolov?"

She twitched, just a bit, like she understood the questions now. "Yes, they were friends."

"Alexi never became a suitor?"

"No, sir. He was much too irresponsible. I couldn't count on him and then he just disappeared."

"Yes, he did disappear, didn't he? Do you know where he went?"

"He didn't tell me."

Again with the careful answer. Not a lie, but not the complete truth, either. Ah, she was a formidable opponent.

"No, of course he didn't. But you didn't answer my question. Do you know where he went?"

If a vampire could sweat, Natasha would be drenched by now. Or maybe not. She raised her head and straightened. "No, I don't believe I do. Because you moved his body."

Dimitri clapped. "Excellent, my dear."

"What is going to happen to me?"

"That depends on you. You've been most useful to me, dear. But I can't have you alerting your friends about what I know. So for now you will be sent downstairs. Ivan!"

The door opened and Ivan entered.

Natasha's eyes widened. "Sir? Could you please have Katya escort me instead?"

"Do you have a problem with Ivan?"

"I do not have a problem if he keeps his hands to himself. However, he rarely keeps his hands to himself."

"Is that so? Well, I'm sorry to disappoint you, but Katya is unavailable."

"Then perhaps someone else from the Committee?"

"Ahhh, yes. The Committee. It no longer exists. I am in charge. And what I say goes."

She stood with her mouth hanging open. Yes, the news would be a shock to his people, but eventually they would come around.

"Ivan, take her. And be careful with that one. She might bite something important off."

Ivan grinned. "Yes, sir." He grabbed the still-speechless Natasha by the arm and practically dragged her out of the office.

Yes, loyal employees. Dimitri needed more of them. But it would take an iron fist to get them in line first. He wasn't sure if he could ever trust Natasha, but stranger things had happened.

Now to find out how Felicks was faring. His loyalty was still up for debate. He'd managed to discover who the pilot was, but if he found Katya and Grigorii, his stature would improve. Greatly.

* * * *

Mandy kept a few paces behind the men as they hiked through the forest. Her father carried the satchel containing their equipment. Perry carried the metal detector. And Oscar led the way, using the map on his mobile for guidance. Which was funny. The only person who would talk to her walked ahead of the other two who wouldn't.

How did she screw up so royally? She'd only wanted to help. Maybe she should have stayed in London. She wouldn't have met

Perry, he would have found his Perfect Mate, and he'd be happy. Instead, he passed up on an opportunity and for what? To prove to her that he meant what he'd said: he wanted to be a couple? Maybe he meant it then, but surely he had second thoughts after the way she'd hurt him. She was such a fool.

She glanced at the time on her mobile. Their plane should be landing in about an hour. Which meant it would be there waiting for them by the time they finished here.

Oscar stopped. "According to Natasha's directions, it should be right up ahead."

Mandy searched the treetops, a mixture of evergreen and deciduous. The lack of leaves on the deciduous trees made the search much easier. "I see two cameras." Both mounted on a naked branch and aimed toward each other, or rather, toward the ground. Each covering one end?

"There's one over here," Oscar pointed. It, too, was on a naked branch aimed at the same spot as the two she found.

And a fourth was located across from that, again on a naked branch, making a nice little box.

"I guess we know where to start digging," Oscar said.

"Hold up." Miraculously, everyone listened to her. "This seems too easy. If you were going to hide cameras, wouldn't you hide them in the evergreens?"

"The one at the entrance wasn't in an evergreen."

"Because it's owned by the government. They probably don't care if you see it."

Oscar pocketed his mobile. "And you think Dimitri cares?"

"I don't know. Do we want to take that chance?" Had they missed an actual hidden camera? She couldn't see any in the evergreens behind them or on the other side of the staged area, but that didn't mean there weren't any. "I'd bet my last quid that Alexi isn't buried over there. That it's a trap."

Oscar looked at the area. "But Natasha saw him."

"And if Dimitri knows she saw him, he would have come back and moved Alexi."

Perry leaned on the metal detector he held. "I get that he's a tricky bastard, and he probably does know Natasha saw him, so why didn't he confront her? Or put her in that jail."

Her father answered, "Because he's using her. Just like he uses everyone else. And we almost fell into his trap, if we haven't already. It makes sense that he would have returned to move the body. We need to hurry."

She didn't know whether to feel shocked or complimented that her father actually agreed with her.

"Well, I hope he didn't move Alexi far." Perry flipped on the metal detector. "It's going to take forever to search this area. If he's even here, he better be wearing some kind of metal or this thing won't work."

Her father took charge. "Since Perry has the metal detector, the rest of us need to sniff the ground. Maybe we can smell Popolov."

Thank goodness the trees kept the area from being completely covered in snow. But a season worth of leaves still covered the ground. The cold also made it hard to smell anything.

She took her shovel and scraped the snow and leaves away. Hopefully the grave would look disturbed, even after all these years. Oscar saw what she was doing and did the same. Her father went around to the other side of the staged area. Perry joined him.

"You and Perry have a fight?" Oscar whispered.

"More like a difference of opinion."

"That's some difference. I've never seen Perry so quiet. Hell, he didn't even play with that detector on the walk over here and I was sure he would."

She was fairly certain he would have, too. Perry had a sweet talent in easing someone's pain, whereas her talent caused it. Especially to those she cared about.

A faint beeping sounded in the area.

"Hey, guys!" Perry said. "I'm getting something."

She and Oscar jogged over to him, as did her father. Even the ground was uneven, as if it had been disturbed.

They all started digging.

"Be careful," she said. "Natasha said Dimitri had used a coffin, but if he moved him, he might not have moved the coffin, too."

"Eeeewww," Oscar said. "That's just sick."

"And burying someone alive isn't?" Perry asked. "The man needs to go. I sure hope Katya can get another Committee together. And soon."

Her shovel hit something soft. "Stop." She got on her hands and knees and started clearing the dirt with her fingers. "There's a body here."

"I sure hope it's him," Perry said. "Be just our luck Dimitri used someone else."

"I wouldn't put that past him, either," her father said as he dug beside her. "I got an arm." He pulled.

"Shit," Perry said.

In five years, the clothes on the man's body were in near tatters. Mandy and Oscar each grabbed a leg while her father and Perry lifted under the shoulders. They laid the man on the ground beside the grave. Her father brushed the dirt from Alexi's eyes, which had been closed. Once they were clear, he opened them. Even after six years, his sapphire blue eyes were alert. There was no way the man could speak. After a significant amount of blood loss a vampire would become too weak to speak. At least aloud.

Her father removed the stake and took who they hoped was Alexi's hand. "Are you Alexi Popolov?" After a few moments, he smiled. "We found him."

"Then let's blow this pop stand," Perry said. "Who wants the honors?"

"I'll take him." Her father lifted Alexi and walked through the camera zone on the way back to their van.

Not exactly the way she wanted Dimitri to know they were here. They still had to get out of the park.

Oscar put the shovels back in the bag and pulled out the crossbow. When they had stopped at a store that had resembled a Bass Pro Shop to buy the shovels and metal detector, they'd also gotten the crossbow, in case they ran into Dimitri's men. Just because her father had tripped these cameras now, didn't mean they hadn't tripped one earlier.

Now the race to the airport began.

* * * *

Dimitri stormed into the computer center just as an alarm blared from his phone. He rushed to a station and accessed the feed from the site. Empty. But what had tripped it off? He rewound the video.

"Damn it!" He slammed his fist on the desk. Should have realized they wouldn't fall for the trap. He pulled out his phone and texted Yevgeni. "Please tell me you are there."

A moment later he received a reply, "We have just gotten in position. Camera's on as requested. Will call you soon."

Yes. Cameras. Dimitri found Yevgeni's feed. The Committee had always denied this basic fundamental need, but now Dimitri was running things. If it was good enough for American cops, it was good enough for the Russian vampires. All his employees would be equipped with cameras.

The black-and-white feed was a bit fuzzy. Best he could do on short notice, though. Later, he would get top-of-the-line equipment. He deserved no less.

A white van was parked in the driveway, pointed toward the exit. They must have noticed the park's camera and didn't take any chances of driving further. Didn't matter. They would be dead soon and Dimitri would be able to watch every lovely second of it.

"What is that, sir?" Felicks asked.

Dimitri stood. He'd forgotten why he came here. "We're on the verge of destroying our enemies. Have you located Katya and Grigorii?"

"Not yet, sir. Destroying? Not capturing?"

"Are you going weak on me too, Felicks?"

"No, sir. They should be destroyed. They have trespassed."

"Exactly. Now go find Katya and Grigorii. I would love for them to witness our freedom from the other Committees. To show them who is king."

"Yes, sir. Right away, sir." Felicks fled the room.

Dimitri turned back to the monitor. He would have to deal with Felicks later, but for now the man was useful. He was afraid of dying, and that right there would make Dimitri a great king. Everyone would do what he wanted for fear of dying. And he would instill fear every second he got.

Killing the foreigners would be a nice start to show his people what he was capable of. Probably should have kept Sergei, too. To show what happened to traitors. But it was too late, now. Maybe next time.

Chapter 21

Perry nearly laughed at Groucho and held out the metal detector. "You wanna trade? You don't look too comfortable with that crossbow."

They still had quite a hike back to the van and Groucho had taken point. Which made sense since he carried the crossbow. What didn't make sense was him carrying the crossbow. He was a pilot and an accountant and right now acted like it.

"You don't mind?"

"Naw. I'm in the mood to shoot something anyway." Especially the person who had buried Alexi alive like that. Without a box. Without a bag. It was unconscionable. But then, did Dimitri even have a conscience? Probably not.

Groucho handed over the crossbow with a grateful smile. "Thanks. All this is way above my pay grade."

Perry took the weapon and packet of arrows. Part of him wanted to shoot some Russian vampires, but the other part just wanted to get home without any issues. The latter did not seem likely, though. "Hey, if you want to hang back, I got this."

Groucho nodded, started to lag behind then caught back up. "It's because of that woman I told you about, isn't it?"

"What's because of what woman?" Was it stupid to play dumb? Because Perry knew exactly who Groucho meant.

"The one at the pool. Is that what your disagreement is about? Mandy didn't want you to go?"

"Naw. She was cool with me going." Too cool. Cold, almost.

"Oh. So you saw her?"

"No. She was gone." Better to lie than explain it all. Although, he should probably tell Barnet about Lily DiMarco. Maybe on the plane. Or back in Atlanta. Yeah, that seemed safest.

"So what's the problem? Anything I can help with?"

If only Groucho could. Perry might be able to change her mind then. But his relationship with Mandy wasn't anyone's business. Not even well-intentioned vampires. "It's personal, okay?" As personal as it could get: he wasn't good enough for her.

"Sorry. You're right. None of my business."

Groucho fell behind, leaving Perry alone on point, following their tracks in the snow. And so far there weren't any additional trails. Just the four leading to Alexi's burial site. All was quiet, too. No inadvertent rustling of the trees. That had to be a good sign.

Perry would have loved to rush ahead, but as Barnet had explained to Groucho earlier, slow and steady made it easier to locate any undesirables.

Yeah, there were undesirables all right. Anyone associated with Dimitri fell into that category.

Ten minutes later, Perry finally spotted the van. He raised his arm to the others to stop as he went to investigate. The only footsteps around the van were the ones they had made. Only one set of tire tracks were leading to the exit and nothing blocked their way. Oh, thank the Great One. Perry turned around and waved them on.

Groucho and Mandy helped Barnet carry Alexi over the wires while Perry kept watch. Although at this point, it almost seemed useless. But being stupid wasn't a recipe for staying alive.

A whirring noise broke the silence. Shit! Someone *was* here.

"Get down!" Perry yelled as he fell to the ground. Some kind of round disc flew overhead and imbedded into a tree with a thunk. What the hell kind of weapon was that?

Groucho had landed beside him. Barnet behind him, covering Alexi. They both nodded. Mandy. Where was Mandy?

Another whirring noise. If they didn't find cover, they'd be downed quicker than blood to a thirsty vampire. "Get behind the van!"

Perry stayed low, the crossbow aimed in front, protecting Groucho and Barnet as they moved Alexi behind the van. Once

Perry joined them, she came into view. Lying on the ground. Blood all around her. Her head nearly decapitated. "Mandy!"

Ready to leap to her rescue, he dropped the crossbow, but Barnet grabbed his arm.

"I'll get her. You get them."

"Is she——?" *Please don't be dead. Please don't be dead. Pleeeease.*

"Get them first."

"Right." There was a dead Russian vampire in Perry's future. He grabbed the weapon, moved to the other side of the van and crouched. Peeked around the front. Yevgeni crouched to the right, in the trees, his focus on where they'd been. No wonder he'd had a clear shot of them, they'd walked right into his line of sight. Perry aimed and let loose an arrow. Perfect heart shot. Yevgeni collapsed.

"Got him." Perry relaxed and stood. The whirring noise sounded again. To his left. Shit, Yevgeni had help. Perry ducked and reloaded as another one of those discs flew above his head and crashed through the side window of the van. As the unfamiliar vampire rushed to his comrade, Perry took aim and fired. Another heart shot. "Bingo! I win."

But maybe not. He waited a beat to make sure all was safe. When no other sounds could be heard, he jogged over to Yevgeni and grabbed the weapon. Those discs were wicked sharp. "What the hell is this thing?"

The man spewed Russian. Perry caught a few curse words, but the rest didn't make sense. Didn't matter. What mattered was the camera on Yevgeni's vest.

Perry yanked the camera free. Stared into the lens. "You better hope we never meet or you'll be a dead man, Dimitri."

* * * *

Dimitri slammed his fist on the table. He might have lost this battle, and his plans for Popolov were now ruined, but he hadn't lost the war as that miscreant Perry Davenport would soon discover. They weren't leaving Russia alive. None of them.

The door opened and Felicks entered.

Dimitri turned off the monitors. "You better have word on Katya and Grigorii."

"Yes, sir. I do. I've discovered they are holding a meeting tonight at three a.m., over at the old Headquarters."

"How did you get word of this meeting? Did they invite you?"

"No, sir. I don't believe they trust me. But I was approached by one of our people. He'd heard of the meeting and questioned me about it. Thought it had sounded treasonous. I assured him he'd done right in reporting it. Do you wish to lead the raid, sir?"

Lead the raid? Was the man a bumbling fool or had he switched sides? Dimitri stood. "Do I look stupid to you?"

Felicks took a step back. "No, sir."

"Can you not see they are setting a trap?"

"No, sir. I read his mind myself. He is telling the truth."

"Then he was being used. They hope to draw me out so they can capture me. Instead, I will send in the army and they can deal with them."

"Army? But sir, we don't have an army."

"The Committee didn't have an army, but I assure you, I do. You think I would be foolish enough to start a takeover if I didn't have the resources?" Dimitri pulled the desk phone over and dialed the number for the prison.

Ivan answered, breathless. "Sir?"

"You still in one piece?"

Ivan chuckled. "Yes, sir. She is a feisty one, though. But I will get her to submit to me shortly."

"I'm afraid that will have to wait. Lock her up and gather the troops. You have a new mission."

"Very well, sir. I'm on it."

"Call me when you are ready." Dimitri hung up the phone. Maybe he would go downstairs and check in on Natasha. If she was close to submitting, he might have a little fun with her.

"We have a prisoner, sir?"

He'd forgotten all about Felicks. "Yes. I caught Natasha aiding and abetting the enemy. She is being detained until I decide what to do with her."

"Natasha Bychkova?"

"Is there another Natasha I don't know about?"

"No, sir. Would you like me to check in on her?"

"No. I want you to report to Ivan. Give him the information about the meeting. I would like you to accompany him on the raid."

Felicks eyes widened. "Me, sir?"

"You are my right-hand man, are you not?"

He bowed. Actually bowed. "Yes, sir. I'll get right on that, sir."

Dimitri nearly laughed as Felicks rushed out of the room. If he was lucky, he'd have a new right-hand man by the end of the night. Because Felicks certainly was not that man.

* * * *

As soon as Perry disabled the shooter, Barnet crawled back to Amanda. Her spine was the only thing keeping her head attached to her body, but she wasn't dead. Not yet.

Thank God.

Barnet adjusted her head so it would start reattaching. But if she didn't have enough blood in her system—and she'd lost a lot of it—there would be no healing. No reattaching. Shit. He couldn't lose her. Not like this. Perry would never believe he hadn't tried his best to save her.

He'd been such a fool. All during the walk back to the van she'd hung back. Just as she had during the walk to the burial site. Probably thinking he didn't love her. Or that she wasn't wanted. And maybe it had been true before, but it wasn't true now.

The more he'd thought about Perfect Mates and Rachel, the more he realized that maybe that's why he'd grieved for so long. Five hundred years was just not normal. And to think it took Perry to figure it out. God, how stupid he'd become.

Didn't matter that Perry and Mandy were at odds at the moment, either. Perry never did say what happened between them. Barnet just knew something had. Something that had broken Perry's heart. Only one thing Barnet could think that could cause a rift between those two: him.

"I'm dying. Just leave me." Since Barnet was touching her skin, she was able to communicate telepathically.

"No one's being left behind." As for the dying part, she might be right, but he'd do all he could to prevent that from happening. And not just for Perry.

"I don't want to be a bother. You can let me go."

She was far from a bother. But if he told her that now, would she believe him? "Hush. We'll get you out of here alive."

"Is Perry okay?"

"He's fine. I think he just took care of our shooters. Hold on. Oscar's going to help me get you to the van."

"Wait. In my backpack. There's the name and address to a Perfect Mate who lives in South Carolina. Give it to Perry. Maybe now he will pursue her."

Barnet switched to telepathy. *"When did he find a Perfect Mate?"*

"Today. Ran into her in the hall. He refused to go to her."

"You told him to?"

"Yes. We both know I'm not right for him."

No wonder Perry was in the dumps. *"I don't know any such thing. I was wrong before and I'm sorry. Can you forgive me?"*

"You're just saying that because I'm dying, aren't you? But it doesn't matter. There's nothing to forgive. You were grieving. I understand."

"No one in their right mind grieves for five hundred years."

"But you loved her. And she was your Perfect Mate."

He would have cried if he'd been able. He certainly didn't deserve her forgiveness but was thankful all the same.

Chapter 22

Mandy wasn't sure this day could get any weirder.

Not only had she nearly lost her head—and it was still up for debate whether or not she would—her father had actually asked for forgiveness.

Asked her. For forgiveness.

Oh, it was highly likely due to the fact she wouldn't see another day, she was sure of it. Without blood to heal her, there was no way they could keep her alive. And without her head, she was a dead vampire.

Perry arrived carrying a strange weapon. "They're taken care of. How is—" He dropped to his knees. "Oh Mandy, no."

Her father gripped Perry's shoulder, getting his attention. "She's still alive. Take her legs, will you? Oscar, support her middle. I'll hold her head."

And she hoped to God she made it to the van in one piece. If the head became completely severed, there might be no putting it back. Except, wait. "*I have some duct tape in my bag.*"

"Stop. She said there's some duct tape in her bag. Do you think it'll work?"

"Can't hurt." Perry patted her hand. "See, even nearly decapitated, you're still thinking." He left her sight, but the van door slid open.

"Can we sit her up?" Oscar asked.

Her father raised an eyebrow. "Well?"

"*Go for it.*"

He nodded to Oscar. Held her head still while Oscar lifted her shoulders upward. Perry returned with the tape.

"Push it down good and tight," Perry said. "I know it's gonna hurt, Beautiful, but trust me, it'll heal faster that way."

"*Tell him I'm not feeling*—" Her father pushed down and woke up every pair receptor in her body. "*Bloody hell!*"

And the squishy noises. There were a lot of squishy noises. Scents never bothered her that much, but noises? Gross noises? Got her every time. Apparently her stomach still worked and it wasn't happy. She couldn't afford to be ill. Which begged the question: could she? Be ill? That was one question she was okay with not knowing the answer to. But if she could take deep, calming breaths, she would. Unfortunately, her lungs were currently disconnected from her mouth.

Perry held the tape in his hand and examined her neck. "I need to dry it off or the tape won't stick." He smiled and winked at her. "Now, don't get all excited."

The man was impossible. Was he trying to get her to laugh? He removed his Hawaiian shirt—without all the fanfare he'd done earlier—and the Union Jack T-shirt he'd worn under it. Ahhh, his lovely chest. Was that what she was supposed to not get excited about? She'd hate to break it to him, but her body wasn't quite working right.

He tossed the Hawaiian shirt toward the van, but kept the T-shirt in his hand. No, no, no. He was going to ruin his souvenir. If she got out of this alive, she'd make sure to replace it.

But silly her. Instead of using the shirt like any normal person, he licked the blood away. His tongue felt so soft. So loving. His saliva would also help in the healing by causing the skin to reconnect. Too bad saliva couldn't connect her internal works.

"Alexi's in the van," Oscar said. "Hey, Perry. You cleaning her or making out?"

Perry was being rather thorough. Too bad her body wasn't reacting the way it should.

Her father chuckled. If she died right now, she'd die a happy vampire.

Perry straightened. "I don't want to ruin my souvenir, okay?" She might have believed him if he hadn't winked at her when he said it. Using the T-shirt, he wiped her neck dry. "Now maybe the tape will stick."

He pulled a strip and ripped it from the roll. Wrapped the tape around her neck. Repeated the process several times. And every time he applied the tape, his face was close to hers.

She figured he would have kissed her if there wasn't an audience. Which was too bad. She wouldn't mind feeling his lips against hers one last time. Because she still wasn't sure she would make it out of Russia alive.

He examined his work. Frowned and placed his hand on her shoulder. "I wouldn't sneeze if I were you."

"Perry!" Her father might be admonishing him, but she just wanted to laugh. If only she could. This decapitation business was frustrating.

"Sorry." Perry cupped her face. "You know I was just joking. Right?"

"*I do. Can't you see me laughing?*"

He grinned. "Cool." He kissed her then. Just a brief touch, a little peck, but it was glorious all the same.

He tossed the tape toward the van. "Hold her head while I lift her. Think she'll be okay on the back seat?"

Her father said, "No. Put her in the back with Alexi. I'll sit with her and hold her head in place."

"I can sit with her."

"I need you up front with Oscar. He'll drive."

Okay, more weirdness. They were now arguing who was going to sit with her?

Perry slipped his Hawaiian shirt back on, sans the T-shirt. "You think there will be more of them?"

"Did you find their vehicle?"

Perry shook his head. "No, I... Shit. Let me go check."

"Oscar, help me get her in the van."

The two of them managed to get her inside with her head intact. Score! Her father sat behind her and pulled her against his body. He wrapped one arm around her collarbone and placed his hand on her head, securing her in place.

It had been too many years since he'd held her last. She hadn't even been a teenager yet. And while the circumstances were dire this go around, she wouldn't have traded it for anything. He cared. He actually cared.

Oscar shut the back of the van.

"Boss?" Perry said from the backseat. "I found their vehicle. It's empty. Do we just leave Dimitri's goons here to burn in the sun?"

"They're still alive?"

"Yeah. Just staked."

"Put them in the backseat and we'll take them with us. I'll not have Dimitri use their deaths against us."

"Got it. She doing okay?"

"She's fine. Now hurry so we can get out of here."

Yeah, she was all for that. *"How's Alexi?"*

Her father took her hand and placed it on Alexi's arm. "Ask him yourself."

She supposed she could make herself useful. Whether she'd be able to pass on the information she learned was questionable.

* * * *

From outside, Perry belted in Yevgeni while Groucho knelt between the front seats and belted in the other goon. The staked vampires both slumped over in their seats, but Perry didn't care. Frankly, he would have left them to burn, but Barnet was right. Dimitri definitely would have used their deaths against them.

Perry yanked on the belt nice and tight. The guy should be thankful that's all he did to him after what he'd done to Mandy. Perry sure hoped that tape worked.

Speaking of which… He grabbed the tape lying on the ground and removed a strip.

"What's that for?" Groucho asked.

"To tape their mouths, what else? I don't want to hear them yammering all the way, do you?"

"Oh hell, no. It's bad enough they're like this."

"At least we don't have to look at them." Perry wrapped a strip of tape so it went completely around Yevgeni's head. Tossed the roll to Groucho, who then did the same to the other goon.

Holding the crossbow—because he wasn't sure he could use the Russian weapon efficiently—Perry climbed onto the passenger seat. They had all received texts from Vic when the plane landed. And that was the only text they'd received, which meant they'd gone undetected. Or at least Dimitri hadn't made his presence known. Could he be waiting to ambush them at the plane, too?

As the van approached the street, Perry rolled down the window and stuck the crossbow out. Just in case.

Groucho braked. "Clear this way."

The SUV was still parked on the road. It wasn't going anywhere even if these two goons had left someone behind. Perry had ripped every cord and belt he could find. It would take a mechanic to put that puppy back together.

"This way, too." Didn't mean they were in the clear. They still had a plane to catch.

* * * *

Dimitri descended the stairs to the jails. Ever since his conversation with Ivan, he couldn't get Natasha out of his head. Or rather, his dick couldn't stop thinking about her. She was one fine piece and it was time he sampled her. She would learn that the best way to be treated—the best way to survive—was to submit. Maybe she would have learned that from Ivan, but Dimitri was king. Time she treated him as such.

He reached the bottom of the stairs. The cells were quiet. He checked each door, all open. Natasha wasn't anywhere to be found. What the hell?

Felicks. That traitor. Dimitri dashed up the stairs and called Ivan from the wall phone.

"We're not quite ready, sir."

"Is Felicks with you?"

"No, sir."

"When he arrives, I want you to detain him. Chain him or stake him, whatever it takes."

"As you command, sir. Anything else?"

Dimitri loved a man who followed orders without asking questions. He needed more men like Ivan.

"Those four vampires who eluded you the last time? They are on the move again. I need one of your men to capture them."

"Do you have coordinates?"

"I have something better. A GPS signal." At least Yevgeni had managed to tag their van. It had taken some tree climbing and jumping, but he'd done it and it appeared they didn't suspect a thing since the signal was on the move.

"I'll get them, sir. I'll make them regret keeping me alive."

"I'm sure you would, but I need you to take care of Katya and Grigorii. They are planning a meeting at the old Headquarters." Although, if Felicks had switched sides... "It might be a trap. So if you have to blow up the building, do it. I want them eliminated."

"You don't need me to destroy a building. I've got men to do that. But it would be my honor to execute the illegal foreigners. For your lordship."

Dimitri chuckled. Destroy. Execute. Lordship! My, how he loved those words. Ivan would make a fine right-hand man.

Chapter 23

Sitting in the front seat while Mandy sat waaaay in the back near death ranked right up there with being buried alive: torturous. Something Perry hadn't anticipated. She might as well be miles away instead of feet. And the few questions he'd asked Barnet were never really answered.

"She's fine," being the main answer. What was that supposed to mean? He couldn't imagine she'd be fine until she fed.

Perry leaned over to Groucho. "We need to find some donors before we get on that plane."

"I agree. You think you can find someone at a gas station? We're going to need fuel soon, too."

The needle on the gas gauge almost touched the red line. Why hadn't he filled up on the drive out here? Oh yeah, because his mind had traveled elsewhere. Damn mind!

Perry straightened in his seat. "Stop at the first gas station you find and we'll hope for the best."

That first station miraculously appeared only five minutes later, with a neon sign in the window that Perry could only assume meant open. Or maybe their beer was on sale. Either way, the lights were on inside. "You take care of filling up. I'll go find someone." Or rather, the first of many someones. Time to try out his Russian once again.

He went into the store. The only person inside was the cashier. Perry worked his vampire powers—and newly learned Russian— and told the man to follow him. Surprise, surprise, it worked. All he had to do was get the guy to the back of the van, and then Mandy could take over.

Perry opened the van. "There you go, Beautiful. Time to heal."

The worker climbed inside. Hey, lookee there. Just like he planned. Except the donor went to Alexi, not Mandy. Placed his arm at Alexi's mouth.

"He was supposed to be for her."

Barnet shook his head. "I don't think she can control anyone, anymore."

No, no, no, no, no! She wasn't going to die. She was *not* going to die! "You can't hear her?"

"No. But she's still alive. She can still blink."

If she couldn't communicate and she could only blink, how the hell was Perry going to get blood down her throat? If her throat was even connected to the rest of her body.

The worker climbed out of the vehicle and went back to the store. Perry was so tempted to bring the man back and use him for Mandy.

"Don't do it," Barnet said, as if he'd read Perry's mind. "No one person is better than another."

Perry lowered his head. He knew that. Didn't mean he liked it.

Alexi licked his lips. Blinked a few times. "I am sorry. When I realized she could no longer communicate, I knew you would need my help. That is the only reason I took that donor."

"Fine. But she needs blood to live. Now. And he's the only one here."

Alexi smiled. "He is not the only one. There is a hospital two klicks down the road."

Oh, thank the Great One. "We'll leave as soon as we fill up."

"Have you interrogated Dimitri's men?"

"Can't. They don't know English and our only interpreter is currently unavailable. Why does it matter? We have them."

"Wrong. You have new interpreter—me. And I can guarantee you that Dimitri is following you somehow. I will find out how."

"They don't have any bugs or tracking devices. Unless Dimitri shoved one up their asses, and I highly doubt those two would allow that. Even from Dimitri."

Alexi lifted his arm. "Help me out. I will interrogate them."

"We don't have time for this. She needs blood."

"And she will get it. There is a vehicle approaching. Use the occupants while I find out what Dimitri's men know."

Who died and put him in charge? *Oh, Great One. No, don't let her die. Please.* Perry helped Alexi out of the back and carried him over to the side door.

Alexi laughed. "They are naked."

"How else would I ensure they had no tracking devices?"

"Leave me with them. Go help your woman."

"She's not my—" Oh, who was he kidding? Mandy was the only woman for him.

* * * *

Mandy had been around death a lot. Most of her friends had been the elderly. They never lived long enough to notice Mandy hadn't aged and Mandy liked to pretend they were family. Grandparents she never had. A father she wanted back so badly. Now that she finally got him back, it was her time to die.

Just didn't seem all that fair.

But one thing she had noticed with all her older friends: when death came for them, it came peacefully.

Mandy was at peace. She could no longer communicate and she was at peace. Her only regret: not telling Perry she loved him. And now she never would.

And yet, she was at peace. Because she was with the people she loved.

After Alexi left, her father laid her on the floor of the van. Gently. Lovingly. He knew the truth. Hadn't said anything to Perry yet. Would Perry freak?

"I know it looks dire, but please, don't give up on us, okay?"

Dire. Now there was a word. She blinked at him, because she could still do that. When would she lose that ability? And would they think she passed before she actually…passed?

That would royally suck.

Perry returned with a female donor.

"Is she the only one in the car?" her father asked.

"Yeah. Is she…?"

"Come in. You sit with her." Her father climbed out of the van.

Perry climbed inside. "Hey, Beautiful. Ready for another rash?"

For once in her life she'd welcome the burn. Mandy blinked. His smile gave her hope. Hope that she'd survive. Hope that they'd be together. And hope that her father's current attitude wasn't an act.

The back door closed. Perry bit into the woman's arm and placed it against Mandy's lips.

The blood tasted sweet and coated her tongue. But swallowing was out of the question. She just couldn't get those muscles to respond. If she could only get it to trickle down…

Whether the channel to her heart was small or non-existent, the blood in her mouth had nowhere to go and it overflowed. Perry removed the donor's arm and sealed the wound. He lifted Mandy slightly, using his elbow to keep her head in line with her body and closed her mouth. "Guess we need to let gravity work today, huh?"

Gravity would be useless if the access to her lower extremities was closed off. And it must be closed or she'd be in some hurt right now.

No need to be a Negative Nelly, though. The blood could eventually open a path. Especially if he kept rubbing her neck downward, like a person did with a cat when they wanted the creature to swallow a pill. She tried to blink to reassure Perry, but no longer could perform that function.

Oh, bollocks.

* * * *

Barnet paced beside the van while Alexi linked into Yevgeni's mind. Everyone was busy except Barnet. It had never bothered him before. He was a leader; he was used to waiting on his people. But now? Now his mind wandered, and not to a good place.

He pictured holding Amanda—okay, Mandy—on the day she was born. Vowing to protect and love her forever. What an utter failure he'd become.

Alexi lowered his hands. "He attached a tracker to the top of the van."

"What?" Barnet opened the passenger door and boosted himself to the roof. He pulled a metal nib free. Instead of destroying it, he jumped down and placed it on the vehicle of the donor. Thankfully, she was headed in the same direction they'd been going, so Dimitri wouldn't notice anything different. Barnet returned to Alexi.

"You are Barnet? Head of US Committee?"

"I am."

"What brought you to Russia?"

Barnet laughed. "Dimitri. He kidnapped me."

"Ahhh. Then I should doubly thank you for rescuing me when you should have just rescued yourself."

"It's not me you need to thank. It's Ama—Mandy. She was so sure you could tell me…" Barnet shook his head. "It doesn't matter anymore."

"Mandy is important to you, too?"

"You could say that. She's my daughter. She's the one who turned me."

"Ahhh. That explains— Sorry. It's just that most men aren't turned—"

"At such an advanced age? I get that a lot."

"What did she think I could tell you?"

Not that it mattered anymore, but the leader in him still wanted answers. "When the first Perfect Mate was discovered."

"The first? Long before I wrote the story."

"So you did write it?"

"I wrote it, but it was told to me."

Told, not experienced. Barnet should have figured that. "So you don't know anything about them?"

"I know plenty about them. When I was told this incredible story, I made it my mission to know more. My source told me about his Perfect Mate two thousand years ago. Plus or minus a century."

"Two thousand?" Barnet's legs gave out and he landed on the ground with a thump. "Just how old are you?"

"Older than you can imagine."

"So they could have existed in 1474? In England?"

Alexi nodded. "Yes. Some could have been born that year. Generations are very sporadic. It's not like they're all born in the same year now, is it? They cover a wide range. And not every year between."

Generations. Exactly as he and Victoria had theorized. "How many generations?"

"Fifteen? Sixteen? Maybe seventeen? Tracking them has not been easy. I knew of the first one and about five hundred years later, more showed up. Unfortunately, those vampires who discovered them killed them out of survival. Which is understandable, I suppose. We must keep our secret, must we not?" Alexi frowned. "That's when I decided to write the story. But most vampires believed I wrote fiction."

"You've never met one?"

"A few, but they were already taken. By then my story had been circulated. Otherwise, those might have met a similar fate. Why do you ask about 1474?"

"It's possible my late wife was a Perfect Mate."

"You were bonded?"

"No, not as lucky as that. We were both mortal then. But Mandy, when she turned me, she tried to turn Rachel. To save our lives. But Rachel didn't make it. The turn wouldn't take."

"And you've been grieving ever since?"

"Unfortunately, I have. But that is in the past. My concern is now. We've found some in the States."

"That would make sense, if my calculations are correct. The latest wave should be well into adulthood now, if they're not still being born. So you found one?"

"More than one."

"You didn't kill them, did you?"

Barnet shook his head. "Once we determined what they were, I put the word out. But that was only a year ago. They're the most wonderful people, though."

Alexi laughed. "I wish you could convince Dimitri of that."

"He calls them freaks."

"He does. The man is pigheaded." He said something in Russian—a word Mandy hadn't taught them—and spat on the ground.

"But can they be dangerous?"

"Perfect Mates? No... Well... Ahhh, Dimitri showed you his little memory, didn't he? She was only protecting her mate. A mate she'd had for four hundred years. Dimitri executed him for harboring her all those years. Wouldn't you have acted the same if you saw the love of your life chopped down? They were unable to subdue her as she'd grown very strong during their bond. Again, I told Dimitri not to go to such lengths, but does he listen to me? Of course not. Maybe I stay in Russia too long. Maybe it is time for a change. You think America will welcome me?"

"You are more than welcome to come to America. We can help you. Provided we get out of this alive."

Perry poked his head over the seats. "Boss? Something's wrong."

Barnet scrambled to the back of the van as the door opened. The donor jumped down and returned to her vehicle. "What is it?"

Although the question was moot. Mandy's jaw and neck were covered in blood as it dribbled from her mouth.

"She's losing more blood than she's taken. We need more donors."

"Oscar, let's go!" Barnet closed his eyes. He wasn't ready to let her go just yet. He moved Alexi to the front passenger seat and climbed into the back with Perry.

Perry stroked Mandy's face as Oscar drove them to the hospital. "Come on, Beautiful. Stay with me, now."

Barnet wanted to ignore the signs. Especially the one big sign: she hadn't broken out in a rash. That meant the blood wasn't getting into her system. And if the blood wasn't getting into her system…

The van came to a screeching halt. About a minute later, the back doors were flung open.

Oscar stood there. "Alexi is feeding again. Told me to wait here while he got some help. Man, I don't know if I could move around as well as he is after being buried for so long. How's she doing?"

Barnet shook his head. It would take a miracle, and he was pretty sure he'd run out of those.

Alexi appeared with a needle filled with blood. "Insert this in her heart."

Perry took the syringe. Stabbed Mandy and pushed the plunger. He cupped her face. "Don't leave me, Beautiful. Please. I love you."

Nothing. No reaction. Not a blink or eye movement.

Barnet climbed out of the van. This couldn't be happening. How could he stop it from happening?

Perry kissed Mandy's lips. Climbed out of the car. "This is all Dimitri's fault. I'm going to kill him."

Barnet grabbed his shoulder. "Perry, she may still come around."

"Don't lie to me. Don't lie to yourself. You have eyes. She doesn't have a rash!"

"A rash?" Alexi asked.

"She's allergic to blood," Barnet said. "She breaks out in a rash when she feeds."

"Let me go, Boss. Let me do away with that monster!"

"That's not going to bring her back."

"He's done nothing but destroy lives. He doesn't deserve to live."

"And if he kills you?"

"I don't care." Perry grabbed the bag containing the decapitating weapon. "I have to try. For her. Go to the plane. Don't wait for me. Just get out of this country. Take her home." He ran off.

"Perry!"

"Let him go," Alexi said.

"I can't just let him go. He's like a son to me."

"And he needs to grieve."

Except his grieving would probably get him killed. Maybe there was something Barnet could do. He found Oscar's phone and made a call.

* * * *

Perry ran. His eyes stung from unshed tears. His heart throbbed as if it had been shredded. So he ran.

Too bad he couldn't run as fast as a car. He'd run all the way to Russian Headquarters, where Dimitri was most likely ordering his goons to do his dirty work for him. But the clock was against him—or rather sunrise—so he required speed.

A man was strolling in the parking lot of the hospital, looking at his phone, not paying attention. Perry took control using English first—a lot of Russians seemed to know the language—and hit pay dirt. The man handed over the keys and then ran back into the hospital with an urge to pee. There was a time Perry took joy in doing that kind of thing, but he wasn't sure if he'd ever take joy in anything ever again. Dimitri had stolen that joy away and he would pay.

Perry pushed the fob. A small sedan lit up. He climbed inside.

She was gone. Gone! The blood should have worked. "Oh Great One. Why'd you bring her into my life just to take her away?" Maybe they were destined to be together in the afterlife. If there was an afterlife.

But first he needed to focus on the here and now. Killing Dimitri. That was all that mattered. Perry would worry about what to do after. Provided he succeeded and survived. And in order to do that, he needed to know where to go. He pulled out his phone. Everyone else seemed to have maps on theirs, and sure enough there was a map icon on his phone, too.

Only problem: Perry didn't have an address. And it wasn't like the map would know where the Russian Vampire Headquarters would be located. A museum! Yes, it was a museum. He typed in the name, found it, and drove like a demon back to Moscow.

He parked a few blocks from Headquarters. Would the building be secure? If Dimitri had his men searching for Barnet, would he have left anyone behind for guard duty? Probably. But probably the minimum: one or two guards. Perry could take care of two guards.

He opened the bag containing the strange weapon. Seemed easy enough to use: fill it with ten discs and press the trigger. When he'd checked out the SUV earlier and spotted this bag with more sharp discs, he'd grabbed it, not thinking he'd actually need them. If he wasn't so disgusted that the Russian vampires had actually created such an ugly weapon, he'd be impressed.

He loaded the weapon to the max. Pulled out his cellphone. Five missed calls. All from Groucho's phone. It would be just like Barnet to call again at the wrong time so Perry shut it off and stashed it in his side pocket. Besides, neither Barnet nor anyone else was going to talk Perry out of this mission. Nope. Not happening.

He exited the car, grabbed the weapon, and slung the bag over his shoulder. It was do-or-die time.

Chapter 24

Was this death for a vampire?

Mandy was aware of her surroundings, could hear just fine, and as long as her eyes were open she saw whatever came into her view. But she couldn't move or communicate in any way, and apparently her heart stopped beating. How many vampires were left for dead in this condition?

Perry had assumed she died. Had said to take her home. For what? Burning? Burial?

Oh God. She'd rather be burned than buried alive. Because she was alive, dammit! But how could she tell them?

The van jostled. Her father's face came into her view.

He caressed her face. "Hey, sweeting. Papa's gonna take care of you now."

Sweeting? He hadn't called her that since she was a child. *"I'm not dead! I'm not dead! I'm not dead!"*

His eyes widened. "Mandy?"

Oh thank God. Maybe some of the blood had gotten through her system. *"Yes! It's me. I'm still alive in here."*

He turned his head toward the opening. "Oscar! Alexi! She's still alive. We need more donors."

For the next hour the back of the van became a mini operating room. Her father plunged blood into her heart, Oscar helped her feed orally, and Alexi… He apparently supplied the donors. After the second donor she could blink her eyes again. They'd gone through a dozen donors before she could finally feel her fingers.

"My fingers!"

Her father smiled. "You can talk again."

She could. She could breathe, too. Oh thank God!

He lifted her hand and rubbed her arm. "But you still haven't broken out in a rash. Strange."

"I'm not feeling the burn, either." Although her neck hurt like the dickens, so she couldn't attribute the lack of pain due to what Perry had done to her brain earlier. "What does that mean?"

"Haven't a clue." He pulled out a mobile.

"Who are you calling?"

"Perry." He frowned. "Damn it. His phone is dead. Or off. Here, leave him a message. He won't believe you're alive unless you tell him."

He put the phone up to her mouth. "How dare you leave me before I died, you doofus. Now get your arse back over to me and show me you love me."

She still couldn't believe Perry had said those words to her. That he loved her. She so much wanted to tell him the same, but not via the mobile, and not with her father staring at her.

He disconnected the call. "Are you going to push him away again?"

"That wasn't what I was doing."

"Wasn't it?"

"I just didn't want him to blame me for keeping him from a Perfect Mate." She almost laughed at the absurdity of that statement. If he had wanted to go, he would have. That he hadn't, should have been enough.

"Yet when you gave him the opportunity, he didn't take it, did he?"

"No."

"Why do you suppose that is?"

"What are you? A therapist?"

He laughed. "No. Just someone who hasn't been there for you in the past and hopes to make up for it now. And I care for Perry."

She liked this version of her father. Had missed this version. The caring man who'd raised her. "Well it doesn't matter what I think if he doesn't hear that message and he gets himself killed."

"Good point. Let's make sure he hears the message." He made another call. "Katya, it's Barnet. Any luck finding Perry?"

Mandy's vampire hearing worked just fine and Katya's voice sounded as if her father had put the call on speaker.

"Not yet. But then we've been busy. Dimitri fell for our trap and sent his army in to do away with our impromptu meeting. We were able to overtake them. Once our people saw the extent that Dimitri would go to, they had no problems fighting for our side. I'm on my way to Headquarters now. We'll stop Perry. We don't need Dimitri to be a martyr."

"When you find him, have him listen to his messages, will you? Mandy is still alive, but he won't believe it unless he hears her voice."

"That is very good news, Barnet. I will definitely have him do that. Are you headed for your plane?"

"Yes. We'll wait for Perry there. Thank you for your help, Katya."

"Don't thank me until you're out of the country. Things can still get fucked up."

Father disconnected the call and handed the mobile to Oscar. "Let's go. Have Alexi sit up front with you. I'll stay back here."

Oscar patted her shoulder. "Glad you're back with us." He jumped out and shut the doors, leaving Father and her alone in the back.

"I sure hope she gets to him in time." It would be just her luck that he'd risk his life before realizing there was no need for vengeance.

* * * *

Dimitri sat in the security office. Thanks to Ivan, Dimitri had two guards who stood outside the closed door. The less they knew about what he was up to, the better.

Numerous screens were mounted on the wall, each showing a different view of the compound. And with a flick of a button, he could change which area surrounding Headquarters he wanted to view. He'd been sitting in this room, waiting for Katya and Grigorii to make their move. But the first person who appeared on the screen was not even on Dimitri's list.

Perry had arrived at Headquarters on foot, alone, carrying the new weapon. Did he think he could get inside unannounced? Dimitri laughed. That would be the day. Just because any vampire could enter the building since all vampires were given the code—even guests such as Perry and Amanda—didn't mean they entered unannounced. The building and its surroundings were heavily monitored. And not just the obvious doors and windows.

Still, Perry hadn't even tried to enter the building. He'd spotted the obvious cameras and kept outside their range, but hadn't found the hidden ones, which Dimitri was using. Was Perry losing his nerve? Or waiting for his comrades?

Dimitri's phone rang. He quickly answered it. "I hope you have good news, Ivan."

"I have good news and bad news, sir."

"Damn it. You lost them, didn't you?"

"No, sir. That's the good news. I had lost them. They found the tracker and put it on another vehicle. So I went back to the place they had stopped. While I was questioning the clerk, the van approached from the town and drove on by. I'm following them now, sir."

"Are they headed toward Headquarters?"

"No, sir. They're going north."

"To an airfield?"

"There are airfields in that direction, yes."

So Perry was on his own. Had someone gotten hurt? Dimitri hadn't seen anyone fall during the failed ambush, but Perry had been mad after he'd ripped the camera off Yevgeni. Maybe his little girlfriend had died already. Wouldn't that be nice.

"Have you heard from your men? Regarding the raid on the Committee meeting?"

"That's the bad news, sir, and why I was calling. They were able to destroy the building, but there wasn't anyone in it. They were ambushed. Some of my men got away and called me. I told them to follow my signal so I'll have backup when I reach the plane. Barnet and his people won't get away, sir."

Dimitri slammed his hand on the desk. Katya and Grigorii knew where all the cameras were situated. Could they be out there now? Willing to help Perry? "As soon as your backup arrives, take out that van. Call me once you've confirmed they're all dead. Do you understand?"

"I understand. Do you realize our men are in that van?"

"That is unfortunate, but their deaths will not go unnoticed. It will be the fuel we need to attack the American vampires. And I fully intend to attack once these miscreants are dealt with. Are you with me on this?"

"Yes, sir. It's an honor to serve you."

And until then, he would have to deal with Perry himself. Or at least get one of his guards to do it for him. That's what they were there for, weren't they?

****

Perry finished his sweep around the building. Every opening had a camera pointed to it. There was no way he could get in unannounced. Unless no one manned the monitors and the inside was just as empty as the outside.

Which was as likely as Atlantis being real.

There wasn't one guard outside. But then, why would they need guards if all the openings were monitored electronically? So he couldn't risk there not being anyone inside, waiting. Dimitri wouldn't be that stupid not to have guards in place.

Perry's nerves were starting to get to him. He'd taken his sweet time checking all the openings. And for what? Oh sure, he could tell himself he'd done it to be careful. But the fact was, he'd never been so scared. He didn't want to screw this up. Mandy deserved retribution. So did Alexi. Dimitri had to die. So why was Perry being such a wuss?

Probably because he'd never had a cause to kill anyone before. He needed to man up. Strike that. Mandy would berate him but good for using that term, and for good reason. She'd been the bravest person he'd known. Certainly braver than him. "Damn it, Mandy. Why'd you have to die?"

He hadn't even known her a week and already knew he didn't want to live without her. What was the point? He'd found his perfect mate, gotten a taste of how wonderful life was with her, and now he was left alone. How did Barnet survive for so long after his mate died? That was a kind of torture Perry had no intention of experiencing.

But first he had a mission to complete. He shot back his shoulders and stood straight. Vampire up. Yeah, that was it. He needed to vampire up. He could do this.

He doubled back to what appeared to be the vampire entrance. It was down a flight of steps, with a keypad beside the door and a sign that probably read "Employees Only" since the words were in red bold lettering. What would happen if he used this weapon to destroy that camera? He knew the code to get in. Could he slip in before anyone noticed the camera went out?

Only way to find out. He aimed the weapon at the camera.

"Perry, stop!"

He lowered the weapon and spun around. Damn it. Barnet had sent Katya to stop him? She and a blond man were standing in the tree line, wearing snow camouflage. She waved him over. Why wasn't she leaving the tree line? That's when he saw it. Another camera, hidden in the trees. Oh shit. How long had he been seen?

Perry stepped up to the duo, out of the hidden camera's range. "It's no use stopping me. I'm going in."

"We don't want Dimitri dead. We can't afford to have him die."

"He doesn't deserve to live, either."

"That is for our people to decide."

Perry eyed the stranger.

"I am Grigorii. What is that weapon you have?"

Perry hefted it up. "It's one of yours."

"It is?" Grigorii took it. "Damn. When did he have this made?"

Katya shook her head. "He's gone farther than we thought. Perry, you need to listen to your voicemail."

"What?"

"Your voicemail. Turn on your phone and listen."

He pulled his phone out and turned it on. "If this is some kind of trick…"

"It is not a trick. Trust me."

"Right. Trust." The display indicated a message from Groucho's phone. Probably Barnet, berating him. Whatever. Katya wouldn't leave him be until he listened to the message. He pushed play.

The sweetest voice in the world came over the speaker. "How dare you leave me before I died, you doofus. Now get your arse back over to me and show me you love me."

He dropped to his knees as his heart soared. "She's alive? How?"

"I do not know. Barnet just said she recovered. And that you are to meet them at the plane."

Perry smiled. Yes. The plane. He looked back at the camera. "He's seen me."

"Maybe not. He hasn't sent anyone out for you yet."

"Or he thought I was waiting for someone. And now that I'm out of view… You need to get out of here."

"No. You need to get out of here. Take that path. It will lead you to a culvert. Cross it. You'll reach a road and will be out of view. Then run. We will take care of Dimitri."

"That's a path?" Maybe for a rat.

She laughed. "We can't have it be obvious, now can we?"

"I guess not." He stood and pocketed his phone.

Gregorii held out the weapon. "Do you want this back?"

"You keep it. I think you'll need it more than I will. Thanks for your help. And don't take this the wrong way, but I hope I never see you again." Perry took the path. Shrubbery branches scraped him and he ducked under low tree limbs. Everything inside him wanted to run, but he advanced slowly so as not to go the wrong way.

Mandy was alive. And he'd left her! But she was dead. He'd been sure of it. Oh, hell. Did it matter? Of course not. She spoke to him. On the phone.

The phone! He pulled out his cell. He needed to talk to her.

Someone slammed into his back and he fell forward. That same someone—Mr. Bulldozer—snatched the phone and crumbled it in his hand. Perry pushed against the ground to stand, but Mr. Bulldozer stepped on him and secured his hands behind his back.

Mr. Bulldozer hefted Perry to his feet and pushed him toward Headquarters. "*Pereyekhat*!"

"Okay, okay. I'm moving." Perry shook the snow from his face. The man held the same type of weapon Perry had just given Grigorii.

Or was it the same weapon? Shit.

Chapter 25

"We're being followed," Alexi said from the front seat.

Mandy could sit up on her own now and was nestled in the back corner of the van, facing forward. Her legs might actually work, too, but she wasn't going to try kneeling anytime soon. Her luck, Oscar would hit a pothole and she'd fall and damage something.

Like her neck.

It was still sore and the tape made it hard to twist her head. Not that she wanted to. She'd rather the tape stay on until they reached the plane. And met up with Perry. He could take the tape off. After he kissed her and told her he loved her again.

Loved. Her. And of course he'd said it when she couldn't say it back. Damn man had the worst timing ever.

Her father sat facing her and spoke over his shoulder, "Are you sure?"

There were no windows in the back of the van, so Oscar and Alexi could only go by what they saw in the side mirrors.

"Fairly sure. They do not have their lights on."

"How the hell did Dimitri find us?" she asked.

"Dumb luck?" Oscar said. "We did pass the same gas station we'd stopped at earlier."

Which they wouldn't have had to do if the other road out of the area had been cleared. Damn snow.

"Can you lose them?" Father asked.

Oscar laughed. "If this thing could go fast, and there were other roads to take, sure."

"Wait a minute," Alexi said. "They just turned their lights on and exited the road."

Father turned around on his knees. "So they weren't following us."

Something thumped the roof, startling Mandy. "That didn't sound good."

"No, it did not." Alexi rolled down his window. "Keep driving." He stuck his head out and sat on the opening. He wiggled a bit as if he was reaching for something. Seconds later, he came back inside and rolled up the window.

An explosion rocked the van and lit up the sky momentarily. Her father fell back, making her doubly glad she'd stuck to sitting in the corner. Wasn't sure how much more her neck could take.

Through it all, Oscar kept on driving.

Father sat upright. "How the hell did they get a bomb up there?"

"Drone. I heard it fly away." Alexi turned to the two captives. "You see how you are expendable now? Do you wish to work for someone who doesn't value your life?" He ripped the tape off Yevgeni's mouth. "And you might as well speak English. She can understand you and will translate anyway."

"They speak English?" Father asked. "All of them?"

"Yes. Dimitri just doesn't like anyone to know. Feels it gives him the upper hand. So what say you, Geno? What did Dimitri promise you that is worth your life?"

"Nothing. I work for Committee. I always work for Committee. I was told Barnet was a threat to our people. That he wanted to take over. And that you had gone rogue and became a traitor to our country."

Her father leaned over the seat. "So you don't know that Dimitri has dismantled your Committee?"

"Dismantled?"

"Katya informed me that he killed Sergei. He would have killed her and Gregorii, too, if they hadn't run."

"Why should I believe you if you are the enemy?"

"But he is not the enemy, Geno. Dimitri is. Dimitri buried me alive. Not because I'm a traitor, but because I'm a threat to his thirst for power. Barnet and his people saved me. Here, see for yourself." Alexi grabbed Yevgeni's hand. Several moments passed.

"Alexi, I…did not know. Dimitri said—"

"Dimitri lied. Did you ever talk to any of the other Committee members?"

"No. He is our leader. I did not think to question his authority."

"What about your friend?"

"Luka was helping me. He does not work for Committee."

Alexi palmed Luka's head for several moments before lowering his hand. "I believe they are no longer a threat. May I remove their stakes?"

Father nodded. He removed Luka's stake and Alexi removed Yevgeni's.

"Guys?" Oscar said. "We're coming up to our exit."

"Pass it and then we'll back track," Alexi said. "We might have to make a stand here."

"A stand?" Her last attempt at a stand had failed miserably and she grimaced. "We can't fight them here. We don't have enough weapons. We should head to their Headquarters where it's more populous. They won't risk being discovered. Would they?"

"At this point I'm not sure Dimitri would care, but I could see it being an advantage. Just because Dimitri doesn't care, doesn't mean his people feel the same. You raised a smart daughter there, Barnet. I would not have thought taking this fight to Dimitri."

And then they could get Perry. If he hadn't already gotten himself killed.

* * * *

Perry tugged on the restraints, but they didn't give an inch. He'd snapped through plastic ties before. Even broke handcuffs once on a dare. But this stuff was vampire proof. Well, normal vampires. "What are these made of?"

But of course Mr. Bulldozer didn't answer. Unless Perry could consider a poke in the back an answer.

Mr. Bulldozer kept poking Perry, steering him to the stairs leading to the vampire entrance he'd seen earlier. Mr. Bulldozer punched in the code, opened the door, and shoved Perry through.

"Do you see me resisting? No, you don't. So stop with the poking and shoving." Were Katya and Grigorii still in the area? Or had Dimitri taken them out, too? If they were still alive, why hadn't they made themselves known?

Perry was poked to descend another flight of stairs. Another door led to a maze of hallways, not unlike his own Committee Headquarters.

No wonder newbies got lost there. Susannah was right. They needed marks on the floor to tell you where to go. Blue strips for the pool, red to Barnet's office. Perry would bring that up at the next meeting.

Positive thinking, and all that.

He was poked to turn the corner, where another man stood in the hallway, guarding a door.

"I'd like to lodge a complaint. Your buddy here has been very rude—" Perry's words were cut off when Mr. Bulldozer whopped him good on the head. Perry stumbled into the wall. "Owww. That was uncalled for."

The guard opened the door, grabbed Perry by his jacket, and threw him inside. He landed on his knees and slid across the black-and-white tiled floor. Security monitors lined all the walls. The door behind him closed.

Dimitri rose from his chair. "So we meet again, Mr. Davenport."

"Hey, Dimitri. Whatcha watching? Got any popcorn?"

Dimitri crossed his arms. "You think you funny man?"

"Funny man? You mean comedian? I've told a good joke once or twice."

Dimitri kicked Perry in the head. "Who were you talking to outside?"

"What is it with you guys and heads?" Perry rose to his knees and shook his head. "Ever think about asking nicely?"

"What fun is that?" Dimitri kicked him again, this time in the side. "Now answer my question."

Perry rested his forehead on the floor while he waited for his lungs to work again. "Well, if you must know... I was talking to the squirrel. He told me to skedaddle, so that's what I was doing when Mr. Bulldozer plowed into me."

Dimitri kicked again, breaking a rib. "You will tell me what I want to know or I will get it from you another way."

Perry rolled into a ball, trying to minimize the damage. "Yeah? You think you're good at the old mind meld thing? Think again. Just remember, the connection is a two-way street."

"Ha! You are not old enough to overpower me."

"I don't think age has anything to do with that." Perry sat up slowly, anticipating another kick. When none came, he relaxed. "I think it has to do with ability. My sire had some wonderful abilities. Not only passed them on to me, but taught me everything I know. And I know how to fry a vampire's brain. You wanna try that mind meld thing now?"

"You are bluffing."

"I wish that I could. You don't know how many card games I could have won. But hey, if you don't believe me, you don't believe me." Perry twisted his wrists inside the restraints. They were connected some way, he just had to find the latch.

Dimitri sat on his chair and crossed his arms. "Who was your sire?"

Genealogy was safe. And just the distraction Perry needed. "I called him J.C. Liked to joke that it stood for Jesus Christ, but it actually stood for—"

"Julius Caesar."

Okay, now that was just weird. "You knew him?"

"You would have me believe Julius Caesar turned you."

"Well, he wasn't *the* Julius Caesar. But I guess you know that."

"Why did he turn *you*?"

"I didn't ask him to. Sheesh. Why does any vampire turn someone into a vampire? He was lonely? Wanted a son?" He had treated Perry like one in any case. JC had been that second father to him.

Perry found the latch. Ahh, finally. He hadn't found a restraining system that could hold him yet. Well, except the burying alive part. But he had been staked at the time.

"A son? I find it hard to believe Julius would want a son. Was he starting an army, was that it?"

"If he was, I knew nothing of it. I'd say ask him yourself, but last I heard he was in South America. Somewhere not very populated." JC had asked Perry to accompany him then, but Perry preferred people to isolation and had turned him down. JC hadn't taken kindly to the rejection and Perry had never seen him again. Maybe if he had gone, he wouldn't have gotten himself buried alive. But then he wouldn't have met Barnet. Or Mandy.

"Why did you come here?"

"To kill you. Duh. What else?"

"But you were leaving. Why? Did you become chicken?"

"I almost chickened out, I'll admit it. But that's not why I was leaving. I no longer had a reason to kill you. You see, I thought you had killed Mandy. Turns out she's still alive. And I was headed toward her when you abducted me. So I didn't have a reason to kill you then, but I do have a reason to kill you now."

Dimitri chuckled. "Another joke? You have reason. But no ability."

"Ahhh, but I do. I told you. J.C. taught me everything he knew." Perry brought his hands around and raised his eyebrows. "See?" He yanked on a cable from the wall. Several monitors went dark. Before Dimitri could stand, Perry had the cable around the man's torso and neck.

The door burst open. Perry dashed behind Dimitri and used him as a shield.

"Perry, don't!" Katya yelled.

"Oh ye of little faith." Perry loosened the cable around Dimitri's neck a bit, but kept the vampire immobilized. "It's about time you got here, though, or I might have done something you didn't want me to." He held up the cable. "Grigorii, will you?"

"I got one better." Grigorii pulled out a stake and stabbed Dimitri in the heart. "He's not getting away."

Dimitri's head slumped to the side as blood bloomed around the stake. "And you will not live once my people have discovered what you have done."

"Your people," Kayta said, "already know. They are ready to help us reform the Committee. One that is not run by an old-fashioned dictator."

Perry rubbed his hands together. "Excuse me, but I don't need to stay for this, do I? I've got some friends and a plane to catch."

Including one sexy Brit.

Dimitri chuckled, which turned into a cough. Blood spewed from his mouth. "Your friends are dead. Or will be soon. You can make your plane, but you will fly home alone."

"What are you talking about?"

"Was I not clear?"

Perry grabbed the man's head. He'd get his answers.

"Go ahead. You can fry my brain, as you so eloquently put it, before you find out anything from me."

Didn't stop Perry from trying. Nothing. He could get nothing. He shoved Dimitri away and faced Katya. "Tell me you can find out who he sent and stop them."

She shook her head. "But I can call Barnet and warn them." Using the landline phone, she punched in Groucho's number. One ring and Groucho's voice answered—voicemail. "I'll try Mandy's phone."

"Don't bother. I have it." He pulled out the cell. No service. She'd dropped her phone in the snow during the ambush. He should have put it in her bag, but his mind had been on other things.

Dimitri laughed. "See? They will all die."

"You bastard!"

"Hold on." Katya went to a computer. "If I know Dimitri, he sent Yevgeni—"

"Yevgeni is with my friends and doesn't have his phone. How about Ivan?"

"Yes, Ivan." Her fingers flew over the keyboard. "Ivan is on the road." She straightened. "Heading toward us."

Dimitri furrowed his bushy brows for a brief moment before he smiled. "If he's on his way here, his job is finished."

Perry didn't believe it for a minute. "Then why did you look confused? Is it because he didn't check in? He would have checked in, right? Which means..." He turned to Katya. "He could be following them here. Where is he? Show me the map."

She pointed to the red dot. Perry chuckled. "You remind me of Victoria. She likes playing with this crap, too."

"It is not crap."

"No, it's not." Not if it got him to his friends in time. "How do I get out of here?"

"Grigorii, go with him. Take some weapons. I'll put Dimitri into a cell. Good luck, Perry."

Yeah, luck. Perry would need boat loads of the stuff. He followed Grigorii down the hall to the weapons closet. Something the American Headquarters did not have. Hell, they didn't even have an army. Hopefully they wouldn't need one after this confrontation, either.

The walls were lined with crossbows. "What? You don't have any more of those head choppers?"

"I didn't even know we had any head choppers." Grigorii held out the strange weapon. "You want this? You know how to use this better than I do."

Perry shook his head. "They're too noisy. Just give me a damn crossbow."

Grigorii grabbed two and filled a white bag with several stakes. "Let's go!"

As soon as they reached the outdoors, they ran toward the highway. About a minute later something ahead exploded.

Chapter 26

"I think I lost them when we turned around," Oscar said.

"You didn't," Alexi said. "They're just staying further back. And I think there are two of them now."

"Two?" Mandy risked moving, crawling over to the seat back and settling on her knees. "Okay, this is seriously fucked up. We can maybe outrun one, but two?"

Father held his hand out. "Oscar, toss me your phone. I'll call Katya and see if she can do something."

"Sorry, Barnet. Phone died five minutes ago. I have no way to charge it."

Her father looked at her. "Where's your phone?"

Her mobile. Yes! She reached inside her pocket. Her empty pocket. "Oh bollocks."

"What?"

"I was holding my mobile when we got ambushed. It's probably back at the park, unless someone picked it up?"

Oscar and Father both shook their head.

"They're gaining on us," Alexi said. "And there are three of them. Not two."

Mandy yearned for a window. Or a mirror. This not being able to see anything was the pits. "They're going to try and blow us up again. Or run us off the road and then blow us up."

Alexi nodded. "Probably."

"We need to bail."

"I agree," Father said. "But they'll notice when the car drives out of control. If it doesn't stop. We'll be sitting ducks, especially with all this snow."

"Not if someone keeps driving. They can get far away and then ditch it." She went to climb over the seat between the two Russians, but her father pulled her back.

"What are you doing?"

"I'm taking my place as driver."

"No, you're not."

She was fairly certain he said it because he cared, but some old wound still surfaced bringing her doubts back into play. "There isn't anyone else to do this and you know it. Oscar didn't sign up for this gig. And you need to make sure Alexi makes it back to the States in one piece. And frankly, I'm not going to be able to help you get Dimitri's men out safely. I can barely walk myself."

"Then I'll drive."

"Like bloody hell you are. Your own Committee would have my head if something happened to you. I'm the one who signed up for this. Let me do my job."

"Mandy, you don't have anything to prove to me anymore."

That he said it made her heart soar and stuffed all those doubts away. "I know that. But don't act like I'm going to die. It's kind of insulting."

He laughed and saluted. "Yes, ma'am."

They played musical passengers. Mandy was able to take over driving. Oscar went to the backseat and held Yevgeni in his lap. Her father held Luka. Alexi stayed in the front passenger seat holding hers and Perry's backpacks as well as the equipment bag.

If they were going to abandon ship, might as well take everything with them.

"I can't afford to slow down," she said. "They might suspect something."

"We'll be fine," her father said. "Just tell us when."

They'd be fine as long as they landed in a snowy area. The overpass ahead might be the best as it wasn't lit. It would not only hide them, the on-ramp might give her more snow to work with, as long as no one was entering the highway. "Get ready. I'll meet you at the plane."

Oscar punched out the overhead light and opened the side door. Alexi turned in his seat, ready to climb in the back.

"Now!"

Oscar jumped. Father jumped. Alexi remained.

"What are you waiting for?"

"Are you sure you want to do this alone?"

"I'm perfectly capable of doing this on my own. Get out!"

"Yes, ma'am." Alexi climbed into the backseat and jumped out the opening.

The three SUVs were still in view in the side mirror. All three continued to chase her as they drove under the overpass. But they were gaining.

The city came into view. On-coming traffic was sparse at best. Most likely Dimitri's men would try something before they reached civilization. Could she get a few klicks away first?

The windshield of an on-coming lorry shattered. The driver turned the truck, breached the road divider, and headed her way. Bloody hell. Those bastards were controlling the driver.

Could she avoid the truck? Granted, the van was sluggish, but the lorry had to be more so. She'd played chicken with cars in the past, but nothing like this. Not when someone else was controlling the other driver. This was not the kind of adrenaline rush she craved. If she ever craved it again.

The van's rear tire blew and the back end swerved. There was no playing chicken now. She abandoned the steering wheel and headed for the side opening just as the van collided into the truck.

* * * *

"No, no, no, no, no!" Holding up the crossbow, Perry ran toward the explosion.

243

"Perry, wait!" Grigorii grabbed his arm. "You can't go out there. They'll spot you right away."

His clothing ranged on the dark side, whereas Gregorii wore a white camo suit. "Then I guess I'll make it hard for them to spot me." In a flash, he stripped naked. One good thing about being a vampire: his pale skin would definitely blend in with the snow.

Underwear would have been smart, but he'd always gone commando. *Oh Great One. Don't let anything freeze. Okay?*

"Was that really necessary?"

"Why? Am I turning you on or something?"

Grigorii rolled his eyes. "We need to approach cautiously. Ivan will most likely be inspecting the wreckage and then we'll have the mortals to worry about."

Perry didn't give a flying fig about the mortals, but Ivan was another matter. "He's just going to kill whatever moves."

"He's not going to be careless, though. This could be a trap for him and he knows it."

Perry gripped his weapon. Why did that have to make sense? His heart didn't care about sense, though. It wanted him to run.

They had to be okay. They just had to.

Gregorii kept to the left side of the road, his weapon up. Perry followed suit. Three SUVs approached the fiery wreck. The van had collided into a trucker, who'd been going the wrong way on the road. The truck driver most likely died. Ivan sat behind the wheel of one SUV. The other two drivers—one blond, one brunette—were unfamiliar.

Gregorii leaned to Perry's left and whispered, "Ivan is our biggest threat. We take him out, the other two will give up easily."

"Whatever you say. You're the boss."

Thing was, Ivan stayed inside his SUV. Was he learning from Dimitri? Spineless bastard. The other two got out of their vehicles, both wearing black suits with white shirts.

"What are they, the Men in Black?"

"They are easy to spot, no?"

The blond shouted in Russian. Lifted someone by the hair.

Not just any someone. Mandy.

"Oh shit. Not the hair."

Snow flew from Mandy's feet as she was lifted. And yes, he was a little relieved to see the rest of her body attached to her head. She grabbed onto Blondie's arm, most likely to loosen the pressure on her neck.

A neck that still needed time to heal.

Perry itched to shoot Blondie, but that would only warn Ivan, who could still drive away. But if Blondie even attempted to hurt her...

Ivan shouted at Blondie.

Gregorii shifted to Perry's right. "Ivan's not getting out of the car. Said to bring her to him. I need to cross the street. Can you distract them?"

"I can shoot out Ivan's tire." Then the bastard couldn't drive away. Not easily.

"I didn't mean expose yourself."

"Too late."

He closed his eyes. "I didn't mean..."

"I won't be exposed long if you can get a clear shot at Ivan."

Sirens sounded in the distance.

"The mortals will be here soon. Ivan's not going to wait. Do it." Gregorii crouched on his feet and waited.

Perry flattened into the snow, aimed and fired. The front tire popped. Gregorii dashed across the street. Ivan poked his head out the window and yelled at the brunette.

Brownie stared in Perry's direction. Blondie dragged Mandy to Ivan. Perry reloaded. Aimed and shot Blondie. He dropped Mandy and grabbed his side. The commotion drew Brownie's gaze away from Perry. He dashed to the left, reloaded and fired. Much better. Blondie was no longer a threat to Mandy.

Brownie got a fix on Perry and charged. With no time to reload, Perry grabbed a stake from the bag. The collision jolted him and the stake flew from his hand. Landed somewhere in the snow. Damn it. Brownie grabbed him by the throat. Perry flipped back, sending Brownie over him. Free from Brownie, Perry lurched for the bag of stakes.

Brownie landed on top of him, pinning him to the ground. "*Dokhlyachka.*"

Probably some weird animal name. But not goat. Nope, not goat.

Damn it. Perry couldn't get free. Had Gregorii shot Ivan? Was Mandy okay? If only he could get this bozo off him.

Perry was twisting to get free when Brownie went limp. Perry scrambled out from under the body.

Mandy fell to her knees, crossbow in her hands. "Got him."

He'd never been so happy to see her. Brownie'd been staked. "My hero! Where's Ivan?"

She pointed over her shoulder. "Your friend got him. Why are you naked?"

Perry rushed to her side. "Camouflage. Come here, you." He yanked her to her feet and planted a kiss on the sexiest lips in the universe.

Her arms wrapped around his neck and she molded into his body while he tasted her sweet, sweet mouth. "I love you, Mandy."

She touched his face. "I love you, too. But we need to get out of here. Sirens."

They were getting louder, but she wasn't going to distract him with logic. "You what now?"

She pushed his chest. "You heard me."

Oh, he heard her. He just wanted to hear it again. And again. And again. But she was right. No time for celebrating. They had a mess to clean before the mortals arrived.

And he had his clothes to find.

✳ ✳ ✳ ✳

Mandy leaned her head back on the seat. At least they had transportation again, and didn't have to hot wire any vehicle. The SUVs Dimitri's men arrived in came in very handy.

Once the wreck and authorities were dealt with, she, Perry, and Gregorii had driven the vehicles to where Father, Oscar, and Alexi had jumped. They'd seen the explosion and had thought the worst. She'd actually gotten a hug from her father.

Gregorii and Alexi had words. Alexi helped put Yevgeni and Luka into the SUV Gregorii took. Gregorii offered Alexi a ride, but he was still interested in going to America and declined. Much to her father's delight. They'd left the third SUV behind for the new Russian Committee to retrieve later.

Alexi drove and Oscar sat up front. She sat on the backseat between the two men she cared the most about. "Is it okay if we go back to the park to get my mobile?"

She did not want to ask for another one. Her Committee would have a fit. She'd lost five last year alone. Okay, she only lost one. The other four had been destroyed. But still...

"You mean this one?" Perry pulled it from his side pocket.

She took it and hugged it to her chest. "My mobile! Thank you."

"You're awfully familiar with that phone. I mean, I didn't even get a hug."

"I believe you got a kiss. Isn't that better than a hug?"

"I kissed you first, though. You just kissed me back. And why did you kiss me back?" He leaned over and cupped his ear as if he couldn't hear the answer. "Huh? What was that you said back there?"

She bit back a laugh. Shook her head. This was what she had to look forward to, wasn't it? Fun with Perry. "I love you."

"You all heard her, right? She said it to me. She loves me!"

She couldn't stop the laugh now. And hugged him. "Thank you for still being alive."

"Ditto. How's your neck?" He fingered the tape. "We should probably leave this on until we get to London." He wagged his brows and spoke telepathically, *"Do you need me to work some of my magic?"*

"Pain's not that bad. Man, I thought my head was going to pop off when that guy pulled my hair, though."

"I had that same thought. You know I wouldn't have left you if I thought you were alive. Right? It's just that you didn't break out in a rash."

"She never did," Father said.

Perry's eyes widened. "Are you saying I cured you?"

"What are you talking about? Cured me how?"

"When you took my blood."

"You took his blood?" Father practically screamed at her, but in a caring way. "Was it an emergency?"

"No. But…" Bloody hell. Was she about to out Perry's secret?

"But what?"

Perry squeezed her hand. "I wanted her to take my blood."

Father shook his head. "But vampire blood to her, to us—"

"Is bad. Was bad. I know. She told me. But you know how I'm so good at digging inside a vampire's head? Well, I can ease the pain, too."

Oscar's eyes widened. "You can do that? Stop the pain?"

Perry nodded.

"Cool."

Alexi glanced in the mirror. "That's a rare gift you have there."

Perry grimaced. "Is it? Or could it be those of us with this gift just don't advertise it. Sort of like being allergic to blood. You don't know how another vampire will take it so you just don't say it. My sire also had this gift and told me that, as I'm sure Mandy's sire said the same thing to her."

"My situation was different. He wasn't allergic. He just created a freak."

"Not true," Father said. "He was allergic. Claimed a witch had cured him. Much to his surprise, the cure wasn't passed down when he turned you. He just led you to believe differently."

She turned toward Perry. Could it be possible he had cured her?

Perry offered his finger to her father. "Want to see if my blood works on you? If it doesn't, I can ease the pain."

Father stared at the offering. "You didn't take much?"

It was a rare day to see him nervous. Not that she blamed him. She'd felt the same when she'd taken Perry's blood. "I just nicked his finger. Barely got a drop."

He nodded, lowered his fangs, and pricked Perry's finger. Licked the blood drop and sat back. "Nothing's happening. Sure I got enough?"

"It never took much for me to get a reaction before. Did it you?"

"No. I ingested some of Frederick's blood by mistake when I killed him. I thought I was going to die."

Oscar turned in his seat and extended his arm toward her father. "Do you want to experiment some more?"

"Why not? I'm all about the experiments, aren't I?" He bit Oscar's wrist and took a strong pull. Licked the wound and sat back.

"Well?" Mandy asked.

He grinned. "Nothing."

Perry sat forward. "Holy shit. You mean all this time I could have cured you?"

Mandy took his hand. "You didn't know, Perry. None of us did."

"I'll let you know how my next feeding goes." Father squeezed Perry's shoulder. "But if it's anything like this, I owe you."

"Oh no, you don't. We're even. Even Steven."

Her mobile rang. Smiling at the display, she handed it to her father. "You might want to take this call."

While he spoke to Katya, Perry lifted Mandy onto his lap.

"Mmmm. This is where you belong." He caressed her face. "Don't ever scare me like that again."

"I'll do my best as long as you don't scare me again."

"I scared you?"

"Yeah. I thought we were going to end up like Romeo and Juliet."

"Okay. No more scaring each other, then. By the way, what did he call me? When he said *dokhlyachka*?"

She rested her head on his shoulder. "You looking to expand your vocabulary?"

"Every chance I get now. Can't have you translating everything for me. So, what did he say?"

"He said you were dead meat."

Perry nodded. "Well, he wouldn't have been wrong if you hadn't shot him when you did."

"I'm sure you would have figured something out. I just didn't want to wait any longer."

"Impatient. I like."

Not as much as she liked sitting in his lap, feeling loved. Best feeling in the world.

* * * *

Barnet answered the phone. "Katya, I take it everything turned out okay?"

"Yes. Dimitri is behind bars and we're in the process of calling an emergency meeting. There are only three of us now, we'll need some volunteers to step up."

"Three? You still have Felicks?"

She chuckled. "Yes. He was instrumental in our cause. Quite by accident, too."

"How so?"

"When he found out Dimitri was torturing Natasha, well, let's just say he's had a crush on her for ages. That was the final straw for him. He was just scared. Didn't know how to fight Dimitri. He's more than happy to be on our side now. And because he saved Natasha, she hasn't left his side. I think there might be wedding bells soon if I am not mistaken."

Barnet looked over at Mandy and Perry kissing and smiled. Probably wedding bells for them, too? But he had more concerns than weddings. "How will this new Committee deal with Perfect Mates?"

"We will follow your lead, Barnet. But we might need to Skype all the Committees and discuss this among ourselves. Not just the Heads. The whole Committee. You understand why, right?"

"I do. Are you stepping up to be the Head Member?"

"That is for our people to decide, but I am not disinclined to hold that position. I just want what is best for our people."

"Your people would be smart to elect you to that position. How will this affect your relationship with Gregorii?"

She laughed. "How did you know?"

"Was he not the man you talked to and kissed when you rescued me?"

"He was. Yes. He's very supportive. In fact, he already suggested I run for Head. So you see, it is for our people to decide. I am sorry you were brought into our fight, but thankful all the same. Without your involvement, we wouldn't be where we are now. On the verge of freedom."

Barnet couldn't help but think the same thing. That because he was brought into this whole Russian mess, he wouldn't have been reunited with his daughter. And for that he would be eternally grateful.

* * * *

Perry loved kissing Mandy. Loved everything about her.

She palmed his face. *"Must I sit on this rock in your pants?"*

"Hey, you turn me on. What can I say?"

"You're also kissing me in public."

"Yes I am." Although, was a car load of people really public?

"What changed?"

"I fell in love."

Barnet handed the phone back to Mandy. "New destination. We can go to the airport here. Katya said their hangar is free for us to use. She's already contacted Victoria who has contacted the pilots. They'll be there waiting for us."

"Home." She closed her eyes. "We're finally going home."

Yes, home. But which one? "Is that invitation still open?"

She grabbed his face. "I would love for you to live in London with me."

"Wait a minute," Barnet said. "You're not coming to Atlanta?"

Oooh, Atlanta would be great, too. And that Barnet asked her was even better. But Perry wasn't ready to share Mandy just yet. "Maybe later, Boss. Or should I call you Pops? Because I plan on marrying your daughter."

Mandy's eyes widened. "Wait. What? You do?"

"It's not every day a vampire finds their perfect mate. And you're perfect for me, Mandy Groves. I'll make sure you never doubt my choice. Because I choose you. I'll always choose you. So let's spend a month or two in London, get married, and then go to Atlanta." Perry stopped when Barnet practically growled. "Or get married in Atlanta. So Pops can be there. What do you say?"

Groucho turned around. "What kind of proposal is that?"

Mandy smiled and her electric blue eyes sparkled. "The one that gets a yes."

"Hallelujah! We're getting married. Can we get married on Halloween? Then we can dress up like vampires."

Laughing, she cupped his face. "It sounds perfect."

Finding his perfect mate had only been a fantasy. Now it was reality. And he was never letting her go.

Epilogue

Multi-colored lights flashed down from the ceiling above. The band—consisting of some fine vampire musicians—played high-energy music. Couples in various costumes jumped and gyrated on the dance floor.

If a mortal walked into this out-of-the-way high school gymnasium, they would see a Halloween dance—sans the food and drink—not a vampire wedding reception.

It was amazing what vampires could get away with on this holiday.

Barnet sat in the back. Near the exit. Alone. He should be with the crowd. Celebrating. But he couldn't quite work up the courage to party. Or explain how he came to have a daughter.

A daughter Perry had fallen in love with. Barnet couldn't be more pleased at that outcome. He wasn't sure who they were supposed to be dressed as, but Perry's long leather coat over black jeans and T-shirt and Mandy's long-sleeved red dress, with a bit of fur around the sleeve openings, really suited them.

Susannah sauntered over wearing the tightest black leather jumpsuit with black boots and her eyes practically glowed blue. "May I?"

"Be my guest." Would it be rude to ask who she was dressed as or should he just enjoy the sight? Because he was enjoying it very much.

She sat in the chair beside him. "I thought for sure I'd meet the great Alexi Popolov today. Wasn't he invited?"

"He was, but he's decided to stay out of the limelight. At least until the Russian vampire mess is under control." Which it would be soon, if Katya had her way. At least she'd been voted in as the next Committee Head. Dimitri's fate was still to be decided, though.

But what Barnet failed to mention was that he'd given Lily DiMarco's information to Alexi. There was a Perfect Mate out there waiting to be claimed. Barnet had found his long ago in Rachel. Thought it only fair to give Alexi a shot. He'd waited longer than anyone.

Susannah folded her arms on the table. "Perry's really pulling off the Spike look, don't you think? I almost thought he'd cut his hair, but I see now he's hidden his ponytail inside his shirt."

"Spike?" It was almost embarrassing that he didn't know all the fictional vampires. Some leader he was.

Her eyes widened. "From *Buffy the Vampire Slayer*. Victoria is dressed as Buffy and Ben came as Angel. Didn't you ever watch the series?"

"Can't say that I have." TV had never interested Barnet. Not even films. Books, now that was the way to spend his time. He just stayed away from the horror genre. "So who is Mandy supposed to be, then?"

"Drusilla." She placed her hands over her heart. "Spike's love."

"Ahhh." That made sense now.

"How come you didn't walk her down the aisle?"

Mandy had asked him to, but he couldn't do it. "Because I'd already given her away once. I wasn't going to do it again." She hadn't married the bastard, and yeah, Frederick had manipulated Barnet at the time, but that didn't matter. The outcome was what mattered. Thankfully, she had understood.

"Is that why she didn't wear white? Because she'd been married before? I thought maybe it was because she was trying to stay in character."

"I don't know about that, but white didn't come in fashion until after Queen Victoria's wedding."

"Really? I guess you would know, huh? If I ever get married, I want the white. And I want Ben to walk me down the aisle. But I doubt it'll ever happen."

"Why do you say that? Anything is possible." Last year he would never have thought he'd finally bury Rachel or that Perry would have gotten married to another vampire. Yet, those happened.

"I suppose." She slouched in her seat as if a great weight pushed her down.

Barnet leaned forward. "Susannah, is everything okay? Job working out for you?" When their last receptionist quit, Susannah had stepped in and took over. He had tried filling the spot with a vampire before, but no one wanted to stay so close to Headquarters. Afraid they were being monitored, even though that was far from the truth. He never cared who ran the business, just that it was manned. And mortals were able to run it fine enough since the assignments usually required mortals.

A grin took over her face and warmed his soul. "The job is great. I'm enjoying it immensely. I was able to place Richard Daugherty in a position last week. He was very thankful. It feels nice to be needed. I can keep the job, can't I?"

"You may work there for as long as you desire." Barnet never thought the business would come in handy for unemployed Perfect Mates, it was just a front that made money. Very good money. Money that was used to help other vampires. "Have you finally met him? Richard Daugherty?"

She laughed. "Yes. Don't know what the big whoop was about, though. Neither one of us got a reaction." Her joy quickly faded and she returned to slouching and frowning. "Do you suppose that's because I'm a freak?"

"You're not a freak." Sure, she had been a susceptible mortal— easily manipulated—but that didn't make her a freak as a vampire. Just like being allergic to blood hadn't made him one, either. Not that he was allergic any longer. Feeding was no longer a chore, and to think he had Perry to thank for that.

"But my powers are weak. I can't even read minds yet."

"Give it time. It took Jack's wife, Sunny, nearly a year to have complete control over her powers."

She sighed and looked out on the dance floor. "Yeah. That's what Perry keeps telling me."

"Are you sad that he got married? To another vampire?"

"What? No. I'm very happy for him. I like Mandy. She helped me pick out my outfit. Said I was the perfect Selene." She eyed him and shook her head. "You don't know who she is, either, do you? From *Underworld*?"

"Sorry. Guilty. But you do look very nice." If sexy could be considered nice. How was it he'd never really noticed her that way before?

"Thank you. I like your red cape. You came as Dracula, right?"

"Yes. Perry's doing." At least Barnet knew that character, although he wasn't the only one dressed as him. Four other vampires also dressed that way. "It's not very original, is it?"

"You look very…regal. I like it." She looked out at the dance floor. The music switched to an old song even he recognized—"And I Love Her"—and she took a deep breath, as if she were working up some courage. To maybe finally say what was on her mind? "Barnet?"

"Yes, Susannah?"

She placed her palm upward on the table. "Would you care to dance?"

Not at all what he thought she'd say. It had been five centuries since he'd taken a lady's hand to dance. Somehow, he felt that Rachel would be okay with him moving on.

"I would love to." He placed his hand in Susannah's and a spark flared in his heart.

Yes. Anything was possible.

* * * *

"This is the best party ever!" Perry grabbed Mandy by her cheeks, planted one messy kiss on her luscious lips, and still hadn't missed a beat to the music. "And all my friends are here, too."

Johnny and Sarah came. As did Sammy and Janie. Perry wasn't sure if they'd be able to make it since Halloween was a busy day at the bar. But when Perry had asked Johnny to be his best man, Johnny had said he wouldn't miss it for anything. Perry wasn't sure he deserved such good friends, but they were all here. Partying with the best of them.

Oh Great One, you are definitely the best. Thank you so much.

"Do you think Dad is having fun?" Mandy glanced over at Barnet, who was no longer sitting alone.

Perry was glad that Mandy could finally call her father "Dad." That their relationship had deepened since they returned to the States. He was pretty sure Barnet dug the name, too. Perry grabbed her hands and swung her back and forth on the dance floor. "Pops is fine. Don't you worry about him."

"You know he hates it when you call him that."

Perry snickered. "I know. Ain't it great? I got immunity now."

Mandy shook her head, but a chuckle leaked out of that pretty mouth of hers. "Is that all I'm good for? Keeping you out of the slammer."

"Oh hell no. You're good for my soul. I ain't lettin' you go."

Perry nodded to the band. The music switched from the high energy number to a more laid-back one. He pulled Mandy in close. "Happy Wedding Day, Mrs. Davenport."

She stared at him with those electrifying eyes of hers. "Are they playing our song?"

Ever since he'd picked that number and danced with her on that deserted Russian road, they'd pretty much considered that Beatles' tune "their song." No matter who sang it, either.

"They are. Thank you for marrying me."

"Thank you for making me want to." She laid her head on his shoulder. "I do love this song, though. You have great taste."

"Of course I do. I picked you, didn't I?" Now to see if their song worked on another couple. Perry grinned as Barnet led Susannah to the dance floor. "Hot damn. It worked."

"What worked?" Mandy glanced in the direction Perry was. "Of course it did. I told you that outfit would do it."

"What are you talking about? It wasn't the outfit."

"Excuse me, but did you not see his eyes practically bug out of his head when she approached?"

"Exactly. She approached. And asked him to dance. To this song. On *my* recommendation."

Mandy laughed. "Have you become a matchmaker now? Is that it?"

"Matchmaker? I'm hardly that. I just brought two people together who have been too scared to admit they had a thing for one another. I noticed when Suzie-Q was freshly turned that Barnet was interested. Just didn't know at the time why he hadn't done anything about it."

"But didn't you try to hook Susannah up with Richard Daugherty?"

"No. I just thought she should meet him. And she did. Eventually. See? Not a matchmaker. Otherwise, that would have worked out. I do love the outfit you picked out for her. And yes, it might have helped...some."

Mandy laughed and snuggled her head against his chest. "Be still my heart. He just gave me some credit."

"Hey, I give you lots of credit." She was still the smartest person he knew, too.

"I just want Dad happy."

"He is happy. And I'm not talking about being with Suzie-Q. Didn't you see him grinning during the ceremony?"

"Ahh, and here I thought you only had eyes for me."

"You have more than my eyes. You have my whole body." And he would prove it to her every ding dong day.

Thank you for purchasing this book.

Sign up for Stacy McKitrick's newsletter to receive new release announcements, sneak peeks of future books, and bonus content. She sometimes even gives stuff away. You can find the signup form on her website: http://stacymckitrick.com

ABOUT THE AUTHOR

Stacy McKitrick always had stories in her head; she just never knew what to do with them. Then one day she decided to give writing a try and discovered the passion she'd been looking for all her life. She waved goodbye to accounting and now spends her time writing romance featuring vampires and ghosts. All with happy endings, of course. Born in California, she currently resides in Ohio with her husband. They have two grown children. You can learn more about Stacy at her website www.stacymckitrick.com.

www.ingramcontent.com/pod-product-compliance
Lightning Source LLC
Chambersburg PA
CBHW021138110726
47900CB00002B/409